ALYSSA DELLE PALME

EVERNIGHT PUBLISHING ®

www.evernightpublishing.com

Copyright© 2025

Alyssa Delle Palme

ISBN: 978-0-3695-1184-3

Cover Artist: Jay Aheer

Editor: CA Clauson

DEDICATION

For my daughter, Rosie.
Your spirit is sunlight—bright and warm.
May your voice always be as steady as the stars and as strong as the ancient pines.

ALYSSA DELLE PALME

SIGNING OFF FOR THE SUMMER

Alyssa Delle Palme

Copyright © 2025

Chapter One

"What do you mean you quit?"

Maggie cringed. She hated it when her father raised his voice.

"Is this about the debacle with that movie star?" he asked.

Maggie sat on the edge of her desk. "I can't go back, Dad." Her voice quivered.

"Do you realize how this makes me look?"

Maggie nodded, even though her father couldn't see her through the phone. She played with the coiled phone cord, wrapping it around her index finger. Her father, a successful television producer, had put his reputation on the line to get her an internship at 880 News Radio in Toronto.

Stay strong, she thought. Maggie always did as she was told, but not this time. Her father's high expectations had become too overwhelming.

"The media world is a small one, Maggie. If you quit now, you won't just be burning a bridge. You'll be blowing it into the stratosphere."

Maggie gulped. She hated disappointing her father. "I'm sorry," she said, her voice barely audible.

"You're sorry?" Her father scoffed at the notion. "How are you going to support yourself?"

"I thought maybe I could come home until I figure things out. I—"

"No. If you do this, Maggie, your mother and I are not giving you a cent."

"I'm not asking for money. I'm sure I could pick up my old shift at the Corner Café."

"With your education? Your big plan is to go back to your high school waitressing job? Do you know how much it cost us to put you through school?"

"It would be temporary until I figure out a better solution."

"No. If you quit, Maggie, you're on your own."

Maggie squeezed the receiver. Panic set in. "Where will I go?" she whispered.

"Well, you're an adult. An adult who is obviously capable of making important decisions on her own." His voice was heavy with sarcasm. "I'm sure you'll figure it out."

"I'm not doing this to hurt you!" Maggie fired back. She squeezed her eyes shut to keep her tears at bay.

Her father paused. Maggie could feel his demeanor softening over the phone.

"Explain it to me, honey. Tell me why."

Maggie swallowed the thick lump in her throat. "I can't."

"Maggie, come on—"

"I said I can't!"

"Damn it, Maggie! If you won't tell me, I guess there's nothing left for us to discuss."

"Wait, Dad, I—"

Click.

Maggie hung up the receiver and pinched the bridge of her nose. The florescent light flickered overhead. She looked at the mess sprawled across her desk and took a deep breath, then grabbed a cardboard box and filled it with her personal belongings—a potted fern, her toothbrush from the top drawer of her desk, and a framed photograph of her boyfriend, Brody. A sense of dread overwhelmed Maggie when she realized how furious Brody might be with her for quitting. She'd made a life altering decision without consulting him first. He wouldn't like that.

Maggie clenched and unclenched her fists, forcing herself to focus on the task at hand. She plugged her USB flash drive into her work computer and saved her best news stories to the memory stick. Maggie had quit the paid internship she had put her blood, sweat, and tears into, and she needed something to show for it. In the midst of her packing, Maggie heard hushed voices in the hallway. She tiptoed to her office door that was opened a crack.

"I heard she was fired," one woman whispered.

"For what? Maggie is the hardest working intern I've ever seen," said another woman.

Maggie's shoulders relaxed. She recognized the voice of the second woman. It was Jenny, the station secretary, who always had something nice to say about everyone.

"She tried to sleep with Andrew."

"What? No way!" said Jenny. "Maggie has a

boyfriend. A cute boyfriend. I've met him."

"Some women will do anything to climb the corporate ladder, even if it means having an affair with their boss."

Maggie gasped. She quickly brought her hand to her mouth and willed the women to continue on their way down the hallway. The women quieted.

"Maggie? Are you in there?" Jenny called.

Maggie didn't move a muscle. She wasn't supposed to be there. After she told her boss, Andrew, that she quit, he instructed her to leave the premises immediately. He said he would have someone deliver her personal belongings to her apartment, but Maggie didn't trust him to save her portfolio of work.

Believing the coast was clear, the women continued with their lunchtime gossip as they slowly meandered down the hallway.

"I just don't see it," said Jenny. "Maggie is so beautiful. Andrew is like ten years older, and he's balding!"

"It's not the first time she's propositioned an older man. Remember the fiasco with that Hollywood star?"

Maggie wanted to stick her head out and tell Jenny's friend to "fuck off," but instead, she bit her tongue until the women wandered out of earshot. Maggie's cheeks burned. It seemed like nobody would let her forget what happened a few weeks back, when her mentor Rooney had burst into her office in a hurry.

"Follow me," he had said in a serious tone.

Rooney was the longtime 880 News music and entertainment reporter. He was a kind, but impatient, man. He didn't have time to teach his interns. He expected them to keep up and demanded high quality professionalism. Maggie thought she was in trouble as she followed him down the hallway to an empty recording studio.

Rooney opened the door and invited Maggie inside. "I'll be right back," he had said.

The windowless studio had a large desk in the center of the room equipped with two microphones, an audio mixing console, and three swivel work chairs with padded backrests. Black soundproof foam covered the walls. Air conditioning blasted through a vent in the ceiling, causing Maggie's teeth to chatter. She wondered what mistake she had made. She bit her thumb nail too short, exposing the delicate skin underneath. Maggie jumped when Rooney opened the door and ushered in a man wearing casual clothes and a baseball cap. Maggie stood to greet them and gave the stranger a half-smile as she shook his hand.

"Nice to meet y'all," he said with a Southern accent.

Confused, Maggie sat back down and dug her nails into the bottom of her chair, bracing for the fall. She wondered if he was from the HR department.

Rooney stared at her with a smile plastered to his face and then tilted his head of dreadlocks back at the mystery man. Maggie followed Rooney's gaze, confused. She cleared her throat. "So, what are we doing here?" she asked.

Rooney's smile fell into a mean line. Maggie intuitively knew she must've said something stupid. Her heartbeat picked up its pace.

"Let's get started," Rooney said, shaking his head. He slipped his headphones over his ears, tapped the microphone, and pressed the record button.

"Henry, it's great to have you here in Toronto to promote your new album, *Henry Cooper Jr. in Concert on Broadway*."

"It's great to be here, Rooney. Thanks for having

me."

Maggie's skin tingled with discomfort. She had been so focused on the idea that she was about to be fired that she hadn't realized she was sitting in the presence of a Hollywood star. She was surprised at how normal he looked. She never would have guessed that he was a Grammy winner or someone who had walked the red carpet at the Oscars. Now, she stared at him like a star-struck fan. Hiding beneath his baseball cap was his movie-star good looks, he had a healthy tan and an easy-going smile. She couldn't take her eyes off him. As the interview unfolded, Maggie noticed that besides his enormous musical talent, he had a natural charm thanks to his native New Orleans.

"I'm giving this album five out of five stars. That's my recommendation," said Rooney, wrapping up the interview.

"Thanks, man, I really appreciate it."

Rooney stopped recording and slipped his headphones around his neck. He stood up and shook hands with Henry.

"That was great. I'll edit it now, and it will air this afternoon. Maggie, could you please show Henry to the elevators?" Rooney didn't make eye contact with her. He was obviously pissed.

"Yes, of course," she stuttered.

Maggie kept her head down as she guided Henry Cooper Jr. down the narrow hallway. As if she hadn't been embarrassed enough, Rooney was making her walk him out. The silence was deafening. Maggie didn't know what to say. She was terrible at small talk.

"So, what are you up to tonight?" she asked casually, pressing the elevator button three times. It arrived seconds later.

Henry gave her a disgusted look. "I'm going

home to my wife and three daughters," he said as he stepped into the elevator.

It wasn't until the heavy metal doors were closing that Maggie realized he thought she was propositioning him. "Wait, that's not what I meant—"

But it was too late. The doors had closed shut. Henry Cooper Jr. was gone, and she had offended him. Maggie slammed the palm of her hand on her forehead. She took a few deep breaths before dragging her feet back to the studio. Luckily, the red light was on above the doorway. Rooney was recording. Maggie tiptoed past the studio and hurried back to her office. She had avoided the wrath of Rooney for the time being. Or so she'd thought. Moments later, Rooney stormed into her office.

"What did you say to him?" Rooney demanded. "I just received an email from his manager saying an inappropriate intern tried to seduce him!"

Maggie looked past Rooney and watched as Jenny slowly walked past the doorway, eavesdropping.

"I simply asked him what he was doing later."

"That's it?"

Maggie nodded. She had never been more mortified in her entire life. She liked to flirt occasionally, but this accusation was unfair. Henry Cooper Jr. sure thought a lot about himself.

"This isn't entirely my fault," said Maggie. "Why did you spring this on me? You never bring me in on your big interviews."

"I was trying to surprise you."

"I thought you were going to fire me."

Rooney threw his hands up in exasperation. "Fire you? I was trying to hand you one of the perks of working in radio. I didn't think you were going to act like a star-crazed groupie."

"I was trying to make small talk!" Maggie argued.

Rooney shook his head slowly. "I know, but I'm going to have to write you up, Maggie. Don't let this happen again."

Maggie blinked, bringing her back to the present moment in her office. She ejected her USB stick and dropped it into the cardboard box with the rest of her belongings. She did one final sweep of her office before grabbing her purse and flicking off the light.

When she reached the elevator, Maggie pressed the button three times.

Come on.

She looked over her shoulder, worried she'd bump into Andrew in the hallway. 880 News was located on the eighth floor of The Press Studios building on Bloor Street in downtown Toronto. The company's radio stations, cable television stations, and magazine publishing operations were all housed on campus. Maggie's father worked on the fourth floor. He was a producer for *Sports News Now!* The building complex was so large it occupied most of the block.

As the elevator doors opened, Maggie came face-to-face with Rooney. His espresso-brown eyes lit up when he saw her.

"Where are you off to on this beautiful day?" he asked in his deep and soulful voice.

"Ground floor, please." Maggie turned to face the elevator doors and breathed a sigh of relief when they closed. She stared into her box of belongings. "I quit today."

"Hold up. What do you mean you quit?" Rooney hit the stop button. He tucked a shoulder length dreadlock behind his ear and raised his eyebrows, waiting for a response.

"I can't do this anymore, Rooney. I'm not cut out for it."

"Bullshit. You're one of the most talented writers I've worked with. This isn't about what happened in the interview with Henry Cooper Jr. is it?"

Maggie rolled her eyes.

"Is this because I wrote you up?" Rooney asked. His face wore the same pained expression it had that day in her office.

Despite the fact she felt Rooney had been unfair that day, she had learned a lot from him. She didn't want him to think this was his fault.

"I'm not cut out for this job," she said. "Please take your hand off the button. I'm not supposed to be in the building."

Rooney dropped his hand, and the elevator resumed moving. "I think you're making a big mistake."

They rode the rest of the way to the ground floor in silence. When the doors opened, Maggie held her head high as she walked out.

"Hey, Maggie," Rooney called.

Maggie turned to him.

"If you ever need a reference, I'd be happy to help."

As the elevator doors closed shut, Maggie's eyes welled with tears. Her cellphone buzzed inside her purse. She balanced the cardboard box on her hip as she dug into her leather saddlebag in search of her phone.

"Hello?" she answered as she pushed the revolving doors forward and walked out of the building. The sunshine was blinding, but Maggie found the warmth of early summer comforting.

"Maggie?"

Maggie stopped in her tracks. "Hi, Mom." She rested her personal belongings on a planter box on the sidewalk that overflowed with shrubs and colorful flowers, part of the city's effort to beautify the gray downtown area.

"Your father told me you quit the internship. What were you thinking?"

Maggie bit her lip. She wasn't thinking. She hadn't planned on quitting. When her boss, Andrew, called her into his office this morning, she was excited. He had promised to review one of her story ideas, and she couldn't wait to show him. She had stayed up late the night before preparing the proposal.

"What are you going to do now?" her mother asked in a gentle tone.

"I want to come home." Maggie's voice cracked.

"Oh, honey. I'm caught between a rock and a hard place."

Maggie swallowed. Her father ruled the roost. She wished her mother would stand up to him just this once. "I told Dad I would get my old job back until I figured out what to do next."

"I wish you had talked to me first."

"There's nothing to talk about! The internship wasn't working out."

"Maggie, you're twenty-three years old. Your father made it clear. If you quit, you're on your own."

Acid rose in the back of Maggie's throat. The stress of long work hours and tight deadlines had left her suffering with bad heartburn for the past few months. She searched her purse for the Tums she'd become accustomed to taking. She opened the blue lid of the bottle and popped a couple of chalky pills into her mouth. The peppermint potion worked quickly, cooling her esophagus, and calming her upset stomach.

"Where am I supposed to go?" Maggie asked.

"Could you contact one of your connections from school? Perhaps another station is hiring."

Maggie ran her tongue against her teeth, thinking.

The radio business was a small one, and news about her quitting would have already spread through the industry like wildfire. No one would touch a junior reporter who quit halfway through an internship.

"Listen, honey, your father and I paid your rent until September. Why don't you go visit Grandma for a couple of weeks? She would be happy to see you and help you talk things through."

Maggie's shoulders relaxed at the mention of her grandmother.

"I'll think about it," she told her mother, but as she hung up the phone, Maggie had made up her mind. There was nothing more to think about. She needed to escape. She would leave the city, her co-workers, and even her boyfriend behind.

ALYSSA DELLE PALME

Chapter Two

"Bridget, are you home?" Maggie shuffled through the front door of their small two-bedroom apartment. Sweat dripped down her lower back. It was early June, but summer had officially arrived. Maggie kicked off her nude high heels and hung her robin's egg-colored trench coat in the tiny hall closet for the season. It was too warm for a spring coat. Maggie heard fiddle music and tapping coming from Bridget's bedroom. Maggie knocked gently at first and then harder. The door swung open, and Maggie came face-to-face with her perspiring roommate.

"Hi," Bridget said, trying to catch her breath. She took a sip from her stainless-steel water bottle. "What's up?"

Bridget was a small-town country girl who had come to the big city to study theatre at George Brown College. She was a talented step dancer who practiced every day for at least an hour. On weekends, she taught kids how to tap at the local community center. Overall, she was a good roommate, but Maggie and Bridget both worked so much they rarely saw each other. They had never managed to become close.

"I'm going to Ottawa to visit my grandmother for a few weeks," Maggie told Bridget.

Bridget tucked an auburn curl behind her ear. Her gray unitard was wet under her arms.

"Okay, have fun." She started to shut the door.

"Wait," said Maggie. "I'm going to leave a note for Brody on the kitchen table. Could you see that he gets it? He's supposed to stop by after his shift today."

"Sure, no problem." Bridget paused. "Is something wrong?"

Maggie shook her head.

"I've got to get back to practicing. I'm in the middle of learning choreography for a class I'm teaching this weekend."

"Right, sorry to interrupt."

As Maggie walked away, the fiddle music blared once again. Maggie's temples throbbed to the beat of Bridget's tap shoes pounding against the hardwood floor.

In her bedroom, Maggie turned on her fan and grabbed her large backpack that she'd used when she and Brody had traveled through Europe the previous summer. They'd had an amazing time exploring Switzerland, Italy, Germany, and France. She felt a sudden pang of guilt for not calling him. If she told him she had quit her internship, Brody would probably say encouraging things and push her to get back on the horse. But he could also react in anger. Lately, if she didn't do exactly what he wanted, he'd flip his lid. He would definitely try to convince her to stay, which was why Maggie couldn't tell him that she was leaving.

Maggie sat down in her oak swivel chair and grabbed a piece of stationery from her desk drawer. She nibbled on the end of her pen as she stared out her open window at the old, red-bricked house across the street. Their apartment was located in a friendly neighborhood, and their street was lined with renovated Victorian homes. After she had received her acceptance letter from Ryerson University's journalism program, Maggie and her mother spent an entire weekend apartment hunting.

"This one is perfect!" her mother had gushed. "It's a short walk away from the subway station, and you're so close to the cute shops and cafés on Young Street."

Maggie's parents had paid for both her apartment and university tuition. They weren't rich by any means, but her father made a good living as a producer, and Maggie was an only child. It wasn't a free ride, though. Throughout high school, Maggie was expected to work hard and earn good grades. Her parents had taken the checks she made from working at the restaurant and put them into a savings account for her. She'd been allotted twenty dollars a week in allowance.

The sheer white curtain in Maggie's window fluttered in the warm breeze. The air smelled of hot gravel and cut grass. Before she could change her mind, Maggie scribbled a vague note. Texting Brody would invite an instant response, and Maggie needed to express herself without being interrupted or manipulated into staying.

Brody,

I quit the internship, and I'm going to visit my grandmother. Please don't be mad. We'll talk when I get back.

Mags

Maggie tucked the stationery into its matching envelope and wrote Brody's name on the front before getting up and going to her closet. She scanned its contents, overwhelmed by the neatly organized rack of clothing, which was mostly made up of blazers and dress pants for work. When she was offered the internship, her mother had wanted to celebrate by taking her on a shopping spree for new workwear attire. It was a big step up from her usual jeans and t-shirt look that screamed university student. Considering the warm weather, Maggie sifted through the hangers of blouses, pencil skirts, and high-waist wide-leg pants until she found her casual summer dresses at the back of the closet. She stuffed her bag full of summer clothes and sandals. She grabbed her makeup bag and blow dryer from the vanity and chucked them into her rucksack. Maggie did a quick sweep of the room. Her bed was made, and her desk was tidy. She picked up the note for Brody and blinked back tears as she looked around her lavender-painted room.

When Maggie first got the keys to her apartment, her dad had spent an entire weekend painting her room the *Morning Orchid* color that Maggie had selected at the hardware store. Her father had beamed with pride when he learned Maggie had been accepted into Ryerson's journalism program, and he wanted her to feel at home in her first apartment. Now, her room was a painful reminder of lost hopes and dreams. Maggie took a deep breath to collect herself. When she was ready, she heaved the bulky bag on her back and flicked off the light switch.

The bus terminal smelled like urine and cigarette butts. Her mother would have been horrified Maggie was taking the bus instead of the train to visit her grandma, but Maggie was on a tight budget, and a bus ticket was all she could afford since the internship only paid minimum wage. When Maggie's stomach rumbled, she realized she hadn't eaten all day. Before boarding the bus, she pulled a ten-dollar bill from her wallet and purchased the lone cheese sandwich from the seedy convenience counter. She showed the bus driver her ticket and handed him her heavy backpack, which he tossed into a compartment under the bus. Maggie found her window seat on the motorcoach. Once she was situated, she dug into her day-old sandwich. The bread was stale, and the cheese had a plastic consistency.

"Excuse me."

When Maggie looked up from her meal, she saw a large man, sweating profusely, standing next to the aisle seat. She quickly realized her purse was on his seat.

"I'm sorry," she said, covering her full mouth with one hand. She moved her purse out of his way.

The man squeezed into the narrow chair. He

smelled like onion rings. Maggie sighed. She had lost her appetite. She wrapped up the rest of her disgusting sandwich and tossed it in the brown paper garbage bag that hung on the seat in front of her. The man placed his briefcase on his knees, opened it up, and grabbed a few tissues to wipe his dripping forehead.

"It's so hot," he mumbled.

Maggie nodded. She leaned her warm forehead against the large, cool window and closed her eyes. Thoughts of her final meeting with her boss came flooding back.

"You can't quit," Andrew had said as he roughly massaged the back of Maggie's neck with his fat thumbs. "You're our best intern."

The passenger bus lurched forward, and Maggie's eyes snapped open. For a split second, she imagined a scenario where she had called Human Resources and told them what had happened, but Maggie quickly scolded herself for envisioning such things. Even if she had stepped forward, it would've been her word against his, and no one would've believed her after the fiasco with Henry Cooper Jr. Maggie didn't care that she was sandwiched next to onion-ring guy for the next five hours. She was relieved to be leaving the city behind.

When Maggie arrived in Ottawa, she grabbed a cab from the line of taxis that were eagerly waiting outside the arrival terminal.

"Where are ye going?" a small, freckled man wearing a Blue Jays cap asked in a Scottish accent. His thick auburn hair stuck out the back of his hat.

Maggie gave him the address to the state-of-the-art rehabilitation center where her grandmother was currently living. Grandma had had hip replacement surgery two months prior and was staying in a luxury accommodation suite for her recovery.

When Maggie arrived, she signed the visitor book, bought a bouquet of flowers from the small gift shop in the lobby, and made her way to the third floor. Her grandmother's name, Rose, was written on the door. Maggie knocked gently before walking in.

"Grandma?"

Maggie found her grandmother lying on top of her made bed, watching her favorite soap opera, *The Young and the Restless*. Even in a rehabilitation hospital, she was dressed immaculately in a beige linen skirt and a cream-colored cashmere sweater.

"Claire poisoned Victor's water," Grandma said, pointing the remote at the television and turning the volume down. "Jordan is Eve's sister!" Grandma spoke about the characters in the show as if they were acquaintances in real life. "Are those for me?"

Maggie nodded and handed her grandmother the bouquet of yellow tulips. "You look well, Grandma."

Grandma closed her eyes and inhaled the grassy scent of the tulips. "Lovely. I'm getting stronger every day. My physiotherapist says I will be out of here in no time. These are beautiful, Maggie. Thank you. Come sit, dear."

Grandma patted the open space beside her on the bed. Maggie dropped her heavy backpack on an empty chair, kicked off her high heels, and joined her in the bed. It felt like old times when Maggie would stay the night at her grandmother's house. She would climb into Grandma's bed, and they would stay up late watching a movie, like *Bridget Jones' Diary* or *My Best Friend's Wedding,* with a bowl of plain potato chips and snack-size boxes of chocolate Smarties. Grandma took Maggie's smooth hand into her wrinkled, arthritic one. "It's so good to see you, dear. Your mother told me you might be visiting."

In the comfort of her grandmother's loving presence, Maggie finally let her guard down. Hot, salty tears rolled down her flushed cheeks. "I've disappointed them."

Grandma reached for the tissues on her bedside table and passed the box to Maggie. "Forget about them. I'm sure you left for good reasons."

Maggie blew her nose and nodded.

"You're smart and talented and beautiful, Maggie. Don't worry. God will take care of you."

Maggie hiccupped between sobs. Her grandmother was a devout Catholic who prayed before every meal. Maggie had been baptized as a baby, but that was as far as she got on the list of the seven sacraments. "Dad won't let me go home. I have nowhere to go."

"That's absurd." Grandma shook her head. "My daughter married a stubborn man, just like her father." Grandma paused for a moment and then reached into her bedside table drawer and grabbed a set of keys. She dangled them in front of Maggie. "Take my car and go stay at the cottage for the summer."

"What? I can't do that. I—"

"Yes, you can. You need a break and some time to think things through."

"Won't you need your car?"

"Where am I going to go?" Grandma laid her head back down on the pile of white featherdown pillows. "I still have a few weeks of rehab before I transition back into my home. If I need you, I will call you."

Maggie shook her head. "It's too generous, Grandma."

"It's my car and my cottage, and I can do with it what I want. Your father can be too stern. All you need is a break, a little time to take stock of your life. You're young, sweetheart. Young people need time to think."

Maggie swallowed. Just the thought of spending her summer by the lake relaxed her tense shoulders. She bit her lip, still hesitant to accept the offer. She was afraid if she said yes, she would be taking advantage of her grandma's kindheartedness.

"Maggie, you would really be doing me a favor. The cottage is in desperate need of a deep clean and could use some sprucing up."

Maggie's face broke into a smile. "I could do that for you!" She would do anything to help her grandma. "Thank you, thank you, thank you!"

"If you need anything at all, an older gentleman has moved into the cottage next door. Mr. McLeod is his name."

Maggie cuddled next to her grandmother and breathed a sigh of relief. Grandma gently patted Maggie's arm and pointed the remote at the television, turning up the volume on her beloved soap opera. As Maggie rested her tired eyes, she could feel the warmth of the sunshine reflecting off the lake and smell the sweet scent of the cedar trees. The more she thought about it, the more she agreed with her grandmother—a summer at the cottage was just what she needed to get her life back on track.

Chapter Three

Maggie awoke when the credits began to roll across the television screen. Her grandmother was snoring softly beside her. Maggie wanted to visit a little while longer, but she didn't want to disturb her grandmother, and she didn't want to drive in the dark. She quietly slipped out of bed, put on her high heels and heavy backpack, and kissed her grandmother's papery cheek goodbye.

The drab cement buildings gave way to flat cornfields and lush green countryside as Maggie drove southwest toward the cottage, which was an hour outside of Ottawa. Her grandmother's dark-blue Buick was twelve years old, but only had a mileage of seventy-thousand kilometers. Maggie rolled the windows down, turned the radio up, and leaned back against the headrest. She didn't know if it was the fresh air or what, but for the first time in months, she felt like she could finally breathe. She was as free as the red-tailed hawk that soared above the farmer's field to her left. Maggie smiled. She hadn't been to the cottage in years, but she remembered how to get there. She had spent her childhood summers at her grandmother's cottage— swimming in the lake, playing in the forest, and paddling around in an old rusty-red canoe. The directions were mapped out on her heart.

As she skirted along the country roads, Maggie's thoughts drifted to Brody. They had met on a pub crawl. Maggie was fresh out of a short-lived relationship with a guy from her journalism program that ended with him cheating on her. She wasn't shattered by his betrayal, but she was disappointed and in no rush to let anyone else in. She carried a fierce resolve to stay single and put herself first. Brody had been standing at the packed bar for a while, impatiently waiting for the bartender's attention. When Maggie appeared next to Brody, the bartender was suddenly available to take drink orders.

"What can I get for you?" the dark-haired bartender asked Maggie.

"Two vodka cranberries with extra lime," Maggie yelled over the music. Maggie looked over at Brody. She was instantly attracted to his kind eyes and the handsome cleft in his chin.

"I'm sorry," she said. "I think I might've budded you in line."

"It's-s-s okay," he stuttered.

Maggie stared into his amber-colored eyes that were as sweet and rich as pure maple syrup. "What are you drinking?" she asked, breaking the spell.

Brody cleared his throat. "I'm getting a pitcher of Stella for my buddies." He pointed to three fit guys seated at a table for four.

"Two vodka cranberries with extra lime," the bartender said, placing Maggie's drinks in front of her. He flashed her a sexy grin.

Ignoring his attention, Maggie slapped her remaining drink tickets down on the bar. "Thanks! I'll also take a pitcher of Stella for my friend here."

The bartender's smile faded. He grabbed a pitcher from beneath the bar, tilted it at a 45-degree angle, and turned on the beer tap. Brody leaned closer to Maggie. "Your friend's name is Brody," he said, extending his hand.

"Maggie." Perhaps it was the cocktails, but she had a sudden urge to do more than shake his hand.

"Thanks for the beer. I've been waiting here forever."

Maggie smiled and tossed her long wavy brown hair over her bare shoulder. "It's the least I could do."

She took a sip of her pink drink. "So, Brody, what is it that you do for a living?"

Brody smiled meekly. "I'm a rookie police officer. I've been trained to remain calm under pressure, but there's something about you that makes me nervous."

Maggie liked his honesty.

"Would you like to join me and my friends? I can grab an extra chair," he offered.

Maggie shook her head. "I have to get back to my roommate. It was nice meeting you, Brody."

Maggie's thoughts returned to the present as she took a right at an old-fashioned gas station with vintage pumps. She pressed her lips together, realizing that the first time she met Brody was the only time in their relationship she had ever ordered for them. Brody believed ordering for your date at a restaurant was a chivalrous gesture. In the beginning of their relationship, Maggie thought his old-school ways were romantic, but thinking back on it now, it felt more like a sexist faux pas.

Brody hadn't asked her out that night at the bar, but he found the courage a few weeks later when they bumped into each other again at Vintage Video, a retro movie rental store. Maggie grew up watching classic movies with her parents. Her dad was passionate about his DVD collection, and he proudly displayed it on a tall bookshelf in their basement. When Maggie went away to university, her dad gifted her his portable DVD player and some of his favorite cult classics from his collection. Any time Maggie missed home, she'd put a bag of popcorn in the microwave and watch a DVD. Bridget made fun of her for it, but it worked like a charm to cure homesickness.

As Maggie waited in line at Vintage Video on a quiet Friday night, she felt a tap on her shoulder.

"Excuse me, miss, I need to check your purse for

shoplifting."

Maggie's eyes widened, but when she turned, she was greeted with Brody's big smile and laughing eyes.

"Brody, hi!" She was surprised, not only to see him in such an unlikely place, but to see him in his uniform. He looked good, and it gave him an air of authority.

Brody ran a hand through his perfectly groomed hair. "You remembered my name."

"I'm good with names," she replied. "You're into retro rentals, too?"

Brody's face split into a wide smile. "Yeah, I am. It looks like we have something in common. I refuse to subscribe to Netflix. Streaming is killing classic film! What are you renting?"

Maggie felt slightly embarrassed as she revealed the cover of the DVD she was holding.

"Ah, *Titanic*. So, you have a thing for older men who only date models."

Maggie giggled. "No! Young Leonardo DiCaprio is hot! What are you renting?"

Brody flashed her the cover of *The Wedding Singer*.

"Ah, so you have a thing for Drew Barrymore."

"Adam Sandler, actually. His old stuff is hilarious." Brody rocked backward on his heels. "I just got off a double shift, and I need to watch something funny to help me wind down."

Maggie paid for her rental and candy and collected her change. "Well, it was nice to see you again, Brody."

As she turned and walked out the front door, Brody left his place in line and jogged after her, setting off the alarm bells with the DVD he hadn't yet paid for. "Maggie, wait!"

She stopped. Everyone in Vintage Video was looking at them. "What are you doing? You're going to get into trouble!"

Brody looked down at his uniform. He held up his hands and shrugged his shoulders. "I am the law."

Maggie rolled her eyes and bit back a smile. "You're making a scene."

"Go out with me."

Maggie paused. Brody was good-looking and funny, and he had a respectable job, but Maggie was hesitant to start anything. She was in her last year of school and wanted to focus on her budding career.

"I don't know, Brody. We barely know each other."

Brody dropped to his knees, pretending to beg. "You'll make me the happiest man alive if you'll let me take you to dinner. Please!"

"Fine," Maggie whispered hastily, "but only if you get up right this instant."

A whole year had passed, and they were still together. To celebrate their one-year anniversary, Brody had rented out the private screening room at the back of Vintage Video to celebrate. Classic movie posters were plastered on the walls, and they had sat side by side in bean bag chairs munching on all-you-can-eat popcorn as they watched the 1939 version of *The Wizard of Oz*. Brody was known for his grandiose romantic gestures, which caused Maggie's friends to swoon with jealousy, but Brody's devotion had always made her a little uncomfortable.

Maggie adjusted the seat belt that suddenly felt like it was trying to strangle her. She turned left at a small log house that was the storefront for a traditional woodfired bakery. The smell of fresh wood oven pizza filled the car as Maggie drove past. Soon, the straight gravel road turned into a winding dirt road. She beeped her horn as she turned a sharp corner. It was tradition to honk at the tight turns to warn other cottage dwellers that you were also on the road.

Maggie's heart sank when her grandmother's cottage finally came into view. The Scandinavian-style cabin, which was once well cared for and loved, looked dilapidated. No one had visited the cottage since her Uncle Johnny's death. Everyone was still grieving his loss, and it had felt wrong to visit his favorite place without him there.

Maggie carefully maneuvered her grandmother's Buick into the driveway that had become overgrown with tall grass and fallen branches. The sun was setting behind the tree line, casting a soft, warm light across the lake. A young, gorgeous guy at the property next door caught Maggie's eye. She slammed on the brakes to get a better look at him. She peered through the sparse tree line that divided their properties. He was wearing jeans streaked with dirt, and sweat dripped down his broad, tanned back as he swung an axe through a piece of wood on a chopping block. He made it look easy, like a hot knife through butter. Grandma had mentioned the neighbor, but Maggie was expecting an old man. This guy looked a bit older than her but was definitely in his twenties. The neighbor turned and squinted his eyes in Maggie's direction. Embarrassed that she had been caught staring, Maggie offered him half a smile and a shy wave. The neighbor gave her a polite nod of his head and went back to chopping wood. Determined to make a good first impression, she got out of the car to properly introduce herself.

"Hi there!" she called. "My name is Maggie. I'll be staying at my grandmother's cottage for the summer."

The neighbor offered a courteous smile before

adding another log to the chopping block. Maggie shuddered uncontrollably. This guy was clearly busy, and she was interrupting him at work. She popped the trunk and hoisted her heavy backpack onto her shoulders. She walked toward the front door of the cottage on an uneven natural path that was surrounded by trees. Maggie watched her neighbor in her peripheral vision. He was tall, six feet at least, with a full head of dark, messy curls. Suddenly, Maggie was flying through the air, having tripped on a root. She landed smack on her stomach. She was sprawled on the forest floor, stuck beneath the weight of her backpack. It was only a matter of seconds before the neighbor was kneeling beside her.

"Hey, are you okay?" he asked. Concern filled his olive-green eyes.

Mortified, Maggie nodded. The neighbor helped her to her feet.

"You might want to get yourself a proper pair of hiking shoes," he said, looking down at her nude high heels.

"I came straight from work," she said, straightening her black pencil skirt. Her outfit looked ridiculous. She tried to brush the sticky orange pine needles off her knees unsuccessfully.

"City girl," he mumbled under his breath. The brilliance of his green eyes twinkled with amusement.

Maggie raised a perfectly manicured eyebrow. "Do you have a name?" she asked.

"Thomas." He held out his calloused hand. His fingernails were stuffed with dirt, but Maggie found his ruggedness attractive.

When Maggie took his hand in hers, a warmth spread up her arm and lit her cheeks ablaze.

"It's nice to meet you, Maggie." Thomas paused suddenly. He slowly brought his hand to her head and tucked a piece of her hair behind her ear. Maggie's body stiffened, but her heart danced in her chest. She held her breath as he leaned in closer.

"Gross," Thomas muttered.

Maggie covered her mouth with her hand, smelling her breath. "What?"

"You have a tick on your neck."

Maggie's hand flew to the side of her neck. "What?"

"A tick. They live in tall grass."

Maggie rolled her eyes. "I know what a tick is! Get it off of me!"

"Do you have a pair of tweezers?"

Maggie unzipped the top of her backpack and pulled out her makeup bag. She dug through her lipsticks and lotions until she found a pair of silver pincers.

"I don't want to get Lyme disease!" she cried, handing Thomas the tweezers.

"You won't. It just attached." Thomas grasped the tick as close to her skin's surface as possible. He pulled upward with steady, even pressure. "Got it!"

Maggie let out a huge breath, resisting the urge to smack the pleased grin off of Thomas's face. "Thanks," she mumbled, rubbing the side of her neck. She felt itchy all over.

"No problem. Make sure you clean the bite area."

Maggie nodded. She packed up her belongings and walked to the front door of her cottage.

"Also, you should cut the grass on your driveway to prevent getting another tick."

Maggie turned to face Thomas. "Okay."

"Do you know how to use a lawn mower?" Thomas looked down at her high heels again.

His arrogance made her wild. Maggie bit her tongue and held her head high. She turned back toward the door. "Of course, I do." Maggie fumbled with her grandmother's keys as she struggled to unlock the cottage door.

"Here, let me get that for you," Thomas offered.

"I got it." Maggie was desperate to get inside before she embarrassed herself any further.

Thomas nodded. "I'll see you around then." He slowly turned on his heel and hiked back through the sparse trees toward his own cottage.

"It was nice to meet you!" she called after him. Thomas didn't turn around but waved his hand halfheartedly behind his head.

Inside, Maggie dropped her heavy backpack on the dusty pine floor. She paused, wondering if Thomas had waved goodbye or if he had been swatting mosquitoes away. She decided she didn't care either way. She found his cockiness unappealing. Maggie slowly walked through the small three-bedroom cottage, opening every window to let the fresh air in. Wispy cobwebs hung from every corner. It was only a three-season cottage because it wasn't insulated, making it unsuitable for Canadian winters. The floors needed to be washed, but the essence of the cottage would be restored after a deep cleaning.

Her grandparents had built the cottage in the early 1980s. Maggie's grandfather was of Swedish descent and designed the cabin to have an overall sense of minimalism. The cottage was small, but the large windows on the exterior walls brought in the natural light and made it feel spacious inside. Built with locally sourced cedar, the cottage blended seamlessly into the surrounding trees, which made Maggie feel like she was immersed in nature. Inside, the cottage had white shiplap paneling throughout the interior walls, giving the cottage a clean-lined and cozy touch. A black, freestanding woodstove stood in the living area beside the oatmeal-colored couch. One large photo hung on the wall. It was an old black and white photograph of her mother's family sitting on the dock. Her grandmother and grandfather were the bookends to their three children—Maggie's mother, Elizabeth, her late uncle, Johnny, and her aunt, Katie. Maggie loved that photo, the vintage swimsuits, the happy smiles. Her grandmother looked like a pinup model in her high waisted retro bikini. Her grandfather, who died of a heart attack before Maggie was born, stared intensely into the camera. He had been a serious man.

"Your grandfather had the most beautiful deep blue eyes," her grandmother had once told her. "The color of the Pacific Ocean."

Maggie's grandparents had met at a summer fair.

"My best friend, Ruth, and I were in line to ride the Ferris Wheel when your grandfather approached us and asked me out on a date."

"What did you say, Grandma?"

"I said 'yes' of course. He was the most handsome man I'd ever seen. We married five months later on Christmas Eve. It was just your grandfather and I, the priest, and the town whore as our witness."

Maggie smiled, looking at the old photograph now. Her grandfather was incredibly handsome with his clean-shaven jawline and full lips. In the photograph, Maggie's mother, the eldest sibling, sat laughing beside Johnny, whose hands were up in a flamboyant jazz-hand pose. Little Katie sat snuggled next to her father. Her eyes looked sad.

"Katie was a sensitive child," her grandmother had told her. "Every few weeks, she liked to crawl into my lap and have a good cry."

"What was she so sad about?" Maggie asked.

Her grandmother shrugged. "She just wanted attention and comfort."

"Your grandma and grandpa spoiled her because she was the baby of the family," her mother had told her. "Katie had nothing to be sad about. She was born a drama queen."

Katie had always been kind to Maggie. When Maggie was a child, the cottage had a revolving door of visitors every summer. Katie and her husband, Uncle Stuart, had twin boys six years younger than Maggie. When the whole extended family visited for a week, people had to sleep on air mattresses, the couch, or in a tent that was set up outside because the cottage was too small to hold them all. Maggie didn't mind. She'd spend the week playing in the forest with her younger twin cousins, Matthew and Joshua. Katie often offered to French braid Maggie's hair or take her into town to buy a new summer dress. Maggie basked in the special attention her aunt gave her.

"Did you ever want a daughter?" Maggie asked one summer evening after Katie had taken her to get her ears pierced.

Katie's eyes instantly brimmed with tears. "I'm so blessed to have my boys and a niece like you."

Maggie's mom said Katie was a drama queen, but in Maggie's opinion, her aunt just had a sentimental heart.

Maggie was weary from her travels. She laid down on the comfy couch that enveloped her in a welcoming hug. She wanted to rest her eyes, just for a moment, before unpacking. A soft wind carrying scents of summer came through the open windows, triggering memories from her childhood. The complex smell of lake water and long marsh grasses brought her back to the summers she'd spent jumping off the floating raft and snorkeling around the bay in search of sunken treasure. For once, there was no city overture of blaring fire trucks or car honks, only soothing sounds of crickets chirping and the sing-song whistles of whippoorwills.

The next morning, Maggie woke with a grumbling stomach. Despite having accidentally fallen asleep on the couch fully dressed, she felt rested for the first time in a long while. She went to the kitchen and opened the fridge. The cool air soothed her warm cheeks, but the empty shelves did nothing for her hunger pains. She'd have to go into town for groceries and cleaning supplies, but first, she needed to get a job. She closed the fridge door and went to the washroom to freshen up. Maggie washed her face, reapplied her mascara and lip gloss, and ran a wide toothed comb through her wavy hair. She examined her neck for any signs of a bullseye rash and applied a dab of clear antibiotic ointment to the spot where the tick had bitten her. Maggie straightened out her pencil skirt and smelled the armpits of her champagne-colored work blouse. She shrugged her shoulders and grabbed her Dove stick from her makeup bag. It was nothing a fresh coat of deodorant couldn't fix. On her way into town for groceries, she planned to stop at the resort on the lake to apply for a job.

Waldhaus, which translated to House in the Forest, was the resort located at the opposite end of Cedar Lake. It was a short 15-minute commute from Maggie's cottage. As she drove into the gravel parking lot, she stared at the large, historic log cabin in awe, despite having seen it many times before. It was magnificent. Waldhaus opened its doors in the 1930s and contained over 100 rustic-style guest rooms and suites. Maggie had only visited the resort once when Johnny had taken her to the Terrace Restaurant to celebrate her champagne birthday.

"Fifteen on August Fifteenth! I'm taking you out!" Johnny had declared.

They'd gotten dolled up in their summer best and drove to the resort in Johnny's classic tractor-green MG convertible. Their table overlooked the lake, and Maggie had felt all grown up as the waiter placed a crisp linen napkin in her lap. Johnny ordered non-alcoholic sparkling cider, which they drank out of crystal champagne flutes. They ate the most delicious seafood linguini for supper and shared a decadent piece of chocolate cake for dessert. After dinner, Johnny surprised her with two tickets to Musical Theater Under the Stars. Every summer, throughout July and August, the local theater company presented a musical at the outdoor amphitheater in town. It was tradition for them to go together.

"Grease! I love that musical!" said Maggie.

"It's the best. I thought it might be a good choice for my next show."

Johnny worked as a flight attendant and traveled around the world, but he was also the director of a non-profit musical theater company in Ottawa.

"There's one more surprise," he said, handing Maggie a Tiffany-blue box. Inside Maggie had found the most beautiful birthstone pendant necklace.

Now, standing in front of the hotel, Maggie smiled, remembering that special champagne birthday. She fiddled with the peridot stone on the white-gold chain around her neck. Maggie never took the necklace off. It was her most treasured possession. She rubbed the stone for good luck and walked through the front doors.

"Hi," Maggie said to the receptionist, "I was wondering if the restaurant was hiring for the summer?"

The receptionist offered Maggie a polite smile and handed her an application form. "Fill this out."

Maggie took the clipboard and sat in a

comfortable leather chair next to the six-sided fireplace. When she was finished, the receptionist instructed her to bring her application to the dining room.

"One of our servers broke her leg in a water-skiing accident over the weekend," the receptionist whispered. "You have experience, and I know the manager, Sadie, is looking to hire someone as soon as possible."

As Maggie approached the hostess stand outside the restaurant, her hands began to sweat. She needed this job. She felt a tickle on her neck and worried she had another tick. The woman standing at the front looked like a blonde Gisele Bündchen. She was tall and slender and wore a professional black blazer with a name tag that read *Sadie*.

Sadie looked Maggie up and down, "Do you have a reservation?"

"I'm here to apply for the server position." Maggie handed Sadie her application and stared at her feet as Sadie examined the page.

"You don't have your Smart Serve certification," she said, handing the application back to Maggie.

"I could get it."

Sadie raised a beautifully defined eyebrow. "This is a five-star dining room. One year of experience in a high-service food and beverage environment is required."

Maggie rubbed the back of her neck. "The Corner Café wasn't located in an iconic resort, but if you contact any of the references listed on my application, you will see I provided exceptional service to our guests."

Sadie opened her mouth to respond but was interrupted by a nervous server.

"Excuse me, Sadie?" The young woman with a mousy blonde ponytail wrung her hands together as she waited for Sadie to acknowledge her.

"What is it?" Sadie asked through clenched teeth.

"Um, Lindsay won't be able to make it into work today."

"Why not?" Sadie hissed.

"She, um, went into labor."

"She wasn't due for another two weeks!"

The server shrugged her shoulders. "The baby had other plans, I suppose."

Sadie sighed and pinched the bridge of her nose. She turned back to Maggie. "When can you start?"

ALYSSA DELLE PALME

Chapter Four

"I got the job!" Maggie told her best friend over the phone the next morning.

"That's great news," June said with a hint of hesitancy in her voice.

"But..." Maggie waited.

"I'm worried about you, Maggie. I think I should come out there. I have vacation time coming up soon."

June had a role in the chorus of an off-Broadway production tour of *West Side Story*. The musical was concluding its run with three sold out shows at the Ed Mirvish Theater in Toronto. Maggie and June had met on the stage when they were preteens performing in Johnny's musical theater company's production of *Anne of Green Gables*. June had delivered a standout performance in the lead role of Anne, while Maggie had played the part of her best friend, Diana Berry. They held hands and cried when the red curtain closed for the last time. They swore they would remain kindred spirits forever and move away to New York City after high school to make it big on Broadway. Even though Maggie's passions had shifted, she was happy that June had pursued their childhood dream.

"I would love for you to visit, June, but seriously, I'm fine."

"You left an amazing opportunity that you've worked so hard for, and now you're living alone in the middle of nowhere."

"I'm not alone. I have a neighbor, who happens to be the most beautiful man I've ever seen, by the way," she said, lowering her voice as if Thomas could somehow hear her. Their cottages were close, but not that close.

"What about Brody?"

43

Maggie pressed her lips together. June, like everyone else, adored Brody. Maggie didn't know how to explain her feelings. They didn't even make sense to her. "I would never cheat on Brody."

"I know you wouldn't. I just don't want you to blow it with a great guy. Brody respects you."

Maggie would never do anything to intentionally hurt Brody, but lately, their relationship had struggled. When they first started dating, Maggie enjoyed the way he pursued her, but now all those sweet moments felt borderline controlling. "I needed a break," Maggie said. "Brody always wants to spend so much time with me, and he wants to know everything about me. He calls constantly to make sure I make it to and from work safely."

"And that's a bad thing?" June asked.

Maggie sighed. "I don't know. I find myself apologizing to him a lot, and most of the time, I'm not entirely sure what I did wrong. I even find myself hiding things from him. Innocent things! Like a few weeks ago, I ran into a friend after work, and we went to an impromptu happy hour. When I got home, I told Brody I had to work late because I wasn't sure how he'd respond."

"Maggie, the guy cooks you elaborate pancake breakfasts on Sunday mornings!"

Maggie bit her tongue. June didn't know the reason Brody cooked her breakfast was because he criticized the way she'd made pancakes. Maggie glanced at the framed black and white photograph hanging on the cottage wall. "Did you know my grandparents had so much passion in their relationship they got married straight away?" Maggie and Brody had been together for a year, but lately she was never compelled to make out with him.

"That's really sweet, but—"

"Shit!" Maggie interrupted, looking at the digital clock on the kitchen stove. "I lost track of the time. I'm going to be late for my first shift. I have to let you go."

"Just promise me you're going to call Brody."

Maggie closed her eyes and took a calming breath. "Yes, I will. I just need time to clear my head."

Maggie rushed out the cottage door, tip-toed through the long grass as fast as she could and hopped into her grandmother's car. When she turned the key in the ignition, the car wouldn't start.

Damn it!

She peered over at Thomas's cottage. Digging her nails into the steering wheel, she hung her head. Thomas was the last person she wanted to ask for help, but she didn't have a choice. She couldn't risk losing her job. When Thomas answered the door, he seemed surprised to see her. He looked effortlessly handsome in a pair of relaxed, straight jeans and a slate-colored, ribbed collared t-shirt. It was the second time Maggie noticed his eyes. Somehow, they seemed greener than the last time she saw him. Maggie's stomach flipped.

"Um, Thomas. Hi." Maggie's palms began to sweat. "My car won't start, and I'm going to be late for my first shift at Waldhaus. I think it's the battery."

Thomas nodded. "I'll bring my truck around and give you a boost."

"Thank you so much! I really appreciate it."

Maggie hurried back to her car and popped the hood while Thomas maneuvered his 1965 Ford F-100 truck into the driveway and parked beside her. Maggie rolled down her window while Thomas retrieved his jumper cables.

"My Uncle Johnny had a thing for classic cars. He would've loved your truck," Maggie called out as

Thomas attached the red and black clips to the appropriate places.

"It's my dad's truck." Thomas reached through his window and turned on the ignition. He let it run for a couple of minutes.

"He's probably going to be mad when he sees how you've been taking care of it," said Maggie, observing the mess of wood debris in the back of his truck. Thomas's tools were thrown about carelessly.

Thomas's jaw tensed visibly, betraying his deep frustration. "My dad is dead. Start your car."

Maggie cringed as she turned the key in the ignition. Nothing. "I'm so sorry, Thomas... I didn't mean—"

"It's fine. You didn't know." Thomas adjusted the clips. "Try it again."

Maggie did as she was told. Nothing.

Thomas went back under the hood of her car. Maggie squeezed her thighs together. She was extremely attracted to the fact that he seemed to know exactly what he was doing under there. When Brody had car trouble, he had to take it to a mechanic.

"I think we just need to give it a minute," he said after walking around to her window.

"How did your dad die?" she asked. As soon as the words left her lips, Maggie brought a hand to her mouth. "I'm sorry, you don't have to answer that." Maggie gave her head a shake. "I'm a journalist and naturally curious. I can overstep sometimes."

Thomas shrugged off her blunt question. "You know, you're the first person to ask me about my dad in a while. He died just over a year ago. Stomach cancer. It actually feels kind of nice to talk to somebody about him, off the record, of course." Thomas winked at Maggie.

Her cheeks caught fire. "I lost my uncle to liver

cancer five years ago," she shared. "Johnny and I were incredibly close."

"I'm sorry to hear that." Thomas put his hands in his pockets and kicked the dirt. "Cancer is a horrible disease. When the doctors told my dad he had six months to live, he bought this cottage and lived out his last good days here."

"Did you move here to be with him?"

Thomas nodded. "I wish I had come sooner. At the time, I was busting my ass, working eighty hours a week for a large wealth management company in Toronto. I was a workaholic who thought the place would fall apart without me. I was so caught up in the rat race in the city that I missed a few good months with my dad." Thomas swallowed and stared off into the forest. "I will always regret that."

"Do you live here now?"

"Yeah. After my dad died, I sold my condo. It's peaceful here."

"What about your job?"

"I'm a contractor now. It doesn't pay like my old job, but I'm happy here. I build decks and renovate cottages in the area." Thomas bent down and leaned his elbows against Maggie's open window. "I'm good with my hands."

Maggie's mouth gaped slightly as she locked eyes with his. He held her gaze as he slowly reached inside her car and turned the key in the ignition. Maggie's car started with a moan. It was music to her ears.

"Thank you!" Maggie wrapped her arms around his neck and gave him a squeeze. The digital clock in the car flashed, catching Maggie's eye. If she left now, she could still make it to work on time. She let go of Thomas's neck.

He slowly backed out of her window and ran a

hand through his loose, messy curls. "You're welcome."

"My shift ends at 7:00 tonight. Would you like to come over for a drink later? I have a bottle of champagne in the fridge, and no one to share it with."

"What are we celebrating?"

"New beginnings!"

Thomas paused and stared into her eyes. Maggie swallowed, hoping he would say yes. She needed a friend.

"All right," he answered. "I'll see you then."

Maggie rolled up her window, watching Thomas as he got back into his truck. She waved meekly when he caught her staring. She put her car in reverse and sped out of the driveway and onto the dirt road.

As she drove to work, Maggie's thoughts traveled to Brody. She took a deep, pained breath. A pang of homesickness engulfed her, and she fought the sudden urge to call him. Maggie still didn't know what she was going to say, and she didn't have the energy to listen to another one of his long-winded speeches about how she disappointed him yet again. Besides, she wasn't doing anything wrong by having drinks with a new friend after work.

When she arrived at the resort, Maggie was pleased with herself because she was right on time.

"You're late," Sadie said in a flat tone.

"But it's 1:00. I—"

"You must arrive ten minutes before your shift starts."

Maggie nodded eagerly. She'd have to work extra hard in order to prove to Sadie that she hadn't made a mistake in hiring her. For the next couple of hours, Sadie went over the standards of service and operational procedures that Maggie had to adhere to. She taught Maggie how to set up and maintain cleanliness of the buffet area, which involved a lot of walking and lifting. Maggie's feet ached in her Mary Jane flats as she tried to keep up with Sadie's quick pace.

"You must ensure guest satisfaction and anticipate their needs," Sadie said.

Maggie worried she wouldn't live up to Sadie's perfectionism as she pulled at the scratchy green vest she had been forced to wear as part of the uniform. It reminded her of an ugly pair of curtains. She felt like one of the Von Trapp children from *The Sound of Music* dressed in Maria's bedroom drapes.

"Stop fidgeting with your uniform," Sadie snapped. "Follow me. I'll introduce you to the kitchen staff."

Maggie did as she was told and marched through the double door that swung both ways. When her Mary Janes hit the grease on the square kitchen tiles, she slipped and grabbed onto the nearest arm to prevent herself from falling.

"Get the fuck out of my way!" said a sturdy man in a white apron. His face was as red as the beets being chopped on the assembly line.

Maggie caught her balance and let go of his arm. Everyone in the kitchen stared. Maggie looked down at her feet. "I'm so sorry," she stammered.

Sadie wrapped her arm around Maggie's shoulders and gave her a squeeze. "That's the head chef," she whispered. "Don't take it personally. He's an arrogant prick to everyone."

Maggie smiled appreciatively at Sadie. Maybe she wasn't so bad after all.

"Everyone, this is Maggie, our new server. She will be filling in as the hostess until she is trained and ready to be on the floor."

"Tell her to get some better fucking shoes," the

chef muttered.

Sadie guided Maggie to the dishwashing station. "I have to make a quick phone call, but I'll be back in five minutes. I'd like you to observe how the cleaning duties work in the kitchen."

The minute Sadie left, Maggie found an empty chair against the kitchen wall and sank her aching body into its welcoming arms. She had forgotten how taxing the restaurant industry was on the body. The backs of her heels pulsed like a heartbeat. She had a blister the size of a quarter on each heel.

"What are you doing?" Sadie asked crossly when she returned.

Maggie showed Sadie the fluid-filled sacs on her heels.

A look of sympathy crossed Sadie's face. She grabbed the first aid kit off the wall and handed Maggie a couple of Band-Aids. "You really do need to get a pair of better shoes."

Maggie nodded. She placed the nude bandages over the blisters. Her feet were still killing her, but the Band-Aids helped reduce the pain enough that she was able to continue the rest of her shift.

Sadie trained Maggie on how to manage the flow of the lounge and buffet area. She also taught her how to deliver room service coffee orders in the mornings. The training session wrapped up with an explanation of more cleaning duties.

"If the restaurant is quiet, you are to come back here and polish the silverware and glassware. It's important to ensure there are no watermarks." Sadie demonstrated by polishing a red wine glass with a rag.

Maggie began the mundane task of polishing forks and handed them to Sadie for inspection.

"Perfect," said Sadie.

Maggie smiled to herself as she continued.

"So, what made you decide to move to Cedar Lake?" Sadie asked.

Maggie's body stiffened. She wasn't prepared to answer that question. She hadn't been able to tell her family why she'd moved, let alone somebody she barely knew. Maggie shrugged. "The city life wasn't for me, I guess." She cleared her throat. "So, how long have you been working here?"

"About five years. I'd die to be back in Toronto. I miss all the excitement."

"Oh, I didn't realize you were from the city."

"I'm not. After high school, I moved away to pursue a modeling career."

That tidbit didn't surprise Maggie. Sadie was gorgeous.

"I modeled for a few catalogues. My mom was so excited when she received a Hudson Bay catalogue in the mail one day and opened it up to see me modeling a swimsuit." Sadie picked up another wine glass. "But I was young and naïve and not at all prepared for the seedy side of the business."

A familiar tightness constricted Maggie's throat. "What happened? If you don't mind me asking."

"In the end, I couldn't do what was asked of me to make it as a top model." Sadie began scrubbing the wine glass so hard Maggie thought it was going to break.

"I'm sorry it didn't pan out."

Sadie sighed and put the wine glass down. "When I ran out of money, I had to come home and get a real job."

Maggie offered her a smile of solidarity. "So, you're saying country living isn't all it's cracked up to be?"

"I mean, the people here are amazing. Cedar Lake

51

is a real community where people look out for one another."

"I totally get that. In the city, people avert their eyes when passing one another on the sidewalks. I literally just moved here, and my neighbor was kind enough to jump-start my car for me today."

"That's exactly what I'm talking about. The men in these parts are kind and courteous."

"And extremely good looking," Maggie added, thinking about Thomas.

Sadie laughed. "That, too."

"Do you have a boyfriend?" Maggie asked.

Sadie tucked a piece of blonde hair behind her ear and shook her head. "No. My boyfriend broke up with me a couple of months ago." She sighed loudly. "I'm still not over it."

Maggie's eyes widened in disbelief. She couldn't imagine why someone would break up with a Gisele Bündchen look-alike. "Was it serious?"

Sadie picked up another wine glass and stared at it closely. "Yes. We were together for a year. He met my family and everything." Her voice trailed off.

Maggie picked up another fork to polish. "Was there someone else?"

Sadie carefully wiped the interior of the wine glass she was holding. "No. Nothing like that. The more I talked about our future together, the more distant he became. When we ended things, he said we didn't have enough in common. Whenever I run into him, though, I can still feel that there's something between us. We're going to get back together. He just doesn't know it yet." Sadie looked up at the clock that hung above the doorway. "This conversation has to be continued. Your first shift is officially over. Welcome to the team, Maggie. I'll see you tomorrow."

Maggie said goodbye to Sadie, grabbed her purse from the staff locker room, and grinned as she walked out into the parking lot. She had passed Sadie's tests and survived her first day of work. Going outside from an air-conditioned resort and into the summer heat felt like stepping into a sauna. Waves of humidity rose from the hot gravel. Maggie couldn't wait to get back to the cottage and go for a swim. She reached inside her purse for her phone. When she glanced at the screen, her heartbeat slowed to a sluggish thump in her chest. Seven missed calls from Brody.

ALYSSA DELLE PALME

Chapter Five

When Maggie got home from work, she exchanged her itchy uniform for a one-piece black Speedo. She grabbed a towel, went outside and down four flights of rickety stairs to the dock. There were eight other cottages in the quiet bay, each with their own floating raft. The lake was significantly longer than it was wide, extending a few kilometers past the bay. Bobbing at the mouth of the bay were two loons, their soft hoots keeping each other in contact as they took turns diving for fish.

The waterfront at her grandmother's cottage was the best in the bay. A birch tree grew out of the mossy rockface and provided shade over a pair of Adirondack chairs to the left side. On the other side of the dock exposed to the sun, there was a small sandy beach and her grandfather's old rusty-red canoe. Down the middle, a long wooden platform extended out into the lake. As a child, she used to spend hours fishing off the end, sometimes catching bluegill or pumpkinseed sunfish. From where she was standing now, she could see Thomas's waterfront. He had a green canoe, and a motorboat tethered to his dock.

Maggie dropped her towel at the end of the dock and dove through the surface of the lake. The plunge was always exhilarating. The shock of the cool water instantly washed away any stress and grease from her workday. Maggie's front crawl was rusty, but she focused on maintaining a steady motion with her arms and alternately kicking her legs from her hips. She had never had the time to work out during her internship, so her stamina was weak, but she was determined to swim across the bay and back.

For Maggie, swimming was like a moving meditation. It helped her organize her thoughts and clear her head. Her lungs burned as she breathed on alternate sides every third stroke. Images of Brody kept drifting through her mind. She was once enamored with his confidence and charming personality, but his persuasiveness had led her to this place where she felt she couldn't trust herself anymore. In the past, she had shared her feelings with Brody only to have him turn things around on her and make her feel like she was a bad girlfriend.

"Brody, I feel like you don't trust me when you tell me I shouldn't go out with my friends!" she told him during a past argument.

"I feel like you having male friends is disrespectful to our relationship," Brody had responded. He had a way of making Maggie feel like she was the one who wasn't committed to the relationship.

Maggie reached the other side of the bay, changed directions, and started swimming back toward her dock. She tried to keep her body parallel to the water to reduce resistance and make it easier on her arms. The sound of her breathing helped her to focus inward. She began to move smoothly through the bay, gaining confidence with each stroke. By the time she reached the dock, the endorphins had kicked in, and she was calm. Swimming allowed her to drown out all the noise and distractions in her mind and focus on what she truly wanted.

After Maggie toweled off, she went inside the cottage and changed into a t-shirt with a wildflower print on the front and a pair of denim short overalls. She sat on her bed, opened her phone, and quickly dialed Brody's number before she could change her mind. It went straight to voicemail, which meant he was working. She cleared her throat and waited for the sound of the tone.

"Hi Brody, it's me," she said, her voice wavering. She rubbed the back of her neck and continued. "I'm sorry I left like I did. I was incredibly overwhelmed, and I needed to get out of the city. I've decided to stay at my grandmother's cottage for the summer. I want you to know I'm safe and everything is okay, but I need a break, Brody. From us. I need time on my own to figure out what my next steps are going to be. I'll call you when I'm ready to talk."

As Maggie hung up the phone, her back slumped against the headboard. Her vision blurred with tears. Even though it was the right decision, it was a difficult one. Maggie still loved Brody, but they weren't right for each other. Maggie sat still, allowing the relief to sink in. When she was stronger, she'd go back to the city and break up with him in person. She owed him that.

Maggie wiped her eyes with the heels of her hands and took stock of her quaint bedroom. The decor was a mix of traditional and modern. Her queen-size bed was from IKEA and the quilt at the end of it was a family heirloom. Her bedside table was a vintage flea market find, and the large curtain-free window allowed maximum light into the room. Sunshine bounced off the floor-to-ceiling wood paneling and filled the space.

Maggie had the sudden urge to get to work sprucing up the cottage. She needed a distraction, or she'd collapse in another heap of tears. Staying busy wouldn't remove all traces of sadness, but it would be a good place to start. Maggie grabbed a pad of paper and pen from her bedside table and walked around the cottage, writing a to-do list. All the windows needed to be cleaned, the floors needed to be swept and mopped, and cobwebs had to be removed. The bathroom toilet needed to be scrubbed, and the shower stall needed shampoo, conditioner, and soap added to its shelves.

Maggie went outside and continued to add to her growing list. The front door could use a fresh coat of paint and the outdoor deck, which was covered in debris, needed to be swept. She put her list down on the picnic table and grabbed the outdoor broom. She was so focused on the task at hand and jumped when she felt a tap on her shoulder.

"I'm sorry. I didn't mean to scare you," said Thomas.

"Hi!" Maggie wiped the sweat from her brow with the back of her hand. "I didn't hear you."

Thomas held out his hand, offering to take the broom from her. "It looks like you could use a break."

Maggie passed him the handle and slumped down on the picnic bench. "Thank you." She had been so wrapped up in her problems with Brody and the overwhelming to-do list for the cottage that she had completely forgotten she'd invited her neighbor over. Maggie was exhausted both mentally and physically. She watched Thomas work for a couple of minutes. His biceps flexed through his sage-green t-shirt as he swept the fallen pine needles and remaining twigs off the edge of the deck. "You know, you don't have to do this," she said.

Thomas stopped, placing both hands on top of the broom stick and resting his chin. "I don't mind. I like to keep my hands busy," he said, holding her gaze.

The hair on the nape of her neck rose. Maggie reached for the peridot stone on her necklace and played with it nervously, sliding it up and down the white-gold chain. She cleared her throat. "Do you mind if we reschedule drinks? It's been a long day and—" Maggie stopped suddenly as she felt the necklace slip through her fingertips. She tried to catch it, but watched helplessly as it fell through a crack in the deck. Maggie dropped to her knees, grasping the sides of her head. "My necklace! Johnny gave it to me!"

"Stay right there. Don't move!" Thomas said. He ran down the first flight of stairs to the platform and leapt onto the cliffside beneath the cottage. "Did you see where it fell through the deck?" he called.

Maggie grabbed a twig from the deck and poked it through the space where it slipped through. "Right here!" She watched Thomas rummage through the plants below the deck.

Moments later, he held his arm up triumphantly. "I got it!" He sprinted back up the stairs with a smile so big it revealed the dimple in his left cheek. "The clasp is broken," he said, barely winded. He reached for Maggie's hand and carefully placed it in her palm. His hand was double the size of hers.

Happy tears sprung to Maggie's eyes. "Thank you so much!" When Thomas didn't remove his hand from hers, Maggie closed her fingers around the necklace and brought her hands to her chest. "This necklace means so much to me. I can't thank you enough."

Thomas shrugged his shoulders. "It was nothing. So, how about that drink?"

Maggie bit her lip. "Rain check? It's been a day, and I have an early shift tomorrow…"

Thomas tilted his head. "Of course. You know where to find me. I'll see you around, Maggie."

Over the next couple of weeks, Maggie settled into her new routine. Canada Day had come and gone, and the lush cottage country landscape was at its peak. Wildflowers were in full bloom and by early July the lake had become busy with vacationers and boaters. Maggie spent most of her days working at the resort or fixing up the cottage. She only went into town to pick up groceries and to get her necklace fixed. When she had down time, she liked to go for a swim across the bay. Sometimes, she'd hike or forage for wild blueberries. She lived for her newfound freedom. Every now and then she'd see Thomas and wave to him from a distance. It was comforting to know that if she needed anything, she had a friend right next door. One day, she returned home from work to find that Thomas had left a tool and a note for her at the front door.

I saw you trying to fix your picnic table with the heel of your boot. Resourceful, I have to admit! I had an extra hammer in my toolbox. I thought you could use it in case you need to remove nails. I didn't think your boots were equipped with a claw for pulling nails.

Maggie smiled so big her cheeks hurt. As a thank you, she decided to bake him a homemade blueberry pie from her most recent harvest. Her grandmother had taught her the secret to making a perfect flaky pie crust was to use a delicate touch when handling the dough. As the pie baked, the cottage began to smell sweet like a country bakery. She had made a lattice pie crust design, and when she pulled the bubbling golden pie from the oven, it screamed state fair blue-ribbon winner. Once it cooled enough to carry, Maggie took it over to Thomas's cottage and knocked on the front door.

Moments later, Thomas appeared with a dishtowel thrown over his shoulder as though he had just been drying dishes. He smiled and tipped his head. "What do I owe the pleasure?"

Maggie couldn't help but notice the dimple in his left cheek. Her hands shook as she held the warm pastry out with both hands. "I baked you a pie. As a thank you for supplying me with tools."

Thomas's eyebrows shot up in surprise. "Wow. This looks incredible. Do you want to come in for a slice?"

As he took the pie from her hands, his fingers brushed against hers, sending tingles up her arms. Maggie quickly put her hands in her pockets. "I can't. I still have quite a bit of work to do at the cottage."

"You know, I am a professional. Just let me know if there's anything I can help you with."

Maggie hesitated. She didn't want to put him out, but there was a job that needed to be done that was above her skill level. "There's a board on the deck that's rotting and needs to be replaced. Do you think you could teach me how to fix it?"

There was a glint of eagerness in Thomas's eyes. "I'd be happy to show you how."

Maggie smiled. "Do you want to stop by after work tomorrow night? Say around 7:00?"

"You bet."

At work the next day, Maggie hummed as she worked on the formal place settings in the restaurant. There was a lot to remember. She placed the bread-and-butter plate above the forks and to the left of the place setting and the stemware above and to the right of the dinner plate.

Saddie stopped at Maggie's table and inspected her work. "Maggie, the water glass stands above the dinner knife, white wine to its right, and red wine is top center."

Maggie bit the inside of her cheek as she carefully rearranged the glasses. "I'm sorry, Sadie. I'll get it right next time."

Sadie laid dessert spoons across the top of each place setting. "Don't worry," she whispered. "It took me a while to get it, too."

"To be honest, I'm a little distracted," Maggie whispered. "My neighbor is coming over after my shift to help me fix my deck, and I don't know why, but I'm nervous."

Sadie walked around the table, inspecting their work. "What's his name? Maybe I know him."

"Thomas."

Sadie stopped in her tracks. "Thomas McLeod?"

"Yes! That's him—"

Sadie crossed her arms. "Thomas McLeod that lives in the orange-colored cabin on Route 1?"

The warm, happy atmosphere in the dining room switched to cold and frigid in an instant. "How do you know Thomas?" Maggie asked.

Sadie's eyes flashed with outrage. "Thomas is my ex!"

Chapter Six

As soon as Maggie got home from work, she stripped out of her greasy uniform and hopped into the shower, rinsing off the disaster of her latest shift. Warm water pounded against her shoulders. She cringed, thinking about how she had tried to rectify the situation by telling Sadie about Brody. Why did she have to open her big mouth?

"It's not a date or anything," Maggie had clarified. "I mean, I'm spoken for. Sort of. I have a boyfriend back in the city … I think."

Sadie looked Maggie up and down with judgmental eyes. "That's a pretty slutty thing to do." Sadie turned up her nose and marched out of the dining room, leaving Maggie to finish the place settings on her own.

Maggie turned the hot water knob up in the shower and let the scalding stream beat against her sore back. Her mind was consumed with thoughts of Brody. Maggie's plan was to break up with him when she was strong enough to see him again, but she still wasn't ready. Brody could be so persuasive. She needed more time and space to think and find her own way. She'd come to the cottage to escape a suffocating relationship. The last thing she wanted to do was get involved with someone else. Why couldn't she have just said that to Sadie?

Maggie turned off the water and wrapped herself in an old beach towel. There was something about Thomas that her heart was drawn to, but she refused to think of him as anything more than a friend. Maggie used a wide-tooth comb to brush out her long, brown hair. She spritzed a detangling spray through her wet locks, which helped achieve chunky beach waves. She opened her makeup bag and grabbed her mascara. Starting at the roots of her eyelashes, Maggie wiggled the wand and swept through the tips. She applied a coat of high-shine lip gloss that made her lips appear full and plump. Pleased with what she saw in the mirror, Maggie adjusted the faded and frayed towel wrapped under her arms and headed for her bedroom to get dressed. As she walked out of the bathroom, she passed the front door and saw a strange figure lurking there. Maggie shrieked, bringing her hands to her mouth. Her towel dropped to her feet. It took her a second to realize that the creep staring at her through the window of the front door was Thomas. And there she was, giving him a free show.

Thomas brought his hand to his brow and adverted his eyes. "I'm sorry! I—uh—"

"What are you doing here?" Maggie yelled. She picked up her towel and haphazardly wrapped it around her naked body.

"I, uh… You told me to come over to help you fix your deck."

Maggie caught a glimpse of the clock in the kitchen. Thomas was five minutes early. "Yes, of course. I just wasn't expecting you yet. Um, why don't you head around back, and I'll be out in just a minute."

Still covering his eyes like a gentleman, Thomas tripped over a broken board on the deck as he made his way to the back with his tools and supplies. "I'll fix that one, too!" he called out.

Maggie broke into a smile as she watched him stumble his way around to the back deck. Through the sliding glass door, Maggie looked on as Thomas organized his tools. When he lifted his head, she averted her eyes and rushed to her bedroom to change into a white, knee-length, cotton summer dress. As Thomas hammered outside, Maggie went to the kitchen and whipped up a charcuterie board with cheese, crackers, and grapes. She grabbed the chilled bottle of champagne from the fridge and went to the sliding glass door. When Thomas saw her standing there with her hands full, he got up and opened the door for her.

"Your deck is as good as new," he said, pointing to the replaced board. "I'll show you how to fix the one out front."

Maggie placed the food down on the picnic table. "I really appreciate your help," she said, handing Thomas the bottle of champagne. "Will you do the honors?"

Maggie quickly ran back inside to retrieve a cloth napkin and champagne flutes. When she couldn't find any, she grabbed a dish towel and a couple of mason jars instead.

Thomas removed the foil from the bottle to expose the cork and the cage. He untwisted the cage counterclockwise and then used the dishtowel to gently pull the cork away from the bottle. When she heard the sound of the cork popping, Maggie clapped her hands in glee.

"To new beginnings!" Thomas said as he handed Maggie a glass.

She smiled, clinking her mason jar against his. The sparkling bubbles exploded in her mouth, releasing pleasing flavors of peach and vanilla.

"You sprang for the good stuff," Thomas said, relaxing into a lounge chair that overlooked the lake.

Maggie sat down on the bench of the picnic table. "My grandma says champagne is the only wine that leaves a woman beautiful after drinking it."

Thomas stole a glance at Maggie, his eyes soft with admiration. "You'd look beautiful no matter what you were drink—"

"Shit!" Maggie said as champagne dribbled down her chin and onto her clean summer dress. Heat rose to her cheeks as she remembered all the times Brody got angry with her for spilling things accidentally. "I'm sorry."

Thomas grabbed the dish towel wrapped around the neck of the champagne bottle and handed it to Maggie. "What are you apologizing for?"

"Thank you," she said, ignoring his question. She dabbed at the wet spot against her chest. "I can be so clumsy. You were saying something?"

Thomas coughed. "Oh, uh, it was nothing." He relaxed back into his chair and stared straight ahead.

The sun was beginning to set. A glowing circle in a grapefruit-pink sky, illuminating a quivering path across the lake. The view from the deck was stunning. Maggie took a moment to soak up her surroundings. She still couldn't believe she was going to spend her entire summer at the cottage. It was almost too good to be true. She grabbed the chilled champagne off the picnic table and went to sit in the lounge chair next to Thomas. She placed the ice-cold bottle down on the deck between them.

Thomas turned to Maggie. "How was work today?"

Maggie took a swig of her drink. "Well, I learned that my boss is your ex."

Thomas nodded and returned his focus to the lake. "So, you've met Sadie."

"You could've warned me, you know."

"Sadie isn't my business anymore."

"She's still in love with you."

Thomas looked at her, baffled. "She told you that?"

"Not exactly. But she did say she wasn't over you."

Thomas nodded his head slowly as though he was

absorbing that tidbit of information.

"What happened between you two?" Maggie asked.

Thomas chugged the rest of his champagne, poured himself another glass, and topped up Maggie's glass.

"I'm sorry. I ask a lot of questions," Maggie said when Thomas didn't respond. "I'm not nosy, it's just the reporter in me. Before moving here for the summer, I was working as an intern for 880 News in Toronto. You don't have to answer."

"Wow. That's really impressive." Thomas traced the rim of his mason jar with his finger. "I don't mind your questions. Nothing happened exactly. Sadie is a great girl. I just didn't see her as the one for me, you know?"

Maggie's mouth hung open. "You think you can do better than someone that looks like Gisele Bündchen?"

Thomas laughed. "It's hard to explain. I know a lot of guys that would kill to be with Sadie."

"So, what was it?"

Thomas's tousled curls ruffled in the breeze. "It's difficult to pinpoint. We had a lot of fun together, good chemistry, too. We got together soon after my dad died. The problem was, she could tell I wasn't really dialed in as much as she was. She started to get insecure. I started feeling guilty."

Maggie nodded. She understood exactly what he was saying.

"It was hard. Sadie is an amazing girl. She treated me well, and I didn't want to hurt her feelings."

Maggie curled her feet up under her and leaned an elbow on the armrest of her lounge chair. She was so enthralled with what he had to say, she began to wonder if her questions were more about her and Brody's relationship. Maggie gave her head a shake. "So, how do you break up with a partner that everyone else is in love with?"

"I was honest with her. I told her I wasn't interested in seeing anyone else, but I wanted us both to have the right to do so in the future. I made it clear I wasn't going to make any promises I wasn't sure I could keep. I've been hurt by broken promises in the past, and I swore a long time ago I'd never reject anybody like that." Thomas stared out across the lake, seeming suddenly distant, like he was halfway there with Maggie and halfway stuck in the cycle of his past.

Maggie had a sudden urge to comfort him. She grabbed the bottle of champagne, poured herself another glass, and emptied the rest of the bottle into Thomas's mason jar.

His eyes settled softly on Maggie. "To being single," Thomas said, raising his glass.

This was the perfect segue to tell Thomas about Brody, but Maggie wanted to forget about all her problems for a minute and live in the present moment. She clinked her mason jar against his and melted into the back of her lounge chair before taking a sip of champagne. Her cheeks were warm and tingly.

"So, what do you do for fun out here, all by yourself?" she asked.

"After work, I like to go for a paddle. Sometimes, I bring my fishing rod."

"I love canoeing!"

Thomas gaped at her in disbelief. "I'm shocked to hear you say that."

"Don't let the high heels and fancy haircut fool you. I spent every summer of my childhood at this cottage."

"You know not to stand up in the boat, right?"

"Oh, shut up!" Maggie playfully smacked his arm.

"Okay, okay." Thomas laughed and rubbed his upper arm, pretending it hurt more than it did.

Maggie was fired up inside. For the first time in a while, she was having fun. "I love that paddling allows you to explore all the hidden corners of the lake."

"Have you ever seen the Algonquin pictographs?" he asked.

"What? On Cedar Lake? No way!"

"Yes," Thomas said, his eyes clinging to hers.

"Where?"

"It's a secret. I'll take you there sometime."

Maggie's warm cheeks turned ablaze with excitement.

"If you're lucky," he added.

Maggie laughed. She couldn't remember the last time she'd felt so effervescent and free. "Do you want to go for a swim?" she asked, jumping out of her chair with gusto. Maggie didn't know if it was the champagne or the easiness of their conversation, but being with Thomas had made her confidence soar.

"You're drunk."

"I'm not!" Maggie paused. "Tipsy, maybe."

Thomas surveyed his outfit. "I'm not wearing a swimsuit."

Maggie grabbed Thomas's hand and pulled him to his feet. She gave him a champagne-sipping, skinny-dipping smile. "Who said anything about needing swimsuits?"

Thomas raised his eyebrows and followed her down the wooden stairs that led to her dock. When they reached the water's edge, Maggie told Thomas to turn around.

"Come on! It's nothing I haven't seen before!"

Thomas teased. He turned toward the mossy rockface, giving Maggie privacy.

Maggie slipped out of her cotton dress, unveiling her white panties and bra. She wasn't revealing anything more than she would have if she had been wearing a bikini, but it felt too intimate to let Thomas see her in her underwear. With his back still turned, Maggie quickly tiptoed into the lake until the water was hip deep and dove in. The lake water washed over her hot skin, cooling her down and rejuvenating her.

"You can turn around now," she called out when she resurfaced.

Thomas took off his T-shirt, revealing his washboard stomach. Watching him undress excited Maggie, but as he unbuttoned his jeans, Maggie peeled herself away and swam deeper into the bay until she heard a splash. The sun had set behind the pine trees, and Maggie saw the faint light of the stars twinkling in the darkening sky.

"Thomas?" she called out when he still hadn't resurfaced. Panic tickled her chest as she treaded water in the middle of the bay. He should've come up for air by now. Suddenly, something pinched her big toe, and she shrieked. It was too dark to see what had bitten her. Maggie splashed around and started swimming for the shore when Thomas emerged.

"Gotcha!"

"You jerk!" Maggie splashed water in his direction, wanting to wash that smug expression off of his face. "You nearly gave me a heart attack!"

Thomas floated onto his back. "Come lie with me. The water feels amazing."

Maggie joined him, and they gazed silently at the distant constellations now shining in the night sky. Maggie's heartbeat thumped in her ears. It was thrilling to stare up at the galaxies from the dark surface of the lake. The stars felt so close that Maggie almost believed she could reach out and touch them. Her pinkie finger gently grazed against Thomas's, spreading sparks up her arm like the flicker of the distant stars igniting in the night sky. Suddenly, an overwhelming feeling of responsibility, triggered by thoughts of Brody, punched her in the gut. She dropped her legs and moved away from Thomas, kicking her legs like an eggbeater to tread water.

"Thomas, I have to tell you something. I have a boy—"

"Maggie?" a woman called out from the shore, waving a flashlight.

Maggie squinted, but it was too dark to see anything.

"Who is that?" Thomas whispered in her ear behind her. His warm breath against her neck sent thrilling shivers down her spine.

"I'm not sure—"

"It's me, Katie!"

Maggie made out the outline of her aunt's wavey, shoulder-length bob. She looked like a young Meg Ryan from the 90s romantic comedies that Maggie used to watch with her parents. Maggie and Thomas swam back to shore. It was quite sobering to be caught in your underwear with the neighbor, who wasn't your boyfriend.

"I saw the champagne bottle upstairs, and I thought you and Brody—"

"What are you doing here?" Maggie interrupted. Thankful for the cover of darkness, she quickly stepped back into her dress and pulled the straps over her shoulders. Meanwhile, Thomas slipped his t-shirt over his head and held his balled-up jeans in front of his soaked boxer shorts.

"Hi, I'm Thomas." He offered his hand to Katie.

"I live next door."

Katie eyed him from head to toe. "Nice to meet you."

"Are Uncle Stuart and the twins here, too?" Maggie asked.

"Uh, no. It's just me. Your mom told me you were here. I'm sorry I interrupted—"

"You didn't interrupt anything. I just wasn't expecting you. Why didn't you call?"

"It was a spontaneous decision to come up here."

"Um, I'll let you two catch up," said Thomas awkwardly. "It was nice meeting you, Katie."

"Don't be silly. Don't let me ruin your evening. Please come back upstairs. I brought a bottle of wine! Besides, I'd love to learn more about Maggie's new … friend." Katie linked her arm through Thomas's.

He hesitated, looking at Maggie for guidance.

Maggie shrugged her shoulders.

"Um, sure, I guess I could have another drink," he said.

Upstairs, Maggie went inside and quickly changed into a pair of jean shorts and a cozy gray hoodie. She grabbed a couple bottles of water from the fridge and a fresh towel for Thomas. By the time she returned to the deck, Katie had polished off half a bottle of wine. The deck was lit up with citronella candles to keep the mosquitoes at bay.

"There she is!" Katie said. She patted the seat next to her at the picnic table. "My favorite niece."

"Your only niece."

Thomas graciously accepted the towel and bottle of water from Maggie. Katie offered to pour Maggie a glass of wine, but she declined. Maggie had had enough alcohol for one night. She took a sip of water instead.

"What made you decide to come up to the

cottage? Does Grandma know you're here?" Maggie asked.

Katie chugged her third glass of wine and then refilled the glass to the rim. Maggie bit her bottom lip nervously. Something was wrong. She had never seen her aunt act this way. Katie took another gulp of wine before she answered.

"I had an affair, and your Uncle Stuart kicked me out."

"What?" Maggie said in disbelief. Stuart worshipped the ground Katie walked on. She couldn't fathom why Katie would cheat on him.

"I had been feeling really blue. Some days, I couldn't even get out of bed, so my doctor put me on antidepressants. Suddenly, the world became as colorful as a milkweed patch in the summer. I felt recharged! I had so much pent-up energy I signed up for a gym membership. That's where I met James."

Maggie glanced hesitantly in Thomas's direction. "Katie, you don't have to tell us—"

"James is a trainer, and he's fun!" Katie said, turning to Thomas. Her lips were stained purple from the wine. "James was nothing like my boring old husband, Stuart."

"Katie, why don't you eat something," Maggie said, pushing the charcuterie board in front of her.

Katie nibbled on a small piece of cheddar. "The affair went on for six months. Do you think I'm a bad person?"

Maggie was at a loss for words. Her aunt had just discovered her in her underwear with a man that wasn't her boyfriend, and *still* Katie worried that Maggie was going to place judgement on her for having an affair.

Maybe infidelity runs in the family, Maggie thought.

"I know, I'm a terrible person," Katie said.

"No! Of course, you're not." Maggie wrapped her arm around Katie's shoulders. "You just made a mistake. You were medicated and obviously not thinking clearly. Stuart loves you. He'll forgive you."

Katie rested her head on Maggie's shoulder. "I don't think so," she slurred.

"What about the boys?" Maggie asked. Katie and Stuart shared seventeen-year-old twins, Matthew and Joshua.

"Oh, they don't need me. Since they got their driver's licenses, they're never home. Matt and Josh both got lifeguarding jobs at a YMCA sleepaway camp for the summer. I'll tell them about the separation when they get back."

It was shocking to hear her aunt mention the word "separation." No one in their family had ever been separated. "Will you be okay financially?" Maggie asked.

Katie sighed, lifting her head. Her eyebrows gathered in. "I'll be fine. Stuart does well for himself, and he'll have to pay me alimony. I have my savings, too. I wish I went to university like you did, Maggie. I married young and had the twins right away. I don't think listing *stay-at-home mom* on my resumé will impress any future employers." Katie closed her eyes and laid her head back on Maggie's shoulder. "Please don't tell your mother," she pleaded. A moment later, Katie drifted off to sleep.

"We should get her inside," Maggie whispered, looking to Thomas for help.

Thomas picked Katie up and carried her like a newlywed into the cottage. Maggie followed and worked quickly to prepare the bed in the back bedroom. Maggie unzipped a sleeping bag, and Thomas gently placed Katie down on the bed. He went to the kitchen to get Katie a glass of water, and Maggie removed her aunt's sandals before tucking her in. When Thomas returned, Maggie placed the water on the bedside table and put a wastebasket next to her, just in case.

"Thank you for staying," Maggie whispered once they tiptoed out of the back bedroom. She slowly walked Thomas to the front door. "I'm sorry you had to see that."

"Don't apologize. All families have their problems. I'm happy I was here to help."

Maggie smiled weakly. She appreciated his kindness, but worried he wouldn't want to be friends with her anymore after what had unfolded that night.

"I'll see you around," she said, opening the front door.

Thomas stepped outside but paused and turned around. "How about tomorrow morning?"

Maggie chortled. "Really? After tonight, you still want to hang out?"

Thomas shrugged his shoulders and kicked his feet in the dirt. "Yeah. What do you say? A sunrise paddle to the Algonquin pictographs."

Maggie's skin tingled all over. "Yes."

"Great. Meet me at my dock at 6:00."

ALYSSA DELLE PALME

Chapter Seven

The next morning, in the dim light of dawn, Maggie stumbled around her bedroom to get ready for her paddle with Thomas. The events of the previous night occupied her every thought. She worried about leaving her aunt all alone. She wanted to call her mother but had promised Katie that she wouldn't.

Maggie slipped into her green floral one-piece bathing suit and pulled her favorite pair of denim shorts over top. She'd had trouble sleeping, not because of her plans with Thomas, but because she was giddy with excitement over them. Brody lingered in her mind and feelings of guilt crept back in. She tied a sweatshirt around her waist and wiggled her feet into her white Keds. As she applied a banana flavored sunscreen balm to her lips, she reminded herself that she wasn't doing anything wrong.

When she was ready, Maggie snuck into the back bedroom to check on her aunt. Katie was dead asleep, snoring quietly. Katie's short blonde hair was matted against her forehead, and her face was streaked with red sleep marks. They looked so much alike, Maggie could almost mistake her aunt for her mother. Katie stirred in the bed. Maggie slowly backed out of the bedroom and silently closed the door behind her.

Maggie found Thomas down by his dock. He wore a pair of navy surf shorts and a bright white sleeveless shirt that showed off his toned biceps. His face lit up when he saw her.

"There you are! Here." He passed Maggie a red lifejacket and a wooden paddle.

"Look who's chipper in the morning." Maggie beamed at his enthusiasm.

"Nothing better than waking up at the crack of dawn to go for a paddle!" Thomas stretched his arms over his head and turned his gaze toward the lake. "Look how calm and quiet the water is. We'll have the whole lake to ourselves."

Thomas's positive attitude in the morning was refreshing. Maggie had always been a morning person herself, but Brody was a night owl. She couldn't even talk to him in the morning until he'd had a cup of coffee. Thomas offered Maggie his hand as she climbed into the bow of his green canoe. The warmth of his hand sent a flutter of butterflies through her. Once she was settled, Thomas carefully placed a small cooler and a backpack in the middle of the canoe before taking his seat in the stern.

They set off on their adventure, silently slipping along the lake and taking in all its rugged beauty. Maggie delighted in the towering rock cliffs and the rich pine forest that she hadn't seen for years. The stunning scenery of Cedar Lake surrounded them and fulfilled Maggie's dreams of solace amid nature's beauty. Fresh air filled her lungs, and birds sang in chorus as the sun slowly rose in the sky. The water was clear, and below the surface, bluegill and pumpkinseed swam along the rocky bottom in the bright spotlights of the sun.

Thomas sighed. "There is no better way to start the day."

Maggie full-heartedly agreed. All her worries dissipated with each stroke away from the dock. Paddling with the sunrise was like hitting the reset button. Thomas effortlessly steered their canoe in between two tiny islands.

"Do you want a cup of coffee?" he asked.

Maggie carefully turned her body to face Thomas. He grabbed a thermos from his backpack and poured her a cup of hot, black coffee. The steaming mug warmed her cold fingertips. She smelled the lightly caramelized brew.

"Mmm, this is perfect," she said after taking her first sip.

"I was surprised when you said you'd come with me." A small smile of satisfaction rested on his lips.

"Who wouldn't want to do this?" Maggie took another sip and admired the beauty surrounding them.

"Sadie would never go on a morning paddle with me." Thomas handed her a soft, buttery croissant from the cooler.

"Really? Why not?" Maggie took a bite of the flaky bun. It was so fresh it melted in her mouth.

Thomas shrugged his shoulders. "I guess we can't all be sunrise seekers."

Maggie lost herself in Thomas's green eyes that reflected the insight of the forest that surrounded them. Thomas held her gaze, it was like she was being seen for the first time in a long time. The depth of his stare took her breath away. Overcome with shyness, Maggie looked away first.

"Well, they don't know what they're missing!" she said. After Maggie finished her pastry and cup of coffee, she repositioned herself to face the front of the canoe. "Where to, Captain?"

Thomas steered them back out into open water and, together, they paddled down the lake.

"Look!" Thomas whispered loudly. He pointed to something slowly swimming along the shoreline. "A beaver!"

Maggie stopped paddling and placed the paddle across her lap. She had seen the lodges the beavers had built out of sticks and mud, but she had never seen the nocturnal animal up close. The lake, tinged with light blue and pink, picked up the reflections of the swimming rodent. When the beaver noticed their canoe approaching, it altered its course and slapped its flat tail against the water. The slap created a powerful noise that echoed across the lake, warning them not to come any closer. Maggie and Thomas silently watched the beaver swim away.

"That was incredible," Maggie whispered when the beaver was a safe distance away.

"There's still more to see. We're almost there."

Thomas guided their canoe to a strip of sand along the shoreline. Maggie was surprised when Thomas told her they had arrived at their destination.

"But I've been here a million times," said Maggie. "I've never seen the pictographs."

"We have to hike in."

Maggie looked down at her bare legs.

"Don't worry. I came prepared."

Thomas took a bottle of bug spray from his backpack and knelt down at Maggie's feet. As he meticulously sprayed the insect repellent on her ankles and upward toward her thighs, Maggie sucked in her breath, quietly thanking her past self for taking the time to shave her legs.

"Let's go!" he said when he finished, putting the bottle back in his bag.

The hike wasn't strenuous, but there were short, steep sections. Thomas led the way and turned around every so often to check on Maggie. He seemed ecstatic to have a hiking partner in tow. Along the way, Thomas pointed out different geological features on the trail.

"See the semicircular depression in the face of this cliff?" he asked.

Maggie nodded, looking up at the carved stone bowl.

"It was a waterfall from the end of the last ice age," Thomas said. "This whole area used to be covered by a glacier. When temperatures rose and the ice began to melt, water probably plunged over the edge of this cliff."

Maggie toyed with her newly fixed necklace. "Wow, you've done your research! It's like having my own private tour guide."

"There's so much more to see!" Thomas turned around and held out his hand to help Maggie step over a boulder on the path. Maggie used Thomas as a railing as she climbed up. He gripped her hand a little longer than necessary, sending a wave of tingles up Maggie's arm.

He let go seconds later and led her further down the trail. Maggie licked her lips. The anticipation magnified the joy she was feeling on their hike. Eventually, the trail brought them through an overhanging caprock.

"This rock shelter has been here for thousands of years," said Thomas. "Wandering groups of people would seek shelter from the rain or cold in here."

"How do you know?"

"There's evidence. Pieces of pottery, bone tools, and the remains of a fire pit."

Thomas was a nature nerd, and she liked it. Maggie swallowed. Avoiding his gaze, she walked closer to the back wall to put some space between them. She knelt down, examining traces of a red pigment.

"Psst. Over here," Thomas said.

Maggie moved over to where Thomas was standing. There, on the wall, were worn red images.

"The First Nations used iron oxide-based pigments mixed with fish oil or bear grease to paint the pictographs."

Maggie didn't dare touch the fading images for fear she would damage them. She strolled along the gallery, admiring the ancient art—an image of two human figures in a canoe, three vertical lines, and an animal that resembled a moose.

"Isn't it incredible?" Thomas whispered in her ear.

The tiny hairs on the back of Maggie's neck stood on end. She couldn't speak. She had never encountered anything quite like the pictographs. She slowly turned to face Thomas.

"Thank you for taking me here," she said in a breathy voice.

A proud smile spread across Thomas's mouth. His teeth were pristine. He leaned one arm against the rock wall, standing tall above Maggie. "Thanks for coming with me."

When her gaze finally locked with his, her nerves fired all at once. She yearned to reach out and touch him, but her instincts immediately reminded her it wasn't a good idea. Technically, she still had a boyfriend. Maggie cleared her throat, quickly moving out from underneath him. "We should head back. I wouldn't want Katie to worry."

A disappointed look flashed from his eyes. After a beat, Thomas nodded. "Of course."

When they reached the canoe, Thomas avoided eye contact as he handed Maggie her life jacket. Her shoulders slumped as her mind struggled to find clarity. She hadn't meant to leave Thomas in the lurch, but she also wasn't willing to cross that line with him. Their friendship was important to her. "So, when are we going on our next adventure?" she asked, forcing her voice to sound bubbly and upbeat.

Thomas's eyes scanned her face as though he were trying to read her. "Soon," he answered. He straddled the stern of the canoe and held it steady for Maggie as she cautiously climbed in and took her seat in the bow. With one foot in the canoe, Thomas pushed off the sand with the other and launched them back into the lake. They paddled in silence until they found their groove.

"There's a bonfire at the resort tonight," Thomas said. "We could go together."

Maggie let out a huge breath. Thomas wasn't jilted after all. A slow smile spread across her lips. "That sounds great! I could use a night out."

"Yeah, Sadie asked me to man the fire."

Maggie's chest tightened. "I—I didn't realize you two were still in contact."

Thomas shrugged. "We're friendly. She still calls me for favors from time to time." Thomas steered the canoe in the direction of his cottage. "So, tell me. Why did you decide to move out of the city?"

Maggie swallowed. "A few reasons." She was glad she wasn't facing him. He would've been able to tell from the expression on her face that something was bothering her.

"Oh, come on, I told you all about my big-shot days in the city. You can tell me."

Maggie stopped paddling. She took a deep breath. "My boss was a dick, and I couldn't stand working for him anymore." It wasn't the whole story, but it felt good to say that part out loud.

"Well, that's one good reason to leave. What's the other?"

Maggie opened her mouth to answer, but suddenly realized she didn't have to. There, standing on her dock, with his arms crossed over his chest, was Brody, watching them as they paddled back into the bay together.

ALYSSA DELLE PALME

Chapter Eight

Maggie's throat constricted with fear. "Brody! What are you doing here?" her voice strained.

"What am I doing here?" Brody asked exasperatedly. "What are you doing here, Maggie?"

Thomas slowed the canoe. "Maggie, is everything okay?"

Maggie nodded. "I'm sorry, Thomas. Yes, everything is fine. This is my boyfriend, Brody."

"Your boyfriend?"

Maggie continued. "Brody, this is my neighbor, Thomas."

Brody uncrossed his arms and leaned down to help Thomas dock his canoe. "Nice to meet you, man. Any friend of Maggie's is a friend of mine."

Maggie quickly clamored out of the canoe, almost tipping the boat in the process.

"Easy!" Thomas yelled.

Maggie glanced down at Thomas. She could tell from the expression on his face that he was angry.

"Thanks for the tour, Thomas. I—I'll see you around."

Thomas paused. He stared past Brody into Maggie's eyes. "Are you sure you're okay?"

"Yes," she squeaked. She cleared her throat. "I'll catch up with you later."

Thomas shook his head in disbelief. "It was nice meeting you, Brandon. I've heard so much about you."

Maggie cringed at his sarcasm.

"It's Brody!" Brody called out after Thomas as he paddled his way to his dock. Brody wrapped Maggie in a tight bear hug. "What a nice guy." His voice dripped with fake sincerity.

"Mmhmm," Maggie muttered against his chest.

"You've put on some weight," Brody said, rubbing his hands up and down her back.

Maggie pulled away. Brody had always been critical of her body. She was either eating too much or not enough.

Brody placed his hands on her shoulders and peered into her eyes. "What I meant to say was you look great, Maggie."

Maggie crossed her arms unconvinced. "What are you doing here, Brody?"

"You left me no choice. You wouldn't take my phone calls. I had to see for myself that you were okay, and I traveled all this way only to find you off adventuring with another man."

Maggie stared at her feet, ashamed. She couldn't stop the tears from falling.

"Don't cry, Mags." Brody wrapped her in his arms and swayed back and forth until her sobs ceased to tiny hiccups. "Let me take care of you like I always do. I'm here now."

Maggie nodded, wiping her nose on the cuff of her sweatshirt. It was time to tell him everything. "I—"

"You know what," Brody interrupted, "let's talk upstairs. Your aunt is making breakfast."

"Oh…"

"She seemed kind of hungover."

Brody grabbed Maggie by the hand and pulled her to the wooden staircase. He turned abruptly, kissing Maggie straight on the mouth and catching her off guard. His teeth had knocked against hers.

"I'm so happy to be here with you," he said before bounding up the stairs.

Maggie sighed and slowly followed suit. Seeing Brody had knocked the wind from her sails.

"Maggie! You should've left a note. I was worried about you," Katie said when the two of them came through the sliding glass door at the back of the cottage.

"Maggie is usually pretty good at leaving notes," Brody said.

Maggie winced. Unbeknownst to her aunt, Brody was mocking her. She was tired of people telling her what to do and how to be. Maggie stood taller. "I'm not a child. I can come and go as I please. I don't need a babysitter."

Katie turned from the stove and brought the frying pan to the three plates laid out on the island. She scooped buttery scrambled eggs onto each plate. "Of course, you don't." Katie tilted her head to the full French Press sitting on the counter. "The coffee is hot."

Maggie grabbed three mismatched mugs from the cupboard and poured them each a cup. Meanwhile, Katie added crisp bacon strips and a piece of buttered toast to each plate.

"I thought we could eat outside," Katie said.

The three of them gathered around the picnic table overlooking the lake. Maggie devoured her second breakfast in an effort to keep her mouth full and avoid conversation. The paddle and hike with Thomas had also made her famished.

"The country looks good on you, Maggie," said Katie. "You have such a nice tan. The sun has added highlights to your hair, and you don't have a single pimple on your face. I'm hoping a bit of time up here will help me look as refreshed as you."

Katie was right. Maggie did feel a lot better, and she hadn't had to take an antacid since she arrived.

"How long do you plan on staying for, Brody?" Katie asked.

"For as long as it takes to get this one to come

back with me." Brody placed his hand on the small of Maggie's back.

Toast crumbs got stuck in Maggie's throat. She gulped her hot coffee and burnt her tongue in the process.

Brody rubbed her back. "Are you alright?"

"Mmhmm." Maggie stuffed a piece of bacon in her mouth. She still wasn't ready to talk.

"Actually, my next shift is in a couple of days," Brody told Katie. "I can only stay for one night."

"You'll have to make the most of your time here then. What do you two plan to do?" Katie asked.

Brody shrugged his shoulders and fixed his eyes on Maggie.

"Um, there's a bonfire at the resort tonight," Maggie suggested.

"Oh! That sounds wonderful!" Katie clapped her hands together. "You know, I used to go to the bonfires when I was in college."

"You should come with us!" Maggie said a little too eagerly.

"Oh, I don't know. I don't want to be the old lady at the bonfire."

Maggie rolled her eyes. "The bonfire isn't just for college kids. All are welcome."

"You know what? A night out is exactly what I need. Thanks, Maggie. I would love to join you guys." Katie stood up and began to clear their empty plates. "I have to run into town. Do you two need anything?"

Maggie shook her head.

"I'll be back after dinner!"

Maggie smiled. It was nice to see her aunt excited about something.

Brody straddled the picnic bench to fully face Maggie. He leaned an elbow on the table and rested his cheek in one hand and traced Maggie's back with his other. "Looks like we're going to have the cottage all to ourselves," he murmured.

Maggie's back straightened. Her heart pounded in her chest. Being intimate with Brody was the last thing she had in mind.

Brody reached into the pocket of his jeans and pulled out a small velvet pouch. "I got you something."

Whatever it was, Maggie didn't want to accept it.

Brody opened the pouch and pulled out a dainty floating diamond necklace. "To replace the old one you're always wearing."

Maggie's hand flew to her peridot pendant protectively. "I don't want to replace it. Johnny gave it to me."

Brody's fury sprang to life. "I buy you a real diamond, and this is the thanks I get?"

"I'm sorry. It's really beautiful, Brody. I just can't accept—"

"Just forget it." His red cheeks smoldered with resentment. He dropped the necklace back in the pouch and stuffed it into his pocket. "You're impossible to please."

A flicker of irritation caused her to snap. "I'm not going back with you!" Maggie bit her bottom lip to stop herself from saying something she might regret. She attempted to soften her tone. "I—I got a job at the resort for the summer. I can't leave. They're already short-staffed."

The muscles in Brody's jawline twitched. "You scared me for a second. I thought you were going to break up with me."

Maggie shifted uncomfortably. "Listen, Brody, my lease is up in September, and I can't afford my apartment anymore. I have to stay here until I figure out my next move. I think it's best if we—"

"Why don't you move in with me?" Brody interrupted, placing his warm hand over hers.

Maggie yanked her hand away as if he had burned her. "What? But we're not ready for that—"

"Why not? We've been together for a year, and we love each other."

"But I don't even know what I'm going to do with my life, yet. Brody, I need to find a more permanent job."

"You can live with me while you figure it out. I have a good job and can pay all the bills."

Maggie studied his pleading brown eyes. In the beginning of their relationship, Brody had made her feel safe and taken care of. Now, his offer felt like a plan to trap her financially. She averted her gaze and shook her head. "That's incredibly generous, Brody, but I want to be able to stand on my own two feet."

"Come on, Maggie, let me take care of you."

Maggie tucked a lock of hair behind her ear. "Life can change in an instant. I need options to fall back on."

Brody tilted his head to the side. "What does that even mean?"

Maggie took a slow, steady breath. "I feel like I need to know who I am before I can have a healthy relationship with anyone."

Brody rubbed his chin. "I know who you are, Maggie. I love who you are. I want to marry you."

Maggie clutched the edges of the picnic table, overwhelmed with sudden claustrophobic thoughts of being trapped in a confined space.

Brody's fingers cupped her chin. "Hey, don't look so shocked. That wasn't a proposal. I just want to be honest about what my intentions are. Do you even want to get married at all?"

"I..." Maggie gulped. "Um, I hadn't given it a lot of thought."

Brody's posture wilted slightly. "Will you think about it?"

Maggie swallowed the acidic bile that had pooled at the back of her throat. Now was the time to tell him it was over, but her words were trapped, imprisoned by her desire to keep things smooth and avoid an explosive argument. All she could do was nod and offer Brody a tight-lipped smile.

For the rest of the day, Maggie and Brody tackled her long to-do list. Brody was eager to help. He was like an energetic border collie who always needed a job to do. As Maggie repainted the front door of the cottage poppy-orange, she watched Brody mow the driveway. When he caught her staring, he waved. Maggie smiled on the outside, but on the inside, she feared he was going to retaliate when she finally told him it was over.

Once Brody finished cutting the grass, he stood over Maggie and inspected her work.

"This is the color you chose?" His voice was full of disdain.

Maggie's shoulders crumpled under his scrutiny. She had chosen the vibrant hue because she felt it symbolized adventure and creativity. The color had made her happy. Now, she doubted her decision. "You don't like it?" she asked.

Brody leaned down and kissed the crown of her head. "Don't worry, when my place needs to be repainted, I'll be in charge of the color palette."

When Katie returned hours later, she was thrilled to see the improvements they had made. "The cottage is beginning to look like its old self!"

A grin tugged at Maggie's mouth. She was relieved her aunt had returned. Brody's big question was hanging in the air and Maggie was desperate to escape having to answer it. "Let's get ready to go to the bonfire."

****

Maggie drove up the long driveway to the resort and glanced over at Brody in the passenger seat. She was nervous but eager to show him this magical place in the forest. Brody looked up from his cellphone as Maggie turned into an empty parking space.

"It's just a giant log cabin," Brody said. There was a critical tone to his voice.

"But ... isn't it beautiful?" she asked, challenging him.

Brody gave an unimpressed shrug.

"Maybe he just needs to experience it to appreciate it," Katie piped up from the backseat. "Let's go!"

Maggie got out of the car and adjusted the spaghetti strap of her ballet-pink cotton swing dress that had slipped off her shoulder on the drive over. The resort had set up a raging bonfire at the back of the property near the lake. The grassy area was busy with adults mingling with cocktails in hand and children running around with sparklers. Teenagers were gathered around the fire roasting marshmallows or avoiding their parents by hiding out in the giant gazebo in the center of the property. Down at the beach, people rented row boats for a romantic evening on the water. Senior citizens relaxed in red Adirondack chairs that were spread throughout the property, taking it all in.

As Maggie stepped through the white iron gate that led to the back of the property, she came face-to-face with Sadie, who was greeting guests as they arrived. "Hi!" Maggie squinched at the sound of her own voice jumping an octave higher. She made a soft sound to clear her throat. "Sadie, this is my Aunt Katie and, um, Brody."

Sadie's eyes widened. "Welcome to Waldhaus!" She offered the group a tight-lipped smile. "Please enjoy the bonfire and cocktail specials at the Boathouse Café."

As Brody and Katie walked through the gate and headed down to the water, Maggie lingered behind. "I know I'm not working tonight, but if you need anything, Sadie, I'm here."

Sadie's spirit seemed lighter after having met Brody. "We're all good! Go enjoy your evening together."

Maggie walked across the grass to join Brody and Katie on the beach. It was one of those perfect summer evenings where the setting sun hit the leaves on the trees, so they flickered in the breeze like candlelight. Amid the perfume of cedar and lake water, Maggie took off her flip flops and felt the cool of the evening wash over her as her toes kissed the sun-warmed sand.

"I'll get us some drinks," Brody said. "Save me a seat around the fire." He gave Maggie a quick peck on the cheek before jaunting off toward the Boathouse Café.

Maggie turned to make her way to the fire, bumping into a passerby and losing her balance. The stranger caught her arm.

"Sorry, I didn't see you," Maggie said. As she looked up, she realized it wasn't a stranger after all. "Thomas! Hi."

Thomas quickly let go of her arm. "Maggie," he said curtly. "Nice to see you again, Katie."

"Nice to see you, too, Thomas! I'm a little chilly… I'll save you a seat by the fire, Maggie."

Maggie waited until her aunt was out of earshot. "I was hoping I'd run into you," Maggie said.

Thomas looked good. His curly hair was perfectly messy, and Maggie could make out his muscular pecs through his moss-green t-shirt. Thomas put his hands in his jean pockets and stared at his feet. "When were you going to tell me about your boyfriend?"

Maggie sighed. "I'm so sorry, Thomas. I should've told you sooner. The truth is, it's messy. We're on a break, and I—"

"No need to explain." Thomas held up his hands. "I get it. Relationships can be complicated." Thomas took a few steps backwards. "I'll see you around, Maggie."

Maggie's heart sank as she watched him walk away. She resisted the urge to run up behind him and wrap her arms around his waist. Instead, she found Katie and sat with a *humph*. The fire crackled. Tiny, orange sparks flew up toward the darkening sky. The music of laughter drifted from the neighboring groups gathered on the property.

"You look miserable," Katie said. She wrapped an arm around Maggie's shoulders. "Want to talk about it?"

Maggie wasn't sure if her aunt was the best person to go to for relationship advice. She took a deep breath. "Brody asked me to move in with him. He even brought up marriage."

Katie gave a knowing nod. "Are you ready to take such a big step?"

"No! I tried to explain that to him, but—"

"Listen, Maggie. I know it may seem like I blew up my marriage for no good reason, but the truth is, I'm being courageous for the first time in my life and searching for my truth. You can't please everybody, so you might as well speak *your* truth. That way, at least you know you're being authentic to yourself."

"I want to break up with him," Maggie said in a clear and confident voice. It felt good to finally say it out loud.

Katie patted Maggie's knee. "Then be honest with him, honey. At the end of the day, you basically have to answer to yourself. Not anybody else."

Maggie bit the inside of her cheek. She was

paralyzed with dread, afraid of how Brody would react when she broke up with him. From a distance, Maggie spotted Brody returning with three cocktails in hand. She shot up.

"Excuse me, Katie. I'll be right back."

Maggie set off, searching for a place to collect herself. She remembered Thomas had said he would be manning the fire that evening and found him gathering wood in the shed. He looked surprised to see her.

"Maggie, what are you doing in here?" Thomas dropped the pile of firewood he was holding into an empty wheelbarrow.

Maggie wrung her hands as she paced back and forth in the small shed. The walls were closing in on her with every passing second. She didn't know why she had decided to seek him out. "I just needed a safe place to hide out for a minute."

Thomas stepped in her way and grabbed ahold of her forearms. "Hey." He opened his mouth to speak again but paused as though he were collecting his thoughts. "Are you okay?"

Maggie needed to escape, to find fresh air. She lifted her head and gazed into his troubled green eyes. His presence calmed her. He smelled like the essence of summer, the perfect mix of campfire smoke, lake water, and sunscreen. She opened her mouth to speak but was unable to.

Thomas leaned in closer, making strong eye contact as he gently massaged her forearms with his thumbs. "I'm right here. I think you might be having an anxiety attack. I—"

"Thomas!" Thomas and Maggie jumped apart at the sound of an intruder. "Maggie?" The girl's voice cracked. There, standing at the door of the shed, was Sadie.

ALYSSA DELLE PALME

Chapter Nine

Maggie was counting the knots in the wood of her bedroom ceiling the next morning when she heard the familiar creak of the pine floors. Somebody was up. She quickly shut her eyes, rolled onto her side, and pretended to be asleep. The truth was, she had been lying awake for hours, reliving the intense moment she had shared with Thomas before Sadie showed up and interrupted them. Maggie had quickly excused herself and rejoined Brody and Katie at the bonfire. She spent the rest of the night avoiding Thomas.

"Mags?" Brody sat on the edge of her bed and gently rocked Maggie's hip back and forth. When he had offered to sleep on the couch out of respect for Katie, Maggie was relieved. Her heart ached, remembering what a thoughtful boyfriend Brody was before the mind games started. He once took her to the mountains in British Columbia for spring break. Maggie had envisioned a romantic trip. She imagined leisurely snowshoeing through the pristine wilderness, warming up in a luxurious hot tub at the resort afterward, and dressing up for a fine dining experience at the hotel's restaurant. However, Brody had a different plan in mind. Maggie could still remember the proud look on his face when he dragged a snowboard, boots, and bindings into her apartment the night before their scheduled flight.

"I bought you all this secondhand gear for an amazing price on Kijiji. It's practically brand new!"

Maggie chewed the inside of her cheek. "All this is for me? But I don't know how to snowboard."

"I know." Brody winked. "I'm going to teach you!"

They ended up spending the majority of their

weeklong holiday on the bunny hill. Maggie had given it her all, but learning to snowboard was no easy feat.

"Snowboarding is harder to learn, but easier to master than skiing," Brody told her.

Snow-tipped mountains soared into the sky all around them. The view from the top was incredible, and the mountain air was so cold it burned Maggie's lungs, but she spent more time on her butt in the fresh powder than she did snowboarding through it, and Brody's encouragement began to waver.

"You're going to make me look like a bad teacher," he said through gritted teeth. "You're not trying hard enough." He spent the rest of the day giving her the silent treatment.

Maggie had tried her best, but at the end of her first lesson, she could hardly move. She was sore from head to toe. Brody was just as exhausted from pulling her up over and over again, but he insisted on giving her a full body massage that night.

"It's not my fault I got so frustrated today," he said, rubbing a knot out of her aching back. "You're capable of doing better."

The next day, Maggie insisted Brody let her hire a professional so that he could go and explore the steep black diamond slopes.

"We didn't come all the way out here for you to cruise the beginner hill," she said.

Brody agreed but stopped by the bunny hill every couple of runs to steal a kiss, cheer her on, and stare down her good-looking snowboard instructor. Every night, he massaged her sore body.

Now, in her cottage bedroom, Brody gently rubbed her hip in an effort to wake her. "Mags?"

Maggie slowly opened her eyes. She'd rehearsed the words in her head all night, knowing it was the right thing to do. "I can't move in with you Brody. I'm sorry." Her voice was groggy.

Brody nodded. His finger traced the pattern on the colorful heirloom quilt that laid atop the white duvet. "I get it. You need more time. Listen, I'll organize a schedule with work so that I can come visit you every other weekend this summer. Maybe you could take a week off in August and come back to the city—"

"Brody, no." Maggie wiggled into a seated position and took his hands into hers. Her mind raced with worry about how he was going to react, but she tried to stay firm. "I care about you, but I think it's best if we break up."

Brody jerked his hands away. "What? You can't be serious."

Maggie's hands shook uncontrollably. She tucked them under the quilt and took a deep breath to steady her racing heartbeat. "I've thought it through, Brody. I don't want what you want. Staying together isn't fair to either of us."

Brody's eyes seemed to be pleading with her. "You don't mean that. You're just afraid because I brought up marriage."

Familiar, anxious feelings of being confined to an enclosed space crept back into Maggie's chest. "No. Brody, I—"

"Maggie, you'll be lost without me. You're making a big mistake. I—"

Maggie held up her hand, and Brody stopped mid-sentence. She was having difficulty concentrating from all the pressure. It broke her heart to see such desperation in his eyes. Maggie struggled between wanting to comfort and reassure Brody and needing to stay strong in her decision. Ending their relationship was best for both of them, even if he didn't see that yet. Maggie swallowed hard, gathering herself. "It's my life, Brody, my choice. I know you love me enough to respect it."

Brody's shoulders slumped. He turned away from Maggie and placed his head in his hands, rubbing his temples in a circular motion. When Maggie placed a hand on his back, he recoiled sharply.

"You'll never find someone like me." There was a mean, disapproving tone to his voice.

Maggie licked her lips and gulped, suddenly mistrusting her own judgement.

"You're unappreciative of everything I've done for you. You're selfish, demanding, and you've single-handedly destroyed everything we have built." Brody stood up from the bed. "You'll never be happy." Without making eye contact, Brody grabbed his belongings and stormed out of the cottage.

It wasn't until she heard his car peel out the driveway that the dam broke. Maggie couldn't fathom how she had just become the most despised person in Brody's life.

The pine floor creaked.

"Maggie, I wanted to talk to you about something important. I—" Katie stopped in her tracks. "Honey, what's the matter?"

"I—I broke up with Brody."

Katie sat on the edge of her bed, and Maggie melted into her arms. Her aunt smelled similar to her mother, comforting like chamomile. Once Maggie's sobs subsided into little hiccups, Katie pulled away. She grabbed a tissue off the bedside table and offered it to Maggie.

"Tell me everything."

Maggie accepted a tissue and told her aunt about how things had ended. "In the beginning of our relationship, Brody was thrilled to have 'won' me as a girlfriend. He always told me how wonderful and perfect I was, but one day that all changed. He started saying mean things to me and would give me the silent treatment. Sometimes for days! When I'd ask him what was wrong, he'd say I didn't understand the stress he was under at work. He'd say I was 'too emotional' or that I was always 'overreacting.' I tried so hard to make him happy, but in his eyes, I was always doing everything wrong. I just couldn't take it anymore."

Katie's eyebrows drew together in a pained expression. "Those things he said to you were thoroughly unfair and wrong, Maggie. Do you regret breaking up with him?"

Moments ago, Maggie was terrified she had made a huge mistake, but now that Brody was gone, she realized that all she felt was relief. "It was the right thing to do. I just can't stand to see him hurt, and I wish I wasn't the cause of it."

Katie nodded. "I think you tried to make things work, even when you realized the relationship wasn't healthy for you. I think you did the right thing, sweetie. You need to prioritize your own well-being and focus on yourself. You know what else you need?"

"A pint of ice cream and a stack of romcom movies?"

A thoughtful smile tugged at the corners of Katie's mouth. "A walk in the woods."

Maggie groaned. She didn't have the energy to get out of bed, but Katie pulled her to her feet. "You'll feel better, I promise."

It had rained overnight, and the smell of the cedar trees was always more abundant after a rain shower. Maggie inhaled the aromatic, woodsy air and hiked down the forest trail that was lined with thick ferns. She dragged her fingertips along various trees as she passed by. Some had smooth, papery bark, while others were rough with deep wrinkles. Small animals scurried through the ferns, hunting for breakfast. Maggie peeked inside a dead, hollow tree trunk and was delighted to find tiny, orange fungi.

Fairy homes!

When Maggie was a child, Johnny had told her such discoveries were magical because they belonged to the fairies of the forest. On their hikes through the woods, he would tell theatrical tales of the fairies and how they were extra busy in the summer, making the wildflowers bloom. Maggie had been determined to befriend the fairies, so Johnny helped her write letters to them. They'd tuck her notes into tiny places that Maggie believed to be a fairy home. When they'd return the next day, Maggie was always delighted to find the fairies had written her back and would sometimes leave special candy for her.

Maggie's heart ached with a sudden pang, realizing her uncle would've had to retrace his footsteps through the forest, in the cover of darkness, to leave candy behind for Maggie to find the next day. A treat from the fairies. Maggie missed Johnny incredibly, but for once, the thought of him didn't make her feel like crying. The memory had made her happy, knowing she was fortunate to have had those special moments with him.

Maggie continued to follow the forest loop until it brought her back to the dock. The sound of the waves gently lapping against the shore soothed the tension she was holding in her shoulders. The fresh air was damp and scented with pine and wet earth. She had learned to swim in this lake. Her uncle would walk the shoreline, shouting instructions, to help Maggie improve her strokes.

"Your hips shouldn't rotate as much as your shoulders! Kick harder!" he'd yell.

Though Johnny was no longer with them, the memory of him was everywhere at the cottage.

Perhaps that's why Grandma hasn't returned yet.

It dawned on Maggie that she would never recover from the loss of her uncle. Time did not heal all wounds. But perhaps, her grief from his loss had integrated into her life and had profoundly changed the way she experienced the world. Maggie couldn't help but grin at the thought. Katie had been right. A walk in the woods had made her feel better.

Maggie scanned the lakeshore and saw Thomas paddling his canoe with his fishing rod hanging out the back. His biceps flexed as he retraced the arc of his arm over and over again as he paddled toward her. Maggie's pulse quickened, remembering the worry in his eyes and how he'd gently caressed her forearms to help calm her down. As his canoe glided in her direction, Maggie's heartbeat pounded in her ears. Thomas seemed relaxed, like the weekend scruff on his chin.

"Hey!" Thomas expertly slid his canoe next to her dock. "Where's your boyfriend?" His voice was edged with control.

"Brody left."

His eyes held hers. "Oh?"

Maggie twirled a wavey strand of hair around her right index finger. "We broke up."

His eyebrows shot up in surprise. "I'm sorry to hear that."

Maggie shook her head and looked down at her feet. "Brody and I should've made it official a long time ago. Listen, I wanted to thank you for helping me last night. I was panicking and I feel a little embarrassed—"

"Don't be. Maggie, I'm here for you." His eyes held hers for a brief, intense moment. Then, almost instantly, he glanced away, nervous laughter escaping his lips. "Love is complex, Maggie, and sometimes being in a bad relationship can cause an irritating itch with other people that's often better left unscratched."

She raised her right eyebrow.

Thomas coughed softly. "What I mean to say is we're friends, right?"

Maggie searched his eyes, relieved to find no traces of anger. The friendly glimmer staring back at her was reassuring. Her mouth twitched with a smile. "Yes, of course we're friends."

Thomas pushed his boat off the dock, flashing a smile. "Good. I'll see you around, Maggie."

As she watched him paddle away, the distance between them growing with every stroke, the relief that had filled her moments ago quickly faded. The lightness in her chest was replaced with heavy longing. The sudden realization that she'd only ever be Thomas's friend hit her harder than she expected, and the weight of that truth stole the breath from her lungs. Maggie pressed her lips together and willed the uninvited thoughts away. Maybe something more was possible in another lifetime, but a friend is what she needed right now, and Thomas was a great one. She swallowed the lump in her throat, refusing to let the yearning take over. Maggie made her way up the stairs to the refuge of the cottage. She opened the sliding glass door and saw Katie standing in the kitchen with her back turned.

"I don't care what people will think!" Katie shouted into the phone.

Maggie stopped dead in her tracks. She hadn't meant to walk in on her aunt fighting with her soon-to-be ex-husband. She slowly turned to tiptoe her way back outside.

"After all this time, I thought you'd be more supportive, Elizabeth."

Maggie's ears perked up at the sound of her mother's name. Maggie never understood the rift between her mother and her aunt, but for as long as she could remember, the sisters had never gotten along.

"I'm doing this with or without your help." Katie tapped her foot as she waited for an answer. "Fine!" she yelled into the phone before spastically stabbing the screen with her index finger and slamming the phone down on the kitchen island. Her eyebrows rounded with surprise when she saw Maggie standing there. "I'm sorry you had to hear that."

"Don't apologize. I—I didn't mean to eavesdrop. Everything okay?"

Katie walked to the freezer and grabbed a bottle of tequila and two shot glasses. "Drink?"

Maggie nodded, a little afraid of turning her aunt down.

Once they were seated outside, they clinked their frosted shot glasses together and swallowed the tipple of burning hard liquor in one gulp. It went down like gasoline.

Maggie scrunched her nose and shivered. "We need lemons!"

"And salt," added Katie as she poured them each a second shot. "So, what has you agreeing to take tequila shots with me before noon on a weekday?"

Maggie spun her overflowing shot glass between her thumb and forefinger. "I think I might have feelings for Thomas."

"And that's a bad thing?" Katie asked.

"Yes! I just broke up with Brody, and my life has no direction. The last thing I need to do is get involved with somebody else."

Katie bit her lip. "I think he likes you, too."

Maggie rubbed her forearm absently. "No, he

doesn't."

Katie raised a single eyebrow and cocked her head. "I can tell by the way he looks at you."

Maggie waved her off. "You're wrong. He just told me he wants to be friends." Maggie winced at the memory and took her second shot in an effort to forget it.

"Does he know that you broke up with Brody?"

Maggie nodded. "I told him. It's for the best. What I need right now is a supportive friend. I'm not going to risk getting together with the only friend I have in this town." She leaned her head into her hand, already tipsy. "So, are you going to tell me what happened between you and my mom?"

"Actually, I've been wanting to talk to you about something for a while."

When Maggie heard the seriousness in Katie's voice, she sat up straight. She tried to ignore the perfect view of Thomas's cottage from this side of the picnic table. She gave her head a shake and tried to focus her attention on Katie. "Is everything okay?"

"I'm worried what you'll think of me once I tell you."

"Katie, you can tell me any—" Maggie stopped short when something, rather *someone,* caught her eye.

"What are you looking at?" Katie leaned across the table and looked toward Thomas's cottage.

Both women watched as Sadie, dressed in a denim miniskirt and a tight spaghetti strap tank top, walked straight into Thomas's cottage.

Chapter Ten

"I'm on my way," said June.

"Seriously, I'm fine," Maggie whispered into the receiver. Katie was listening outside her bedroom door.

"Liar. I can tell you've been crying," said June, matter of fact.

Maggie glimpsed her bedside table that was littered with damp balls of used Kleenex. "What time will you be here?"

After Maggie had watched Sadie waltz into Thomas's cottage, she surprised both herself and her aunt when she burst into tears. She quickly excused herself and sought the solace of her bedroom. When she hadn't emerged the next morning, Katie came knocking on her door.

"Honey? Is there anything I can do for you?"

"I'm fine!" Maggie yelled from underneath the crisp white duvet. "I'm just tired."

"I'm here if you need me."

A sharp pang of guilt gripped Maggie's chest. Katie had wanted to tell her something important, but Maggie couldn't control the waterworks long enough to listen. Her emotions had already been teetering on the edge from quitting the internship, disappointing her parents, breaking up with Brody, and then her sudden, unexpected feelings for Thomas. Seeing Sadie was the tipping point and there was no stopping the tears that followed. Maggie determined the tequila was the culprit of her mini breakdown, and she would apologize to Katie once she could pull herself together.

As Maggie hid under the blankets, she wondered if the intensity she had felt in certain moments with Thomas were completely one-sided. She scolded herself for being so upset in the first place. She had no right.

She'd had a boyfriend and withheld that from Thomas when they were first getting to know each other. Thomas himself had said love was complex. Maybe this whole debacle had made him realize he still had feelings for Sadie, who was loyal and still madly in love with him. It was immature, embarrassing even, for Maggie to be this affected.

"I'm going into town. I've prepared a camp care package for the boys, and I need to drop it off at the post office. Do you need anything?" Katie asked through the closed door.

Maggie came out from under her duvet. "No, thank you!"

" A pint of chocolate ice cream it is!"

Maggie's lips curled in a quiet, sad smile. She was lucky to have such caring friends and family. After she heard Katie's car leave the driveway, she crawled out of bed, washed her face, and grabbed a cold bottle of water from the fridge. She headed to the dock to sit out in the sunshine in her pajamas—a pair of Brody's old boxer shorts and an oversize Taylor Swift t-shirt she had bought at a concert when she was in middle school. Maggie sat down in a beige rattan lounge chair. The body-long cushion was warm from sitting out in the sun. Maggie settled back, closed her eyes, and luxuriated in the sun's heat, soaking up its rays and vitamin D. The waves gently lapped against the dock, stirring up a familiar scent of lake water and seaweed. The wavering call of a loon echoed across the lake, and a small smile tugged at Maggie's mouth. Nature always had a way of relaxing her and allowing her to forget her problems, at least for a moment.

"Long time no see."

At the sound of Thomas's voice, Maggie opened her eyes and shot straight up. Blinded by the sun, she had to blink a few times before her eyes could focus on his tall frame. If she had known she was going to be seeing Thomas, she would have brushed her hair, put on a bra, and changed out of her tear-stained t-shirt.

"Thomas, hi." Maggie crossed her arms over her chest.

Thomas walked to the end of the dock, kicked off his navy flip-flops, and sat down. He put his feet in the water and looked back at Maggie, patting the empty space beside him. His full lips welcomed her with a warm and confident smile.

Maggie hesitated. "What are you doing here?"

"What? A guy can't come visit with his friend?"

Maggie regretted leaving the safety of her bed. A soft, reluctant sigh escaped her lips as she got up and joined him at the edge of the dock. When she sat down beside him, she couldn't resist being drawn to his profile. His straight nose complimented the strength of his jaw that was covered in a light, rugged stubble. Maggie dipped her feet into the lake, the coolness offering a brief escape from the heat that had made its way to the tips of her ears.

"How are you doing?" Thomas asked. His eyebrows knit together in a frown. "With the breakup, I mean."

Maggie was captivated by his green eyes that flickered like the sunshine that filtered through the leaves on the trees that surrounded them. She looked away first. "I'm fine."

Thomas placed his hand on her forearm. "Really? Because it looks like you're struggling."

The warmth of Thomas's hand sent a spark down Maggie's arm to her fingertips. She quickly pulled away. "That sounds like a nice way of saying I look like crap."

"That's not what I meant. I—"

"No, it's okay. I am struggling. To be honest, I feel overwhelmingly guilty because I'm relieved! I know Brody was upset, and the fact I feel so much better seems unfair. It feels selfish."

Thomas stared out into the distance. "Listen. From personal experience, if you're unhappy in a relationship, it's selfish to stay."

Maggie raised her right eyebrow and held it for a moment. "I'd think it would be even more selfish to break up with someone and then continue to hook up with them afterwards. Especially if you know that someone is still into you," she said, referring to Sadie.

Thomas cocked his head. "I mean, if you had clearly defined guidelines, I guess it would be all right. I—"

Maggie put her hands over her ears. She couldn't stand to hear any more about Thomas and Sadie's friends with benefits guidelines. "Enough!"

Thomas stopped, taken aback. His eyes studied her quizzically. "Well, you were the one who brought it up."

Maggie waved her hands. "Can we just stop talking about this?"

Thomas nodded. He was quiet for a moment. "Do you want to go for a paddle? You seem a bit tense. Getting out on the water always helps me when I—"

Maggie rose abruptly and dusted herself off. "I don't think Sadie would appreciate that."

A look of puzzlement crossed Thomas's face. "What are you talking—"

"My best friend is driving up from the city, and she'll be here any minute," Maggie interrupted. "I have to go get ready. I'll see you around, Thomas."

Maggie bolted up the stairs, a deep sense of disappointment spreading throughout her chest. Being friends with Thomas was proving to be more difficult than she'd thought.

"Hello?"

Maggie's shoulders relaxed the moment she heard June's singsong voice. When she reached the top of the stairs, Maggie couldn't hold back a laugh when her best friend walked around the wrap-around deck, pulling two overstuffed suitcases on wheels.

"How long are you planning to stay?" Maggie teased, eyeing the amount of luggage June had brought with her.

The women embraced and excitedly rocked back and forth. June was so tiny at five-foot-two that Maggie could almost rest her chin on the top of her head. June's silky brown bob smelled shampoo-fresh and lovely like peonies.

"It's so good to see you!" Maggie said. She held June at arm's length, admiring her high cheekbones, which June claimed were a gift from an Indigenous relative on her mother's side. She looked trendy in a pair of high-rise black denim shorts and a white short-sleeved crop top.

June's hazel eyes sparkled. "It's so good to be here, Maggie! Where should I park these things?" She pointed to her suitcases that were threatening to explode at any moment.

"In my room. You'll stay with me." Maggie guided June to her bedroom. "You packed lightly." Maggie's voice strained as she heaved one of June's suitcases on the bed. "Why did you bring so much?"

"I wanted to tell you in person. I got a role as a performer on a cruise ship! We sail away next Monday."

"June! That's incredible. Where are you going?" Maggie flopped on the bed and rolled onto her side, enthralled by her friend's big news.

"It's not that big of a deal. I didn't get the lead."

"Oh, come on, June! You're going to travel the world! This is a huge accomplishment. What part did you get?"

"Cassie in *A Chorus Line*."

"I love *A Chorus Line*! You do know there's no real leads in *A Chorus Line*, right? Hence the title."

"I know, I know—"

"Where's the ship taking you?"

June collapsed dramatically onto the bed next to Maggie. "Europe. We'll be traveling from London to France then Germany and then Norway to Copenhagen."

Ever since they were twelve years old, Maggie and June had dreamed of touring the world as performers. They used to sit on the floor of June's bedroom, cutting up magazines to create large vision boards of their futures. Their posters were collages of images like the Empire State Building, their favorite movie stars, and colorful sofas from the IKEA catalogue, which they planned to buy for their New York City apartment.

Maggie sighed, remembering her preteen dreams of becoming famous and traveling the world with her best friend. "I'm proud of you, June. You're really doing it!"

A big smile spread across June's face. "I am, aren't I?"

"Johnny would be so happy for you."

June sat up and pressed her hands to her cheeks. "Stop! You're going to make me cry."

Maggie covered her eyes with her hands. "Don't! Or then I'll start." Maggie peeked through her fingers and made eye contact with June. They burst into a fit of giggles. "Let's go for a walk," Maggie said once she was able to collect herself.

Outside, the sun was shining, and a gentle breeze blew through the treetops. There wasn't a cloud in the sky. It was hot, but the humidity was low.

"It's the perfect summer day," June said, linking her arm through Maggie's. As they strolled down the winding dirt road, they peered at the different cottages as they passed by, making up stories of those who lived there.

"This one is owned by movie stars," June said. She pointed to a red two-story cottage at the bottom of the hill. The large retreat had the best view of the lake.

"Yes, a celebrity couple and their three beautiful children vacation here every summer," Maggie added.

"Except nothing is as it seems. The husband is having an affair…"

"With the au pair!"

The women erupted in laughter. Maggie marched on with a satisfied grin. Having June by her side brought her a sense of comfort and happiness. As they continued on their walk, Maggie found wild grapes at the side of the road and harvested two long vines, which she tied into two small wreaths. She handed one to June. "Now we just have to add wildflowers."

A gentle smile curled on Maggie's lips as she watched June gleefully pick wild daisies, purple asters, bluebells, and yellow black-eyed Susans. When she was finished, June placed the flower crown on her head and did a twirl to model it for Maggie.

"What do you think?" June asked.

"You look like a forest queen!"

When the women reached a fork in the road, they veered to the left, eventually reaching a dilapidated building on their right-hand side.

Maggie slowed her pace. "This is the old schoolhouse! I totally forgot this place was here. When I was little, Johnny would let me hop the fence and look through the windows. It was a mess inside, but the antique desks were still standing. I'd beg him to let me go inside to explore, but he always said no. He was worried the roof would collapse at any moment."

"And your mother would've had his head!"

Maggie and June sat on the old wooden fence in their flower crowns, facing the old schoolhouse.

"I can't believe you live here now. It's such a beautiful spot, Maggie."

Maggie shooed a hungry mosquito off her thigh. "I know, but it's only temporary."

"Yeah, but what a way to spend your summer."

Maggie uncrossed her ankles and leaned forward. "I truly love it here."

June bumped her shoulder against Maggie's. "Do you think you could still patch things up with Brody?"

"What? No!"

"Why not? He's perfect. I still can't believe you broke up with him."

Maggie hopped off the fence. "You only saw the side of Brody where he'd bombard me with affection and gifts."

June scratched her face. "Are you saying there's a different side to Brody?"

"Sometimes, he'd treat me like a child. He'd talk down to me and he wouldn't let me do the simplest of tasks. He'd act as though I were incapable. He'd also hold grudges for days, and when I asked him about it, he'd invalidate my feelings."

June jumped off the fence. "Why didn't you tell me any of this?"

Maggie shrugged. "I guess part of me liked that you loved my boyfriend. I thought if I just tried harder to do better and be better, then things with Brody would improve."

June wrapped her arm around Maggie's shoulders.

"I'm sorry I didn't see it. He certainly pulled the wool over my eyes."

Maggie leaned her head against June's shoulder. "The thing is, Brody was also all of those things you believed him to be. I think that's why I was confused a lot."

"Two things can be true at once." June rubbed Maggie's arm. "You didn't need to change, Maggie. You're incredible. I'm sorry he treated you that way. He didn't deserve you. Fuck him."

Maggie lifted her head and adjusted the flower crown. "Yeah. Fuck him!"

June snickered. "So, what's next?"

Maggie sighed, taking in the nature scene that surrounded her. A yellow butterfly fluttered above the wildflower field in search of flight fuel and eventually rested on a petal landing pad to probe for nectar. "I don't know what's next. I wish I could stay out here forever."

"If you stay here too long, you'll turn into one of those people that builds a tiny home and has chickens for pets."

Maggie hesitated before speaking. "That doesn't sound so bad."

"Maggie! Are you serious? I hope this isn't about that guy."

Maggie shook her head. "Thomas wants to be friends. Besides, I think he might be back together with his ex. Anyway, this isn't about Thomas. I promise. It's hard to explain. When I'm out on the lake or in the forest, I feel the most like me."

"Are you sure you're not running away from something?"

Maggie licked her lips. "At first, yes. I needed to escape Brody and the internship, but I'm happy here. I feel a joy and steadiness in my heart that wasn't there in the city."

"But, like you said, this is temporary. You can't stay here forever. What about your career?"

Maggie paused before answering. "It didn't work out, June."

June stepped in front of Maggie and crossed her arms. "Are you ever going to tell me what really happened?"

Maggie hung her head. June was the type of trusted friend you could tell anything to, but Maggie didn't have the energy to get into it. "The internship wasn't all it was cracked up to be."

"You barely gave yourself a chance to acclimate. Any new job can feel overwhelming. Sometimes there's a learning curve that—"

"I put everything I could into it. I didn't need more time."

"You do realize that even a 'dream job' is never going to be perfect, right?"

"Of course, I know that." Maggie cringed at the defensive tone in her voice. June was only trying to help. "I think I wanted the job so badly that I just assumed things about the position, and I dismissed some warning signs."

June cocked her head to the side. She was waiting for Maggie to explain further, but when she didn't, June gently placed her hand on Maggie's shoulder. "Have you thought about why you wanted the internship in the first place?"

"I wanted to write! I thought I could contribute. I allowed myself to imagine where the internship could lead me in the future." A single tear fell onto Maggie's flushed cheek. She quickly wiped it away and pulled the flower crown off of her head. "I feel ridiculous."

June gave Maggie's shoulder a gentle shake.

"You're not ridiculous. You're Maggie Taylor! A talented journalist. I've read your writing and heard your reports. You're good. Like really good. You can't let all that talent go to waste."

Maggie adjusted June's crooked flower crown. "You're a good friend, you know that, right?"

June took Maggie's crown from her hand and placed it back on her head. "The best!"

Maggie giggled. June always had a way of cheering her up when she was feeling down. "I'm trying to put everything in perspective, I promise. I'll figure it out. I just need more time."

As they walked back to the cottage, arm in arm like two kindred spirits, Maggie was inspired for the first time in weeks. June understood her on a deeper level, unlike anyone else. Maggie had allowed herself to sink into despair over the internship, and June had known just what to say to help Maggie realize what she wanted and how she could continue working toward her goals. Maggie could reveal the messiest parts of herself to June, and June would always love her anyway.

Chapter Eleven

"I still can't believe you live here," June said. She rolled from her back to her stomach in her watermelon-pink, v-neckline bikini with ruffles. The movement rocked the floating raft that bobbed gently in the bay in front of the dock. Maggie and June had slept in and were now tanning in the midday sun, enjoying a strawberry smoothie for brunch. It was Maggie's first day off since June arrived, and she was relieved to finally have a break from Sadie's angry glares.

June exhaled in satisfaction. "Lake life is the best life." She took off her sunglasses and hid her face from the sun in the crook of her arm.

"You're beginning to sound like the decorative pillows they sell at the gift shops in town," Maggie said. She was seated at the edge of the raft, watching the boats as they passed by from time to time. She splashed her feet in the cool water. Droplets sprayed onto her legs, magnifying the sunlight onto her already bronzed skin.

"Well, I am a tourist after all. Let's go into town this afternoon! We could go shopping and to a restaurant for dinner. You can be my personal tour guide." said June.

Maggie looked down at the red sweetheart-neckline one piece bathing suit she was wearing. "I'd love to, but I'm on a tight budget, remember?"

June lifted her head from her arm pillow and squinted from the brightness of the sun. "It will be my treat," she said, putting her sunglasses back on.

Maggie took a sip of her pink smoothie and shook her head. "I can't let you do that."

June turned from her stomach to her back. "Of course you can. I've been here all week on vacation, eating all your groceries. It's the least I can do."

Maggie grinned, suddenly lost in a happy memory. June's idea reminded her of when she was younger, and Johnny would take her into town on rainy days.

"There's nothing like the charm of a small town," he would say.

They'd link arms and skip down Main Street, which was filled with locally owned shops and diners. Residents stopped to say hello and let Maggie pet their dogs. Remembering the smell of fresh bread and hot fries that would drift out of the mom-and-pop restaurants was enough to make Maggie's stomach grumble.

"I'd love to show you around!" she said. Maggie also needed a break from looking over at Thomas's dock every couple of minutes.

Cedar Grove was a short fifteen-minute drive from the cottage. The little town was established as a military settlement in the early 1800s, but today its small-town charm was a combination of its history, natural beauty, and ever-expanding collection of unique shops, art galleries, and restaurants. The locals were very involved in community activities, festivals, and outdoor recreation, but they were also keen on preserving the town's authentic, relaxed cottage lifestyle.

"Cedar Grove is so vibrant!" said June. She rested her arm on the car door frame, gazing out her open window as they drove through town. The sleeves of her tropical print romper fluttered in the wind.

Maggie was thrilled June could see what she saw in Cedar Grove. Maggie reclined back as she slowly cruised down Main Street, enjoying the warm summer breeze that blew in through the open windows. She was happy that June appreciated the town that meant so much to her.

"Tourists from all over the world come to town in

the summer," said Maggie, pulling into a parking space overlooking the river that flowed through downtown. She unbuckled her seatbelt and removed a pine needle from her smocked, pinstriped maxi dress.

"What's the plan?" June asked.

"First, I'm going to take you to the Farmer's Market, where we can get a good cup of coffee. Then, we'll shop in all the best boutiques, explore a gallery, and grab a bite to eat at an outdoor patio. What do you think?"

June's ear-to-ear smile said it all. "I'm in!"

Maggie and June spent the day visiting all the independent shops on Main Street that operated out of century-old stone buildings and sold clothes, soaps, and beautiful glass pieces. Maggie thought she saw Thomas twice that day and was disappointed both times when the men turned out to be strangers. Maggie tried to push thoughts of Thomas to the back of her mind and focus her attention on June. They explored a local thrift shop and bought fresh produce from a farmer's stand, only stopping to eat when their arms were laden with heavy shopping bags. Maggie decided to take June to her favorite waterfront patio, *Rocky River Cafe*.

Maggie collapsed in her chair, sighing. "They have the best fish tacos!"

"Could this day get any better?" June carefully placed her shopping bags on an empty chair at their table and sat across from Maggie. "It's been so fun."

"It has!" Maggie's feet throbbed from their day of shopping. "I wish I could afford a trip to the spa for a pedicure."

"That would be nice! Do you remember that time I had a spa sleepover party for my thirteenth birthday, and we all ended up with lice?"

Maggie's head was suddenly itchy. To celebrate

officially becoming a teenager, June had invited a few girls over for a slumber party. They had stayed up until 4:00 in the morning, making their own face masks out of sugar and egg whites, and laid around talking about the latest celebrity gossip with cucumbers on their eyes.

"Do you think Harry Styles is gay?" their friend Sophie had asked, referring to her favorite boy band member from *One Direction*. She flipped the page of a *Teen Vogue* magazine.

"No, because I'm going to marry him," said their other friend, Alana, with a deadpan expression.

Somewhere between face masks, manicures, and talking about boy bands, someone had suggested makeovers. They played with each other's hair and made up their faces and took photos with a disposable camera. It was a fantastic party, one of the best, but was spoiled when a few days later Sophie's mother called the other mothers.

"Sophie has lice. We think her little brother brought it home from daycare."

Maggie scratched her head at the memory. "Ew, June. Please don't remind me!"

June giggled. "I still remember having to help my parents pack all the stuffed animals in our house into garbage bags. We had to leave them in the garage for weeks."

"I remember my mom, who I never heard swear a day in her life, cursing her head off as she scrubbed my head with the lice treatment."

Maggie and June laughed until tears fell from their eyes. They could barely keep it together when the waiter came to take their order.

"We should have a spa night tonight!" said June.

Maggie raised an eyebrow at her suggestion.

"It will be fun, I promise. We can go to the drug

store and pick out new summer nail polish colors. I'll grab us a clay face mask and a couple bottles of champagne, too."

Maggie broke into a wide, excited smile. June had a way of making life fun. "Let's do it! Would you mind if I invited Katie to join us?"

June rolled her eyes. "Do you even have to ask? Of course, I wouldn't mind."

Maggie relaxed against the back of her chair. "Thank you. It's just that I know she's been struggling, and I've been wanting to do something nice for her."

"Has she told you anything else about her situation?"

"She tried to before you arrived, but I've been so busy with work and focused on my own problems that I haven't been a very supportive niece."

The sun had already set by the time Maggie and June returned from town. Maggie couldn't resist glancing at Thomas's cottage. Fireflies lit up the sparse pine grove that divided their cottages like strings of twinkle lights. It was a relief to see his truck was the only vehicle parked in his driveway.

When Maggie and June walked through the front door of the cottage, Katie was sitting alone in her bathrobe at the kitchen table. A cold cup of tea sat in front of her. Her eyes were glassy, the rims red. Maggie could tell it took a lot of effort for Katie to offer them a weak smile.

"You're back! How was your trip to town?" Katie asked.

Both Maggie and June piled a mountain of shopping bags on the kitchen table to display their success.

"Cedar Grove is just the cutest little town," said June. "I'm going to go freshen up."

"Everything okay, Katie?" Maggie whispered once June was out of earshot. She sat down beside her aunt and placed a hand over top of hers. Katie's fingers were cold.

Katie pulled away and rubbed her eyes. "Everything is fine. I'm just tired."

"Then you're going to love what we have in store tonight," said June, skipping back into the kitchen. Maggie bit her lip. She could tell Katie wasn't doing very well.

"I'm not really up for doing anything tonight," said Katie. "I just need a night to relax and—"

"Exactly! We're going to pamper you with a do-it-yourself spa night," said June.

Katie hesitated. "I don't know. I—"

"Oh, come on, it will be fun," Maggie promised. She didn't know what was wrong with Katie, but she hoped a little pampering would make her feel better and take her mind off the separation.

"We have champagne!" said June in a playful sing-song rhythm. She took the heavy green bottle out of the brown paper bag and waved it around, trying to entice Katie.

Katie gave an exaggerated sigh. "All right, I'm in."

"Yes!" Maggie and June said in unison.

They changed into their pajamas and took their time setting up the spa. They wanted it to feel authentic, which was enhanced by the atmosphere of the cottage. They filled three buckets with steaming hot water and Epsom salts for foot baths. They lined the coffee table with their new nail polish colors, lit candles throughout the cottage, and June hit play on a Zen playlist on Spotify. Once the champagne was chilled, Maggie poured them each a glass.

"To girls' night!" Maggie cheered in her buttery-soft, modal pink bathrobe.

"I needed this," said Katie. She settled back into the couch and let Maggie paint her face with a thick, gray clay mask. Clutching her champagne in one hand, she allowed June to go to work on her other hand.

"You take great care of your cuticles," June said, admiring Katie's left hand. "Wow! Your ring is beautiful."

Katie immediately withdrew her hand.

June smacked her hand against her forehead. "Katie, I'm sorry. I didn't mean to bring it up—"

Katie waved her off. She chugged the rest of her champagne and handed her empty glass to Maggie. "It's fine, June. It is a beautiful ring. It was Stuart's great-grandmother's. Maggie, could you pour me another glass, please?"

Maggie nodded. She placed two slices of cucumber over Katie's puffy eyes and went to the kitchen. She pulled brie, aged cheddar, and grapes out of the fridge. She arranged them nicely on a wooden charcuterie board before adding crackers, red pepper jelly, and stuffed green olives to the platter. Thomas's porch light turned on, catching Maggie's eye.

Suddenly, her mind flashed to that moment in the woodshed, standing nose to nose with Thomas. His touch unexpectedly buzzing through her again.

"Maggie?" Katie waved her champagne glass around blindly.

Maggie shook her head, breaking the spell. "Coming!"

Maggie placed the charcuterie board down on the coffee table and poured everyone another glass of champagne. "I'll be right back."

Maggie hurried into the kitchen and turned off the

light to see better and to remain inconspicuous. Thomas was alone, playing his guitar in the screened porch. Maggie yearned to walk across her property to join him. She imagined cuddling up next to him as he strummed her a song that he had written just for her.

"Who are we spying on?" June asked. She placed her chin on Maggie's shoulder. "Oh."

"I'm not spying."

"Mmhmm. Is she there with him?"

"No. He's alone."

"I don't know why you're doing this to yourself."

"Doing what?"

"Pining over a guy who might be getting back together with his ex."

Maggie paused. "You know, when Thomas and I were hanging out, I never got the feeling that he was still into her or anything. And when we did talk about Sadie, he was respectful. It didn't feel like any part of him hoped to keep a connection with her."

June snapped her fingers. "Aha! Thomas is your bad pancake."

"My what?"

"You've never heard about the bad pancake theory? It was on that hit TV show—"

"No."

June rolled her eyes. She grabbed Maggie's hand and led her back into the living area and sat her next to Katie. June filled Katie's empty glass with more champagne before she sat on the edge of the coffee table across from Maggie. She patted her lap, and Maggie begrudgingly placed a foot on top of her thigh. As June went to work painting Maggie's toes salmon-pink, she explained the bad pancake theory.

"Thomas is the first guy you liked at the end of a serious relationship."

"Yes, so doesn't that make him the first pancake?"

"Yep, which always gets burnt."

Maggie crossed her arms and sunk deeper into the couch. The truth was, she'd always liked eating the crispy pieces on the first pancake.

"James, that guy from my gym, was my bad pancake," Katie said, her dry mask cracking across her face as she spoke.

June removed the cucumbers from Katie's eyes and handed her a warm, wet towel. Katie gently wiped the clay from her face, revealing soft, glowing skin beneath it.

"James was a mistake. I've ruined everything." Katie hiccupped. She chugged the remaining champagne and leaned forward for a refill.

June topped her up. "Do you think you could work things out with Stuart?"

Katie's bleary eyes fixated on June with a look of utter disbelief. "Would you forgive someone who had an affair for six months?"

June offered Katie a sympathetic smile before putting her head down to concentrate on finishing Maggie's pedicure.

Maggie pressed her lips together, gathering the right words to comfort her aunt. "We're not married, Katie. We don't have kids. We can't answer that. Your situation isn't so black and white. It's complicated. Have you talked to Stuart since you've been up here?"

Katie shook her head. "He's screening his calls. I left him a message to let him know where I was staying, but he never called me back."

"Well, you can't stay here forever. He'll have to talk to you at some point," said Maggie.

Katie hiccupped. "I don't know how he'll ever forgive me. I can't even forgive myself."

Maggie watched nervously as Katie polished off the bottle of champagne. June chewed her lip. Maggie could tell she was concerned, too. June gently placed Maggie's foot down.

"Don't move. Your toes need to dry," June told her. June quickly fixed a plate of cheese and crackers and passed it to Katie. "Here, eat something."

Katie nibbled on a cracker, deep in thought.

"People make mistakes, Katie. Uncle Stuart is obviously upset, but he has to talk to you eventually. After the dust settles, he'll remember how much he loves you, and he'll want to work it out."

Katie placed her plate back on the coffee table. "Even if he forgives me for the affair, he'll never forgive me for sharing the other secret that I've been hiding."

Maggie gave a small, confused shake of her head. "What other secret?"

"I tried to tell you before. I'm so ashamed, but I…"

"You can tell us anything," Maggie encouraged.

June sat on Katie's other side and placed a hand over top of hers. "We won't judge you."

Katie sucked in a steady breath. "Do you remember when I used to tell you stories about my high school sweetheart, Dan?"

Maggie nodded, but there was no way Katie could've possibly have had an affair with him. He had come out of the closet later in life. "Isn't Dan gay?"

"Yes, but this happened before all that."

"From when you two were together?" Maggie asked.

Katie nodded.

A cold wave of unease flooded Maggie's stomach. Her heart went out to her aunt. Katie was obviously devastated by something that had happened in her past.

"That's an awful long time to keep a secret."

Tears streamed down Katie's flushed cheeks. "The weight of it is unbearable. I'm having trouble sleeping. I can't keep living like this."

Maggie and June made eye contact over top Katie's head. June looked back and forth between Maggie and Katie in a way that silently said she didn't know what to do. Maggie wrapped her arm around Katie's shoulder. Worry bubbled in her chest, but she needed to stay calm for Katie's sake. "It's safe to talk here."

"I did a terrible, terrible thing. I think about her every day."

Her? June mouthed silently to Maggie.

Maggie shrugged, equally confused. "Who are you talking about?"

Katie drew in a ragged breath. "When I was in high school, I put my baby girl up for adoption. I gave her away."

ALYSSA DELLE PALME

Chapter Twelve

The cottage was still. Hours had passed since her aunt had revealed her secret. Maggie had tucked an exhausted Katie into her bed before crawling into her own bed with June, who happened to be quietly snoring in a restful sleep. Maggie sat in the dark wide awake as if she had taken two shots of espresso before bed. She couldn't stop thinking about Katie's baby, who would now be a few years older than herself. The evening replayed in her mind, like an unending loop.

****

"You had a baby with Dan?" June had asked. Her eyes were as big as saucers.

Katie nodded. "When I found out I was pregnant, we both agreed to put the baby up for adoption. Luckily, I didn't show much for the first six months, and I was able to hide my pregnancy for a while. When I started to show at the end of our senior year, Dan and I skipped out on graduation and got summer jobs at a resort in Alberta."

"Did you tell Grandma you were pregnant?" Maggie asked.

"No, I couldn't. I was so ashamed. I knew she would've been angry with me. I had a scholarship to Queens University. She would've been so disappointed. Dan's parents were strict Catholics, too. He made me promise to keep it a secret."

"Why did you choose to work in Alberta?" June asked.

"Well, for one thing, we wouldn't have to worry about running into anyone we knew. Also, at the time, Alberta had different adoption laws. As long as you were eighteen years old, you could place your baby up for adoption without your parents' written consent. I turned

131

eighteen just two days before my daughter was born. I always wonder what would've happened if she were born a couple of weeks early. Maybe I wouldn't have given her away…"

"Do you know where she is now?" Maggie asked.

Katie shook her head. "I contacted the adoption agency, but due to privacy laws, they can't give out her information." Katie fiddled with a loose string on her bathrobe. "After I placed her for adoption, I tried to move on. I met Stuart, and he didn't judge me for having had a baby out of wedlock. We got married young, had the boys, and created this wonderful life together, but I have trouble sleeping at night because I'm up worrying about her. A few months ago, I was watching a news special about Canada's child-welfare system. Inspection reports from the Ministry of Social Services found instances of children sleeping on soiled mattresses and a lack of access to medical care, and I lost it." Katie's voice faded. She took a deep breath, twirling the loose string from her bathrobe around her index finger. "When I told Stuart that I wanted to find her, he asked me not to, saying it would ruin our family. That's when I fell into depression. I begged Stuart to reconsider, but when he refused, I began to resent him. That's when I got involved with James, and everything crumbled from there." Katie snapped the string off her bathrobe. "I'm tired of living up to everyone's high expectations and having to keep this secret to not embarrass anyone or disrupt their lives. It's time to find my daughter. I need to know that she's safe."

Maggie was in awe of her aunt's strength. Tears spilled from her eyes.

Katie turned to face her. "I'm sorry, honey. I've upset you. I—"

"Katie, these are happy tears. I have a cousin out in the world somewhere! You don't need to be ashamed.

We just need to find her."

Katie wiped her eyes and grabbed Maggie's hands. "I've tried. I had it approved with the adoption agency so that if she ever comes looking for me, she will have access to my contact information, but she hasn't come forward yet. She probably hates me and thinks I abandoned her."

Maggie wiped her nose on the cuff of her terry cloth bathrobe. She embraced her aunt in a tight hug. Katie's body relax into hers, the weight of her secret finally lifted. "When we find her, you can tell her how much you love her."

"You have to believe me, Maggie. I did what I did because I love her so much. I was a child myself. I wasn't ready to be a mother."

****

June tossed restlessly in the bed, snapping Maggie out of her recollections of the conversation with Katie. Once June settled, Maggie grabbed her cellphone and tiptoed out the front door. She used the screen as a flashlight and hiked to the top of the driveway where she'd have the best reception.

"Hello?" her mother answered. Her voice was full of sleep.

Maggie spoke quickly. She only had a few minutes remaining on her cellphone. She was frustrated with herself for not purchasing more minutes in town. "Mom, you have to come to the cottage. Katie is in a dark place, and I need your help."

"Maggie? Is that you? What's wrong?"

Maggie envisioned her mother turning on the bedside lamp and struggling to bring her tired body to a seated position. She heard her father mumbling in the background.

"What is it, Elizabeth?" he groaned.

"It's nothing. Katie is bringing Maggie into her dramatics. Go back to bed."

"Mom, did you hear me? Katie needs you."

Her mom cleared her throat, irritation evident in her tone. "Grandma told me what she did to your poor Uncle Stuart. She made her bed. Now she can lie in it."

"This isn't about the affair. Something happened to Katie a long time ago, and I think you should come here so she can explain."

"Maggie, darling, I don't have time for Katie's drama. There's always something with her. She—"

"Twenty-five years ago, Katie put a baby girl up for adoption!" The words came out like vomit. Maggie flinched, immediately regretting telling her aunt's secret, but like a bad stomach bug, she couldn't keep it in any longer.

"I know about the baby."

The hair on the back of Maggie's neck stood on end. "What?"

Mom let out a heavy sigh. "I know, and Grandma knows. Katie didn't want us to tell you or the twins. She thought it would be too complex and emotionally heavy. We respected her wishes."

"When did you find out?"

"When Katie and Dan moved back from Alberta, they broke up. She was depressed, and we thought she just needed time to get over it. This went on for months. Finally, one day, Grandma asked her if something had happened in Alberta. I guess she had an inkling that whatever was wrong with Katie was about something bigger than Dan. That's when Katie told her."

"What did you say?"

"I wasn't there for that conversation. A few days later over breakfast, Grandma, who must've been in shock, told me that Katie had given a baby away. I couldn't believe it."

"What happened next?" Maggie asked.

"I remember telling your grandma, 'We have to go get her!' You see, back then, a birth mother had a year to revoke her decision. It had only been six months."

"So, did you?"

"No, Grandma said it had been too long, and we couldn't do that to a baby."

The operator interrupted their conversation. "You have one minute remaining."

"Shit. Mom, I'm out of minutes."

"Out of what?"

"Minutes. I'm on a budget now, remember? I can't afford a phone plan."

"Have you given the internship any more thought? I'm sure your father could pull some strings—"

"Mom, I can't talk about that right now. What are we going to do about Katie? We need to help her."

"Listen, honey, Katie is a grown woman. The decision was hers to make. She needs to move on."

Maggie couldn't wrap her head around what she was hearing. "It's not like she suffered the loss of a pet hamster, Mom! Katie has a daughter. You have a niece you've never met. I have a cousin—"

"I think it's best for everyone involved to leave the past in the past."

The line went dead. Maggie kicked the dirt. She didn't care what her mother thought. One thing was for certain—she would help her aunt in any way she could.

The next morning, Maggie awoke to the smell of coffee brewing. She put her robe on over top her floral print pajama set and rubbed the sleep from her eyes as she joined Katie and June at the kitchen table.

"Good morning, sleepy head," said Katie. She seemed chipper for someone who had spent the prior evening crying herself to sleep.

June got up and checked the steaming waffle iron on the kitchen counter. "You hungry?"

Maggie's stomach growled. "I'm starving."

June plated a steaming waffle with a square of butter on top and placed it in front of Maggie, drizzling maple syrup all over until the tiny squares were overflowing with the amber sugar. "Eat up."

Maggie used her fork to cut a piece of waffle and shoved it into her mouth. It was crisp and as light as a feather. "Mm," she hummed.

"I'm leaving in half an hour," said June.

"Don't go!" Maggie mumbled with her mouth full. Maple syrup dripped down her chin. "You just got here."

June chuckled as she handed Maggie a paper napkin. "I've been here for over a week! The cruise is only for three months. We'll see each other again soon."

Maggie wiped her face. Her throat tightened as tears threatened. "I'm going to miss you. It's been so nice having you here. What am I going to do without your support? I need help trying to navigate my way through the mess that is my life."

Katie poured Maggie a cup of coffee. "I'm here, and I'm not going anywhere."

Maggie smiled warmly in appreciation. There was a closeness with her aunt now that she had never felt before.

"And I'm just a phone call away," reassured June.

After the dishes were washed and her clothes packed, June got dressed in a sage-green mini flounce dress and set off on her adventure around the world. Maggie couldn't wait to hear all about it. Katie joined Maggie at the end of the driveway, and they waved goodbye until they could no longer see June's car.

Katie wrapped an arm around Maggie's shoulders. "Everything is going to be okay," she said with an air of confidence, but there was a subtle hesitation in her voice, as if the reassurance was just as much for herself as it was for Maggie.

Maggie needed space to think. "I'm going to swim to the island. After that waffle, I could use the exercise."

When Maggie reached the small beach to the right of the dock, she dropped her heavy, striped Hudson's Bay towel on a pine-green Adirondack chair, revealing her flirty, black one-piece bathing suit with scalloped detailing around the neckline and leg openings. She gathered her hair into a high ponytail. As she stepped onto the sand and smooth rocks that lined the bank of the lake, she squinted at the water, which danced with the sunlight under the reflection of the blue sky. The bay was still quiet. Maggie imagined the other cottage dwellers on the lake were sleeping in or enjoying a hot cup of coffee and a good book in bed. She stepped into the clear lake and paused, allowing her body to acclimatize to the water's cool temperature. Small waves gently lapped against her legs. Her plan was to swim across the peaceful bay to the island with the lonely jack pine.

Maggie dove into the water, and the lake nurtured the mermaid within her. As she swam, she wished she could stay in the underwater world. She was as free as the waves, flowing without restraint. When she tired, she flipped onto her back and rested. With her ears under the water, the only sound she could hear was her heartbeat. By the time she reached the island, the shock of Katie's news had washed away.

Cedar Lake was littered with little islands, but the one with the lonely jack pine was probably the smallest of them all. You could walk the perimeter in less than a minute. The island sat between the bay and a narrow channel that brought you to a public access boat launch. On one side of the island, there was a beaver lodge, and on the other side, there was a giant flat stone, perfect for sunbathing. Maggie climbed out of the water and sat on the rock bed, letting the heat of the stone warm her cool skin. She closed her eyes, soaking in the peace of the moment.

"Maggie?"

Her eyes opened in a flash. She quickly ran a hand over her head in an attempt to tidy her hair that had already began to frizz in the humid summer air. Without her towel, Maggie felt exposed. She hugged her knees to her chest. "Thomas, hi."

Thomas confidently steered his green canoe from the narrow channel, around the flat rock, and into the bay. He looked incredibly good with his Bass Pro Shops cap worn backwards. He docked his canoe beside a rock and secured it by tying it to a fallen tree with a yellow rope. He joined Maggie on the flat rock. It was just big enough for them both. Maggie resisted the urge to reach out and touch his untamed, yet perfect, curls that were peeking out from under his hat.

Maggie nodded toward the fishing gear in Thomas's canoe. "Catch anything?"

"A couple of small bass. Too small to eat. I released them."

Maggie's breath caught as Thomas's gaze met hers. The depth of his green eyes seemed to change with the sunlight, flickering between shades of lichen and pine. Sitting next to him ignited a craving she had, but she quickly brushed off the longing. Thomas was back with Sadie.

"What have you been up to? I haven't seen you around," said Maggie.

Thomas grinned. "Checking up on me?"

"I, uh, well I—"

Thomas bumped his shoulder against hers. "I'm only kidding. I got a job renovating the Evans's cottage. You know the rustic cabin on the point?"

Maggie nodded.

"They haven't done anything to it since it was built in the sixties. Some of the floorboards are rotting. It's a big job, but it will be beautiful once I'm finished working on it. What's new with you? You looked deep in thought when I came paddling around the island."

"Well, I have a cousin that I've never met. Katie gave her up for adoption twenty-five years ago." Maggie hadn't meant to blurt out the entire story, but she was desperate to tell someone who would listen with more empathy than her mother. Thomas was that shoulder she could lean on. That friend who would offer understanding, without judgement.

"Whoa. I was not expecting you to say that. Wow. Here I was thinking you were still reeling from your breakup with Brody."

"What?" Maggie said, incredulously. "No! That chapter is closed. Forever."

Thomas gave a thoughtful nod. Maggie wasn't sure if she had imagined it, but she thought she saw the corners of Thomas's mouth turn upwards slightly.

Thomas cleared his throat, his smile fading. "That's heavy stuff, about your aunt, I mean."

Maggie was grateful he had steered the conversation away from her ex. "It explains why Katie has been acting like a hot mess lately."

"Does she want to find her daughter?"

"Yes, but the adoption agency won't release her records."

"That's so sad."

"I mean, I understand the agency has to protect my cousin's privacy, but my aunt just wants to know she's okay. She wants to tell her she has family here that loves her, too." Maggie's voice wavered.

Thomas put his arm around her shoulder. Maggie ached to relax into the warm nook of his arm, but the image of Sadie waltzing into his cottage the other day drifted into her mind. Maggie's body went ridged, and he must have sensed her discomfort because he quickly removed his arm.

The air between them felt as thick as the humidity. The shared awkward space was filled with unspoken words as they sat together in the quiet of nature. Thomas fiddled with a twig. Maggie shifted her weight, unsure of how to break the silence.

"Enough about me," she started. "How are things with Sadie going? Maggie glanced at Thomas but quickly looked away when his eyes met hers.

"Sadie? Not sure. Why do you ask?"

"I—I thought you two were back together. Or at least hanging out again—"

Thomas scoffed. "Why in the world would you think I was back together with Sadie?"

"I saw her at your cottage the other day."

Thomas chuckled. "Wait, is that why you were acting so weird and bolted from the dock that day?"

Maggie looked down at her newly manicured toes.

"You thought I was hooking up with Sadie?"

Maggie refused to look at him. Her cheeks burned. From his tone, it was obvious she'd read the situation wrong. She was consumed by the sting of her own absurdity. Avoiding eye contact, Maggie stood up and dove off the end of the flat rock into the lake. The water cooled her fiery cheeks.

"Sadie called and asked to borrow some of my tools. That's all," Thomas called out.

An almost imperceptible smile tugged at the corner of Maggie's lips. Even though Thomas was only interested in being her friend, Maggie's heart held the tiniest spark of hope. She swam closer to the rock and playfully splashed his legs. "Get in here! The water is beautiful."

Thomas stood in a hurry and quickly removed his hat and t-shirt, revealing his impressively toned midsection. "You're going to get it!"

Maggie tried to swim away, but Thomas's cannonball created an unavoidable splash. Her laughter came to a halt when he resurfaced, meeting her face to face. For a moment, time stood still. The lake shimmered, and Maggie was acutely aware of every ripple in the water between them. Her breath caught in her throat when he gazed into her eyes.

"I've been meaning to tell you I'm interested in someone new," he said.

Maggie's smile wavered as she treaded water, disappointment washing over her. "Oh, yeah?" she said, trying to mask the twinge of hurt. Maggie didn't have the heart to listen to him express his feelings for another woman, but at the same time, she wanted to be a supportive friend. "Who?" she asked half-heartedly.

"Come on, you're going to make me say it?"

Maggie cocked her head. "Who?"

"I'm interested in you, Maggie."

His confession hung in the air as his words echoed throughout her chest, causing her heart to flutter. A mix of elation and fear flooded Maggie's body. "I thought you were only interested in being friends."

Thomas swam a lap around Maggie. "That's when I thought you were still in love with your ex-boyfriend.

So, what do you say? Will you go out with me?"

Chapter Thirteen

"Which one?" Maggie asked Katie. She held out two hangers, presenting her aunt with two dress options. The burgundy dress on the right hanger was a linen smock dress with flirty ruffled sleeves. Its short length showed off Maggie's tanned legs. The sunflower-yellow dress on the left hanger was flowy and accentuated Maggie's feminine physique.

"Where are you going again?" Katie asked.

"Thomas invited me to a traffic light party at the staff housing at the resort."

"What's a traffic light party?"

"Basically, just your typical house party, but you dress in the color that best suits your relationship status."

"I don't get it."

"Green means you're single and looking for a relationship. Red means you're in a relationship or you're not looking for one. Yellow means maybe. You're interested in meeting new people."

"You're going with Thomas?"

Maggie's arms were getting tired. She gave the hangers a little shake. "Yes."

"Like on a date?"

Maggie chewed the inside of her cheek. "Yes."

"So, shouldn't you wear the burgundy dress?"

Maggie dropped her arms. "It's just a date. He didn't ask me to be his girlfriend. I don't want him to think I don't know the difference. Besides, what if he wears something yellow? Or worse, green? I would be mortified."

"Yellow is a safe bet."

"But what if he takes that to mean I'm open to meeting new people at the party? I'm only interested in him."

"My advice is to wear the color that expresses what you want your relationship to be."

Maggie nodded. She would risk humiliation and wear the burgundy dress. She didn't like to play games. Despite her mind urging her not to date again so soon, Maggie's heart wanted Thomas to know she was all in. Maggie went back to her room to finish getting ready. She slipped into her demi-coverage black lace bra and matching panties before stepping into her pretty burgundy dress. She moisturized her tanned skin and dabbed her favorite vanilla perfume behind her ears. She scrunched her natural beach waves one last time and looked in the full-length mirror that hung behind her bedroom door. She looked nothing like the stressed-out version of herself who'd arrived at the cottage weeks earlier with dark bags under her eyes and a Costco size bottle of Tums in her purse. She much preferred her current reflection of sun kissed cheeks and eyes that glittered with excitement.

"Maggie! Thomas is here," Katie called.

Maggie inhaled deeply, gathering her composure before meeting her date. A sense of relief washed over her when she saw Thomas was also wearing red. His mahogany-colored t-shirt accentuated his messy brown curls. He had aced the whole untamed-hair thing. Thomas's green eyes lit up as they met hers.

"Wow. You look incredible," he said. His subtle, yet sexy dimple appeared in his left cheek as his smile broadened.

Maggie swooned. She couldn't take her eyes off of him. "So do you."

Thomas ran a hand nervously through his hair. "Shall we?"

Thomas was an old-fashioned date, which Maggie appreciated. He opened the passenger side door of his dad's old truck for her and, as they drove down the country roads to the party, he reached for her hand.

"Thank you for saying yes," he said. He kissed the back of her hand, sparking a surge of electricity up her arm. Maggie squeezed her thighs together. She found Thomas incredibly good looking and it was taking all her willpower to resist jumping him while he was driving.

Maggie cleared her throat. "Is it hot in here?"

Thomas tilted his head back and laughed. He rolled down the windows, and the fresh summer air flowed over Maggie. Her favorite indie folk band, Hollow Coves, came on the radio. She turned up the volume, and as the intro to "These Memories" filled the car, Maggie settled back into her seat and looked out her open window. There was something about driving with the summer breeze blowing through her hair that made Maggie feel more in touch with the landscape. She tried to steal a glance at Thomas, but he caught her, and she immediately looked away. Thomas squeezed her hand. Maggie had never felt more nervous about a date in her life, and yet, Thomas had a way of making her feel at ease.

When Thomas pulled into the staff housing parking lot, the traffic light party was in full swing. The large three-story building looked like a log cabin with a sloped red roof. It housed over one hundred employees in dorm-style rooms. The open concept apartments accommodated up to four people during the summer season and included a bathroom and kitchenette. Just like any other college or university dormitory, the staff building at Waldhaus was party central on Friday nights. It was far enough away from the resort so not to disturb any guests.

"Ready?" Thomas asked.

"Let's go!"

The front lawn of the staff housing residence was a sea of green, yellow, and red. Kegs were set up outside, and music blared from a speaker that was strategically placed on a second-floor balcony. At the back of the building, partygoers were gathered around a campfire that overlooked the lake. Maggie recognized a few kitchen and wait staff, but she didn't know most of the people attending the party.

"Keep warm by the fire. I'll go get us a drink," Thomas whispered in her ear. His closeness ignited a shiver that traveled down her spine.

"Maggie!" a drunk girl cried from around the fire. "Come sit with me!"

"I'll be right back," said Thomas. He squeezed her shoulders and headed for the keg.

Maggie walked toward the girl she now recognized as Kristin, the nervous waitress with the mousy brown ponytail that she had met on the day she'd applied for the position at Waldhaus. Kristin clearly had had a few drinks and wasn't as timid as usual. When Maggie sat beside her on the empty bench, Kristin held out a mickey of Fireball, offering a shot to Maggie. Maggie took a swig. The spicy cinnamon liquid coated Maggie's throat. Its taste reminded her of Big Red chewing gum.

"Spill. Are you and Thomas an item?" Kristin asked.

Maggie took another swig from the bottle to avoid answering the question that she herself didn't even know the answer to. Yes, she was on a date with Thomas, but they weren't officially *together.*

"You are, aren't you! Girl, you've got guts." Kristin lit a cigarette.

Maggie tilted her head. "How so?"

"You're dating your boss's ex-boyfriend. Sadie

can be mean. I would never cross her. I'm scared of her."

A frown tugged at Maggie's lips as she processed Kristin's words. "They've been over for a long time."

Kristin passed the cigarette to Maggie. Maggie held it between her index finger and her middle finger, watching the smoke rise. She wasn't a smoker, but the smell of burning tobacco was oddly comforting. She took a small puff before handing it back.

"They may have broken up a while ago, but she's not over him. Have you seen the way she looks at him?" Kristin asked.

Maggie had heard enough. "Thanks for the intel and the shots. I'm going to go find Thomas. It was nice talking to you. I'll see you at work, Kristin!"

Maggie walked through the darkness toward the keg. When she found it, she stumbled upon Sadie and Thomas in deep conversation. Thomas held two red plastic cups that were overflowing with beer foam. Maggie observed as Sadie seductively stepped closer to him and took one of the beers from his hands. She brought it to her lips entrancingly. Maggie couldn't watch anymore. She turned to leave.

"Maggie!" Thomas called.

She stopped in her tracks. He had spotted her. She turned slowly, her face plastered with a fake surprised smile. "Thomas, Sadie. Hi!"

Thomas held out a beer. "I got you a drink."

Maggie accepted and took a sip to avoid Sadie's glare. The beer was flat, much like the date with Thomas was turning out to be. She was about to ask him for a ride home, when to her surprise, he took her hand. A wave of tingling warmth spread up her arm.

"So, the rumors are true. You're hooking up," said Sadie.

"It's more than that, Sadie. Maggie is my

girlfriend."

Maggie didn't know if it was the alcohol kicking in or the pure elation of hearing Thomas tell his ex that she was his girlfriend, but suddenly the ground beneath Maggie was unsteady. She swayed slightly, leaning into Thomas for support. Her constant heart-head conflict locked her in place. Rushing into a new relationship too soon meant she might end up getting hurt again. But if she waited too long, the opportunity for love could pass her by. Maggie looked up at Thomas, and his green eyes probed the depth of her heart. In that moment, she decided that without risk, love was impossible. She trusted her feelings for him would lead her to something wonderful. Something that logic could never predict. Maggie's pulse raced with a mix of fear and ecstasy. She covered her stupid happy grin with her beer cup. She didn't want to rub her excitement in Sadie's face.

Sadie chugged the rest of her beer and tossed the empty cup in a nearby trashcan. Maggie could tell she was buying herself time before having to speak.

"I'm happy that you're happy, Thomas. I better get home. I'm working the early shift tomorrow. I'll see you at work, Maggie."

A nervous lump formed in Maggie's throat as she awkwardly waved goodbye.

"I hope that wasn't too much," said Thomas.

"I mean, it's a bit uncomfortable talking to Sadie, but I can't really avoid it. She is my boss."

Thomas stepped in front of Maggie and placed his hands on her shoulders. "I meant it when I called you my girlfriend. I hope that's okay. I know we hadn't discussed it, but I—"

Maggie placed her hands on top of his forearms. "It's better than okay. It's great."

"Really?"

Maggie licked her lips and nodded. She was eager to know what it would be like to kiss Thomas. Sweet and gentle or perhaps hot and wanting, Maggie desired both.

Thomas cupped his hands around her cheeks and looked into her eyes. "Is this okay?"

Maggie didn't answer. She wanted to show him that it was more than okay. She closed her eyes and leaned toward him until her mouth met his. The warmth of his lips felt like sunshine after days of rain. The heat from his body traveled through to her own, awakening every nerve ending. The soft pressure of his lips intensified, and a wild spark ignited deep within her. She was suddenly lost in the sweetness and want that flowed between them. When he finally pulled away, Maggie was left breathless and needing more.

"Hey, Thomas!" someone called out. "We need two more for flip cup. Come play!"

Thomas gazed down at Maggie with the biggest smile she'd ever seen him wear. His eyes sparkled. "You up for it?"

Maggie was up for anything with Thomas. "Yes! Let's do it."

Thomas grabbed her hand, and they jogged toward a small crowd gathered around a long, empty folding table. Maggie recognized the guy who had called them over. His name was Marco. He worked as a dishwasher.

Marco handed each of them a full cup of beer. "Do you know how to play?" he asked Maggie.

She shook her head.

"It's a relay race drinking game," Marco explained. "When it's your turn, chug your beer, place the empty cup on the table, and using your index finger, try to flip it one-hundred-eighty degrees so that it lands open side down. If it doesn't land right, try again. Once you flip your cup, the next player in line starts drinking. Got it?"

Maggie nodded. Marco placed her and Thomas at the end of the table on opposite sides.

Thomas rubbed his hands together. "It's on!" he teased.

Maggie raised her right eyebrow and placed her beer on the table. Though nervous, she was mostly excited. "You better be ready."

"Go!" Marco yelled from the other end of the table.

Maggie's team was off to a rough start. The first player on her team, a tiny young woman, obviously didn't like the taste of beer. She pinched her nose as she tried to drink it as fast as she could. Meanwhile, Thomas's teammates didn't have any trouble slamming back the foamy beer. However, they were already three sheets to the wind and struggled to flip their cups. This is when Maggie's team was able to catch up. As the relay made its way down the table, it became a head-to-head match between Maggie and Thomas. They were both the anchors of their teams and began racing at the exact same time. Thomas polished off his drink first, but he flipped his cup sideways and it rolled off the table. As he went to retrieve it, Maggie slammed down her empty cup and ever so gently, flipped it over on her first try. Her team roared with cheers. Maggie raised her hands to celebrate, jumping up and down.

Thomas retrieved his cup from the ground and went over to her side of the table. He grabbed Maggie from behind and spun her around. "Ahhh! Beginner's luck!"

Maggie couldn't stop laughing. "I beat you! I beat you!"

Maggie was having the time of her life. When

Thomas placed her feet back on the ground, she turned to him and pulled him in for a victory kiss. In the distance, she heard her favorite dance song come over the speakers. A sudden surge of courage coursed through her. "Let's go dance!"

She grabbed Thomas's hand and walked backward, leading him into the staff residence, which had been transformed into a makeshift nightclub. Thomas didn't resist. He seemed transfixed by her and followed her right in. Maggie had never felt more confident in her own skin than she did in that moment. Inside, they were handed red glow stick necklaces to match the color they had decided to wear. Someone else offered Jell-O shooters. Maggie happily accepted.

Thomas kindly refused, yelling over the music. "No, thanks, I'm driving!"

The couple made their way to the second floor of the residence, where the dance party was well underway in one of the common areas. Maggie dragged Thomas onto the middle of the dance floor. Colorful strobe lights flashed across the room, and arms waved around the humid, sweat-stained air. The loud bass thumped in Maggie's chest. Thomas grabbed her from behind, and their hips began to sway in unison, perfectly in tune with the beat. Maggie was pleasantly surprised that her outdoorsman could dance. Now, she was more curious than ever to find out if his amazing dance moves would translate into the bedroom. Maggie lost herself in the song and let her body move freely to the rhythm. Her hips grinded with his, moving back and forth or in slow sensual circles. When Thomas began kissing her neck, it was about all she could take.

"Do you want to get out of here?" he whispered in her ear, sending a rush of warmth from her neck to her pelvis.

Maggie turned to him. His eyes glittered seductively in the flashing lights. Her breath was short, and her body trembled, but she had danced away all her inhibitions. "Yes."

Outside, the cool night air sent a shiver down Maggie's spine.

"You're cold. Do you want to go sit by the fire?" Thomas asked.

Maggie shook her head. "I was hoping we could go somewhere more private."

"I have a sweatshirt in my truck…"

Maggie nodded and followed him back to the parking lot, but her plan had nothing to do with putting more clothes on. When they reached his truck, he grabbed a gray hoodie from the back. Maggie peeked over his shoulder, looking into the bed of his truck.

"Wow, you cleaned it up."

Thomas turned around and slipped the neck of the sweatshirt over her head. "Well, someone gave me a hard time about it."

Maggie slipped her arms through the hoodie. "What? Me?"

Thomas leaned back against his truck and placed his hands on Maggie's hips. He looked her up and down. "Mmhmm, that day I gave you the boost."

Maggie remembered, but she could tell Thomas wasn't interested in talking anymore. Neither was she, for that matter. She pressed herself against him and brought her lips to meet his. As he kissed her back, a rush of heat traveled between her legs. A soft moan escaped her lips. Thomas draped his strong arms around her body and pulled her in closer. With every breath, his presence filled Maggie's senses. His scent was intoxicating, a mix of pine and leather. When they finally came up for air, heat was radiating off Maggie's cheeks.

"I'm not ready to go home just yet," she murmured into his ear.

"I know somewhere we can go," Thomas answered.

ALYSSA DELLE PALME

Chapter Fourteen

Thomas drove cautiously down the dark dirt road. Maggie was eager to get to their destination, wherever that might be. "You drive like an old man," she teased.

Thomas tilted his head back and laughed. "Hey! It's hard to see. I don't want to hit a deer. Besides, I've got precious cargo aboard."

Maggie giggled. "So, where are you taking me?"

"Guess."

"Back to your place?"

They reached a fork in the road. Left would take them to their cottages, but Thomas turned right.

"Guess again," he said.

"To be honest, I'm not sure I've ever driven down this road."

It was too dark for Maggie to see anything. She gave up on the guessing game and settled back into her seat. It didn't matter where Thomas was taking her. She was incredibly happy just being with him. They were having an amazing time together. Eventually, his truck lights lit up an old sign on the abandoned road. A clue. The sign read *Dark Sky Preserve.*

Maggie was instantly transported back to her childhood, to a time when Johnny was still alive. She was sitting at the kitchen table in the cottage, eating her breakfast and watching her uncle read the newspaper. She remembered the smell of her soggy Golden Crisp cereal.

"Cedar Grove is set to open their dark sky preserve this weekend," Johnny read to her.

Suddenly, Maggie sensed a warm hand on her thigh, bringing her back to the present moment with Thomas.

"Have you been here before?" he asked, pulling

into the empty parking lot.

Maggie gave a small nod, holding back the happy tears of nostalgia.

Thomas's jaw dropped. "Really? I've never seen another soul here. I didn't think anybody knew about it. The field is overgrown."

A knowing grin tugged at her lips. "Back in the early 2000s, the town was committed to eliminating light pollution and preserving the night. Some wildlife and many insects rely on darkness to forage and breed, so the town created the dark sky preserve to protect ecosystems."

"Damn, I wanted to surprise you. It's the best place to see the—"

"Stars," Maggie finished, glancing up at the night sky through the windshield. "I used to come here when I was little. For as long as I can remember, I've been fascinated with the stars and their constellations. My uncle taught me how to use a star chart and identify Polaris, the north star." Maggie turned and met Thomas's gaze. "Looking up at all those shimmering stars reminds you it's such a gift to be here, right now, in this moment."

A warm smile spread across Thomas's face as he looked at her. "I have blankets and a cooler in the bed of my truck. Do you want to go look at the stars with me?"

"Yes," she answered without a second thought.

Thomas layered a navy plaid button up over his t-shirt, and reached for her hand, curling his fingers around hers. The warmth of his touch steadied Maggie's heart. They walked down the dark trail that led them from the parking lot to the dark sky preserve at the top of a hill. When Maggie stepped out of the forest and into the wildflower field, she gasped. The fabric of the black sky was splattered with silver sparkles, the Milky Way manifesting before her eyes.

"It's incredible, isn't it?" Thomas asked.

Maggie exhaled in wonder. "The stars are so bright!" She appreciated how the stars kept their familiar patterns. They were a constant in an ever-changing world, really, especially with Maggie's ups and downs lately. She no longer needed a chart to locate Polaris. Its position had been etched in her memory forever.

Thomas squeezed her hand. "I knew you would see the magic in it."

Maggie and Thomas laid the blanket out and sat to enjoy a late-night picnic together. The spread included barbequed chicken drumsticks, a French baguette, a Tupperware of washed grapes, and a potato salad from the grocery store deli.

Maggie was impressed. "Wow, you came prepared."

Thomas smiled sheepishly. "To be honest, I didn't know if the party was going to be our scene. I was a little worried about how Sadie was going to react seeing us together. So, I came up with plan B, just in case we had to escape from any drama. I was determined to have an amazing first date with you."

"It has been pretty amazing."

Thomas reached into his jeans pocket to retrieve his Swiss army knife. He used it to pop the cap off of two ice cold bottles of Steam Whistle. "I totally agree."

Maggie lifted her beer. "To first dates."

"And to many more."

Maggie took a sip. The crisp bitterness of the beer tickled her tongue.

Thomas ripped off a small piece of the baguette and popped it into his mouth. "Tell me more about your life in the city."

"Well, I didn't have much of a social life because I was always working. The work, though, was exciting."

Thomas offered the Tupperware of grapes to Maggie. "What was it that you loved about being a reporter?"

Maggie bit into a firm green grape, savoring its sweet, juicy center. "I loved the thrill of a breaking news story. The newsroom would literally buzz with excitement. I loved the chase of tracking someone down to interview them. I loved editing the piece together. It felt like a challenge to complete a complicated puzzle. Meeting a deadline was incredibly satisfying."

"It must have been hard for you to leave it all behind."

"It was."

"I mean, everyone has experienced a bad boss in their life. Do you regret not pushing through and finishing your internship? I mean, if you had, you could've gotten a job somewhere else eventually."

Maggie shook her head. She wanted to tell him everything, but if she talked about it now, it would ruin the best date she had ever been on. "If I had stayed in the city, I wouldn't have met you, and we wouldn't be here."

"Well, when you put it that way..." Thomas smiled, the warmth of his eyes made it clear how he felt about her.

Maggie tried to steer their conversation away from her. "What do you miss most about city life?"

"Honestly? Nothing."

"Come on! You must miss something."

"Well, there was this amazing hole-in-the-wall Lebanese restaurant that sold the best shawarma."

"That's it?"

Thomas shrugged. "I hated the traffic, the pollution, the materialistic life."

"So, you'll never move back?"

"I don't plan to. I'll visit from time to time. I still

have friends there, but Cedar Grove is where I want to be." Thomas opened his arms, inviting Maggie in. She settled in between his legs and leaned back against his chest. Thomas wrapped his arms around her waist and kissed the top of her head. The symphony of crickets was comforting. They watched the night sky in silence until a shooting star revealed itself. Maggie squealed with girlish delight when the unexpected flash of opalescent light shot across the sky.

"Did you see that?" she whispered.

"I did. Did you make a wish?"

Maggie responded with a silent nod. She had wished for something important. Something she wanted more than anything. "What do you wish for in your future?" she asked.

"Honestly, I'm truly happy with my life, but if I had to make a wish, I guess I'd wish to share that happiness with someone. I'd like to get married one day, have some kids, and grow old with someone."

Maggie paused, waiting for her stomach to lurch like it did when Brody brought up marriage. But, unlike with Brody, Maggie's body wasn't repulsed at the idea of a lifelong commitment to Thomas. Instead, a warm feeling of elation washed over her. She still had to figure things out. Her life plans didn't include working as a hostess forever, but the idea of making a life with Thomas intrigued her. In this moment, Maggie was exactly where she was supposed to be.

Thomas stroked her hair. "What did you wish for?" he asked.

Maggie peered back at him. "I can't tell you that. If I tell you, it won't come true."

Thomas smiled, revealing the dimple in his cheek. "Come on, give me a hint."

"Okay, one hint."

Maggie turned and slowly crawled up his body like a vixen ready to pounce. She straddled him on the blanket, catching him off guard, but she could tell from his subtle smirk that he was pleased. He leaned back on his hands, taking her in, and seemingly enjoying the view. She peeled his flannel shirt off his shoulders, and he wrestled it off his arms while still managing to keep Maggie balanced and upright in his lap. He tossed the shirt aside, his eyes lingering on her.

Maggie shimmied out of the gray hoodie she was wearing and dropped it next to them. She shivered from the sudden exposure to the cool night air. "I want you," she said, wrapping her arms around his neck and pressing her lips against his.

Thomas's muffled moan against her mouth, sent a vibration of anticipation to her pelvis. He kissed her back passionately, open-mouthed, and soft lipped, his rough stubble scratching her chin in the sexiest way. As he traced his fingers up and down her back, her nipples hardened. Maggie sighed in delight. Her reaction to his touch encouraged Thomas to keep going. He cupped her butt with both hands and swiftly flipped her over, crushing the wildflowers beneath them and releasing the melon scent of bluebells into the air. Thomas's strength turned Maggie on. She wrapped her arms around his waist, eagerly pulling him to her. The rapid beat of his heart pounded against her chest and the hardness in his jeans revealed how aroused he was, too.

He ran his tongue from her collarbone to her ear. "I've wanted you since the first time I saw you," he said.

Unable to resist any longer, Maggie peeled his t-shirt up his torso, exposing his chiseled midsection. Thomas assisted her efforts by pulling his shirt off the rest of the way, adding it to the growing pile of discarded clothing. He loomed above her on his knees breathing heavily.

"You're so fucking beautiful," he said, slowly running his hands from her knees up to her mid thighs. He gently pushed her legs open wider, making more room for himself. He leaned down on his forearms beside her head and his eyes locked with hers. His gaze was full of tenderness and trust. "Are you sure?" he asked.

Maggie had never been more sure of anything in her life. "Yes," she answered breathlessly.

Thomas cupped her cheek, and their lips met in a tender, unhurried kiss. He tasted like Steam Whistle, crisp and refreshing. The warmth of his touch quickly spread from her mouth to the spot between her legs that pulsed with desire. She kissed him harder, guiding his hand to the damp pocket of her panties. She wanted to show him just how sure she was.

"You're so wet," he groaned as though he were in agony.

Maggie traced her index finger inside the waistband of his jeans from his hip to the button in the front. "Take these off," she demanded.

Thomas got up on his knees. He unbuttoned his jeans and reached inside his pocket. As he removed the condom from the wrapper, Maggie watched, wide-eyed as he slipped it down his perfect length. Maggie's urgency became too much. There was no time to undress further. She quickly lifted the bottom of her dress and pulled her black lace panties aside. Thomas's green eyes darkened with hunger as he positioned himself. Maggie inhaled sharply when he pushed into her. Thomas paused, his gaze holding hers.

"More," she pleaded.

Thomas groaned and whispered her name as he continued to thrust. There, in the meadow, under the stars, his eyes never left hers as they made love for the first time.

Chapter Fifteen

After the most unforgettable night with Thomas, Maggie drifted off to sleep in his arms under a ceiling of stars. She awoke the next morning, feeling refreshed and ready for more. Maggie didn't have the words to describe how amazing their night had been, but it was as satisfying as drinking enormous gulps of water when one has been extremely thirsty for a very long time. Maggie played with the buttons on Thomas's plaid shirt, which looked like a welcoming blanket for her to lie down on. She snuggled into him and wrapped an arm around his waist. He was safe and stable, like a tall tree with deep roots.

Thomas slowly opened his eyes and pulled her in closer. "Mmm, good morning."

"Good morning," she murmured against his chest.

"How long have you been awake?" he asked.

"Long enough to watch the sun rise."

On top of the hill, the beauty of the sunrise was breathtaking. The valley below was bathed in its yellow light, and the birds sang into its shine.

Thomas rolled onto his side to come face-to-face with Maggie. "Last night was incredible," he said.

The ambience of the starry sky was gone, but looking at Thomas in the morning light was just as sensual, if not more so. Maggie wanted to see every part of his body in the daylight, and she planned to bare it all for him, too.

Thomas glanced at his watch. "Damn, I've got to get moving. I'm meeting the electrician at the Evans's cottage later this morning."

Disappointed, Maggie lay on her back and crossed her arms, pretending to pout. "I'm not ready for this date to be over."

Thomas rolled on top of her and started kissing

her neck. "Let me take you to breakfast. I have time for a quick bite to eat."

It wasn't the morning quickie Maggie had been hoping for, but it would have to do. The anticipation would make the next time all the sweeter.

Thomas took her to Peter's Restaurant and Bakery on Main Street. It was a family-owned diner that served breakfast all day and used fresh, local ingredients. The hostess, who Maggie assumed was the matriarch of the family, greeted Thomas by name.

"Good to see you, honey. A table for two?" she asked.

Thomas nodded. "Gail, I'd like you to meet my girlfriend, Maggie."

Gail offered Maggie her hand. "Pleased to meet you. You'll have to tell me, what's the secret behind your skincare routine? You are absolutely glowing."

Gail led them to their table and Maggie followed, blushing. "Thank you, Gail. It's wonderful to meet you."

Thomas sat down with a smug smile on his face.

Maggie felt like everyone in the restaurant was staring. "What?" Maggie whispered.

"Nothing."

Maggie kicked him under the table. "Tell me."

"Ouch. Okay, okay. I just happen to know the secret behind your skincare routine."

"Excuse me?"

Thomas leaned across the table and lowered his voice. "Did you know climaxing releases chemicals that can help improve the tone of your skin?"

Maggie tilted her head back and let out a hearty laugh. "With you around, I'll be able to skip my makeup routine altogether!"

Now it was Thomas's turn to laugh. Flirting with him was effortless. Thomas always made friendly, lasting eye contact, which made Maggie feel sexy and adored, even when she was wearing his oversized gray hoodie. She reached across the table and lightly touched his hand. Though they were great at flirting, the real magic of their attraction was in the ease of their conversations.

"I really like you," Thomas said. His green eyes danced with admiration.

"I really like you, too."

"You're like the coolest person I've met … in this restaurant, anyway." A muscle twitched at the corner of his mouth.

Maggie's jaw dropped. It was abundantly clear that Thomas was teasing, but she pushed his hand away, pretending to be upset. He made her crazy, but in a good way. Suddenly, she realized she happened to love a lot of things about Thomas—

"What can I get you?" Gail said, interrupting Maggie's thoughts.

Maggie shook her head and focused on her menu. "I'll get the basic breakfast with over easy eggs, bacon, white toast, and coffee please."

Thomas closed his menu and handed it to Gail. "Make that two."

As Gail walked their order back to the kitchen, Thomas reached across the table and held Maggie's hand. "You're beautiful."

Maggie glanced down at the gray hoodie. The skirt of her burgundy dress was wrinkled from sleeping in it. Her hair probably needed taming, too. "I'm walking around town, after an unplanned sexual encounter, dressed in the same clothes as last night!"

"Hey, at least we're in this walk of shame together."

"What if we run into someone from the party?"

Thomas shrugged. "Maggie, I want the whole

world to know we're together."

Maggie could tell from Thomas's arched eyebrows and smile that he was truly happy. In high school science class, Maggie had learned that happiness could be detected through the eyes. Thomas's large pupils revealed that he liked what he saw in front of him. His eyes had the clarity of the lake on a sunny day. Suddenly, Maggie was aware she didn't just like Thomas. She was falling head over heels in love with him. The realization sent a rush of euphoria through her body. She wanted to spill it out, but she bit her tongue, refusing to say "I love you" for the first time in a diner. It had to be special.

"What?" Thomas asked.

Maggie raised her eyebrows. "Hmm?"

"You're smiling."

"No, I'm not."

Thomas nodded his head as though he had it all figured out. "You were thinking about last night again, weren't you?"

Maggie was about to playfully wipe the proud smugness off his face when their meals arrived. Gail placed steaming plates piled high with eggs and hashbrowns down in front of them. "Two basic breakfasts. Can I get you two love birds anything else?"

"No, this is great," said Thomas.

"Thank you, Gail," added Maggie.

Maggie and Thomas settled into their breakfasts, talking, and laughing as they ate. Maggie was so enamored with Thomas that she didn't hear her phone ringing in her purse.

"Someone's calling you," Thomas said, biting into a piece of buttered toast.

Maggie fumbled through her purse for her cellphone. It was Katie. "Hello?"

"Maggie! You'll never believe it."

"What's happened?"

"The adoption agency called. My request for information was approved, which means they released her name to me! My daughter is Carrie Smith."

Maggie was so overwhelmed with excitement she could hardly take a full breath. "Oh, my God! When are you going to call her?"

Katie paused on the other end of the line. "They will only release her post-adoption birth information, like her name, birthplace, and the doctor who delivered her. No phone number. No address."

Maggie's shoulders dropped. "That's disappointing."

"I was hoping you could put your old investigative reporting skills to good use and help me find her."

Maggie sat up straighter. "Yes! I would love to help you find her."

Maggie filled Thomas in on what had happened, and after Thomas had paid the bill, they slowly made their way to the parking lot hand in hand. When they reached his truck, Maggie stood on her tiptoes, wrapping her arms around his neck, and kissed him. His lips tasted like citrus from the freshly squeezed breakfast orange juice. "Thank you for an incredible time."

"I can't wait to take you out again. Are you sure you don't need a ride?" Thomas asked.

Maggie shook her head. "I'm going to walk. The library is only a couple of blocks away. Katie's going to meet me there. She'll give me a lift home."

After one final kiss, Maggie waved goodbye and headed down Main Street on foot. The morning sunshine reflected off the shop windows that lined the charming street. Maggie enjoyed the slow summer stroll, browsing the windows. All the reminders of decades past, like the towering antique clock that stood outside the jeweler's storefront, evoked feelings of nostalgia. The clock dated back to the early 1900s and was stationed a block away from the Cedar Grove Public Library.

When Maggie was younger, Johnny took her to the library on rainy days. He never hurried her. She was allowed to take her time as she browsed the children's section at the back of the building. She'd carefully select each book and leave with a stack piled so high she needed to use her chin to help balance the books.

Maggie's lips curled upward in a wistful way as she stepped through the front door of the library. It still smelled the same, a mix of old leather-bound tomes and freshly printed paperbacks. The library was housed in an old schoolhouse, and though it was small, it had a catalogue of over two thousand books. Maggie perused the community bulletin board while she waited for Katie to arrive. There was a poster advertising yoga in the park classes and a sign-up sheet to register for Cedar Grove's upcoming annual kilt run. The town's goal was to set a Guiness World Record this year for the largest traditional kilt race.

"Maggie!" Katie shuffled through the front door of the library, carrying two heavy laptop bags.

Maggie quickly took her black leather tote to relieve Katie's small shoulders. They approached the information desk, and the librarian, who had white, wispy hair like Albert Einstein, ignored them until she was finished typing something with her two index fingers. Katie shifted from one foot to the other.

"How may I help you?" the librarian finally asked. She pushed her glasses up her nose.

"We'd like to access the internet please," said Maggie.

The librarian nodded. She handed them a card

with a username and Wi-Fi password. Maggie and Katie thanked the librarian and went to find an empty table in a private corner to set up their laptops next to each other.

"I think it's time to get internet installed at the cottage," Katie murmured under her breath as she turned on her computer.

"I already asked Grandma," Maggie whispered. "She said over her dead body."

"I'm not surprised. She believes the cottage should be a place to unplug from the busyness of city life."

This summer, Maggie had missed the ease of connection the internet could bring. But, after the initial social media withdrawal, she realized there were plenty of benefits to being offline. She couldn't fault her grandmother's decision, and even though she didn't always have the best reception, Maggie still had use of her cellphone.

Once Maggie logged into the library's Wi-Fi, she typed *Carrie Smith* into the search engine. It rendered over 74-million results. Maggie tried again, typing *Carrie Smith Alberta* into the search bar. 5-million results. Maggie bit her lip. This was going to be harder than she thought.

"Why did she have to have one of the most popular surnames in the world?" Maggie muttered under her breath.

Katie looked up from her laptop. "Have you found anything?"

Maggie chewed the nail on her right thumb. She wished she had better news for her aunt. "I think we're going to be here for awhile."

Maggie continued her search. There was a doctor named Carrie Smith from Alberta, a teacher on staff at a Catholic elementary school, and another woman with the same name who had been arrested and charged with fraud. None of these women were her cousin. They all had graying hair and looked old enough to be her grandmother.

"Did the adoption agency give you anything else to go on?" Maggie asked.

Katie took a piece of paper from her purse. "She was adopted by a teacher and a farmer."

Maggie's ears perked up. She could work with that. She typed the new information into Google. "Look at that! Did you know there are only seventy-thousand farmers in Alberta?"

Katie's shoulders slumped. "We're trying to find a needle in a haystack. It feels like an impossible task."

Maggie reached for Katie's hand. "I'm here every step of the way. We're going to find her."

Katie nodded. "They changed her name."

"Who changed her name?"

"Her adoptive parents. When she was born, I named her Kaylee Elizabeth. I wanted her to have the same initials as me, Katherine Edwards. And I wanted her to carry a family name, so that's why I named her after your mother."

"That's really beautiful, Katie."

"You know, some biological mothers deliver their babies and leave the hospital at their earliest opportunity. It's too painful for them to stay. But I stayed for as long as I could. I got three whole days to hold her and tell her how much she was loved." Katie wiped a tear that escaped down her cheek. She quickly ducked her head, focusing on her computer screen. "Let's get back to business."

Maggie placed her hand on Katie's back. "You're going to have the opportunity to tell her all of this. I promise."

Katie stared down at her hands. "I wrote her a letter in the hospital."

"You did?"

Katie nodded. "I tried to explain to her why I was placing her up for adoption. I wanted her to know I wasn't abandoning her."

"Do you think her parents would've given her the letter?"

Katie shrugged.

"If they didn't, you'll be able to tell her yourself. We just need to find her first," Maggie said.

Maggie and Katie went back to work. While Katie searched for small-town schools located near farms, Maggie flipped through endless pages that included *Carrie Smith Alberta*. Maggie worked until her eyes watered from staring at the screen so intensely. She grew increasingly uneasy, worried they wouldn't be able to find her after all. Maggie closed her eyes and said a little prayer. She wasn't very religious, but Grandma, a devout Catholic, would have told her to pray to Saint Anthony. In the past, any time Maggie had lost or misplaced something, like her keys or her wallet, her grandmother would say, "St. Anthony will help you find it!"

Maggie opened her eyes. In a last-ditch attempt, Maggie clicked the images tab on Google. She flipped through page after page until she landed on a photo that looked exactly like her aunt. Maggie swallowed and clicked on the photo. It led her to an old Facebook account. The owner of the account had posted a picture of her volleyball team. The names of the girls were listed below the photograph. *Carrie Smith*. There was no doubt in Maggie's mind that this was her cousin. She was Katie's clone with the same blonde hair and matching blue eyes. She zoomed in on the photo to inspect the jerseys. The team was called the Predators from Fox

Creek High School.

Maggie stood up quickly, knocking her chair backward. She gaped in astonishment. "I–I found her!"

Chapter Sixteen

Maggie picked up a piece of silverware and polished it thoughtfully with an old rag. She imagined she was married to Thomas and preparing the table for a dinner they were hosting for their friends and family.

"Maggie!"

Maggie jumped, snapping out of her daydream. Sadie stood at the doorway of the backroom.

"Is this all you've done?" Sadie asked. A tiny purple vein bulged in her forehead. She inspected the small, polished pile on the table versus the much bigger pile of cutlery that still needed some attention.

Maggie swallowed. "It's heavily tarnished."

Sadie crossed her arms. "Work faster, Maggie. I need you to polish the wine glasses next."

Maggie nodded. "I will."

In an attempt to show Sadie how quickly she could work, Maggie picked up a fork, applied the paste and furiously worked it into the crevices. This seemed to be enough to satisfy Sadie. She marched out of the room without saying goodbye. Maggie sighed. She could've finished this task already, but thoughts of Thomas kept distracting her. Anytime she closed her eyes, she could feel the warmth of his breath on her neck.

"Hey, Maggie!"

Maggie's eyes snapped open. Kristin, the waitress with the mousy brown ponytail, carried in a crate of washed wine glasses. Maggie offered her a cheerful grin.

"Dozing off on the job, are you?" Kristin teased. She picked up an extra rag and a spoon and began to polish.

"No, I'm just bored. This has got to be the most monotonous task ever."

"Sadie said you were having trouble keeping up

and needed some help."

Maggie rolled her eyes. "Leave it to Sadie to make it seem like I'm an idiot who can't complete an easy task like polishing silverware."

"Why are you back here anyway? This is a job usually left to the kitchen staff."

"I think we both know why I've been banished to the back room."

Kristin gave an affirming nod. "Ah, yes. You're the other woman. She probably can't stand looking at you."

"I'm not the other woman! Thomas and Sadie broke up before I even arrived in Cedar Grove." Maggie resisted the urge to smack some sense into Kristin. She really didn't like her.

"But they were together for a while, right?" Kristin asked.

Maggie let out an irritated sigh. "What's your point?"

Kristin added her spoon to the polished pile. "My point is there's history there."

"Yes, ancient history."

Kristin's gaze focused on something behind Maggie. Her eyes bulged, and she erratically picked up a knife and began to polish.

Maggie slowly turned her head toward the doorway. Sadie was leaning against the frame. Maggie gulped. She wondered how much Sadie had heard. "Sadie, I—"

"I'm literally counting down the days until your relationship fails, and I will be there when it does."

"Excuse me?" Maggie's voice rose in defiance.

"He loved me first."

Maggie's jaw dropped, but no words came out. She was speechless.

"You know, I regret the day I hired you. You better watch it, Maggie. One mistake, and you're fired." Sadie turned and marched down the hotel hallway.

Maggie's heartbeat pounded so hard it reverberated in her ears.

"I told you she was scary," Kristin whispered.

The echo of Sadie's high heels click-clacking down the corridor faded away. Maggie picked up a spoon and began to heatedly polish it.

"I wish someone had the guts to stand up to her," Kristin said.

Maggie nodded in agreement, but she wouldn't be the one to tell Sadie off. "I can't. I need this job." Maggie held her head high, trusting Thomas with a steady heart, but deep down, a quiet doubt lingered, planted by old wounds from cheating and narcissistic exes.

It wasn't until she was on the road, with the car windows rolled down, that Maggie's anger melted away. After working in an air-conditioned building, Maggie welcomed the warm summer breeze on her face. It smelled like the end of July—freshly cut grass and sizzling barbeques. The closer she got to the cottage, the better she felt. She couldn't wait to see Thomas. Despite what Sadie had said to her, Maggie was confident she had a strong connection with Thomas. Over the past couple of weeks, Maggie and Thomas had been so busy with work that they'd hardly seen each other, but Thomas had been making an effort to let Maggie know he was thinking about her. Before he left for work, he'd sometimes hide little notes for her to find on her windshield or under a rock on her dock. *Find the Note* was always written across the front in his messy penmanship. His notes were sweet or funny. Never cheesy. Sometimes, a blush swept over her as she read his flirty comments. Their sexual tension was building, and Maggie couldn't wait to be alone with him again. His most recent note was an invitation to go canoe camping. *Circle yes, no, or maybe* it read. Maggie was ready to tell Thomas how she felt about him. This would be the perfect opportunity. He made her so happy. She didn't want to sweat the Sadie stuff and refused to obsess over it. Maggie wanted to focus on what was important—her and Thomas.

When Maggie pulled up to the cottage, she was surprised to see her dad's SUV parked in the driveway. She hurried into the cottage, worried that something was wrong. Her parents weren't the type to make unannounced visits.

"Mom? Dad? Katie?" Maggie called as she stepped through the front door. She heard laughter coming from the back deck. Maggie walked through the sliding door to discover her parents sharing a bottle of wine with Katie.

"Maggie, honey, that uniform is awful!" said her mother.

Maggie glanced down. She looked disheveled. Her hair was a windblown mess, and she had untucked her white shirt, which had wrinkled on the drive home. She walked over to her mother and kissed her on the cheek. "Nice to see you, too, Mom."

Dad offered a tight-lipped smile. "I brought the projector and a few of your favorite movies from my collection." He pointed down below the deck to the campfire pit that overlooked the lake. "If you hang a white bed sheet between those two big pine trees, you could enjoy a movie under the stars!"

Maggie looked from her mother to her father, trying to comprehend what they were doing at the cottage. "Um, wow. That's really nice, Dad. Thank you."

"I still can't believe you left your internship to work as a hostess," her father said under his breath. He swirled the red wine in his glass and took a sip.

Her mother nudged him in the ribs with her elbow. "Jerry, we said we weren't going to bring that up."

"Maggie, would you like a glass of wine?" Katie piped up. She poured a generous glass and handed it to her.

Maggie was thankful for both the subject change and the drink. "What are you guys doing here?" she asked her parents.

Mom patted the empty space on the picnic bench beside her. "We missed you, honey. I convinced your dad to take a long weekend so we could come visit you. I wish we had come sooner. I forgot how peaceful it is here."

Maggie sat down beside her mother. "It really is something special. I love it here."

"You know, the last time we were here, Johnny had just been diagnosed," said Mom.

Maggie nodded, remembering. She'd been a teenager, and her mother had given her strict instructions not to talk about the C-word on their vacation.

"He wants a normal family trip up at the cottage. Don't even mention the word 'cancer,'" her mother had said.

Despite everyone's best efforts, the vacation was anything but normal. The whites of Johnny's eyes were yellow and his skin jaundice, common side effects of liver cancer. Their family vacation lasted for two weeks, and during that period of time, Johnny lost thirty pounds. Maggie was terrified he was going to die on their holiday. She woke up frightened one night and couldn't go back to sleep. She tiptoed out to the kitchen and poured herself a glass of Grandma's homemade iced tea. The sliding glass door was open, and a skunky smell drifted in through the screen door. Johnny was outside, smoking marijuana. It helped with his pain. Maggie joined him on the deck.

Johnny took a long drag. "There's my favorite girl," he said, holding the smoke in. When he exhaled, he pushed small amounts of smoke out at a time to make rings.

Maggie tried to catch one with her index finger, making Johnny laugh. "I love you, kid."

"I love you, too, Johnny."

They sat in silence for a long while after, watching the fireflies dance in the night. It was as though they had been choreographed by the magical memories of the forest fairies who used to leave notes for Maggie in the woods when she was a child.

A soft tap on her shoulder brought Maggie back to the present moment.

"Are you hungry, honey? Dad is going to barbecue."

Maggie nodded, struggling to keep the tears from the memory at bay. "Yes. I'll go freshen up for dinner."

Maggie hurried to her bedroom. She didn't want anyone to see she was upset. That was the thing about grief—it hit you when you least expected it. Her father rarely took a day off from work, and Maggie didn't want to ruin her mother's long weekend. Once she was able to pull herself together, she changed out of her stiff uniform and into a flowy bohemian-inspired caftan. She untangled her wind-blown wavy locks from the drive home, spritzed her face with a soothing rosewater facial spray, and applied a coat of clear gloss to her lips. She emerged from her room a new woman.

Katie and her mother were standing at the kitchen island, preparing a salad for dinner. The scent of steaks sizzling on the barbeque drifted in through the open windows. Mom stopped tearing lettuce leaves when she saw Maggie. She wiped her wet hands on a dish towel.

"You've never looked more beautiful, honey. I think this break has been good for you," she said.

Maggie beamed. She was pleased her mother had noticed. Living at the cottage had been good for her. She no longer suffered from terrible heartburn, her skin was clear, and her clothes fit comfortably again.

"It's been good for both of us," Katie said, smiling at Maggie. "Actually, Elizabeth, I have some exciting news to share."

Maggie braced herself. It was obvious how much her mother's support would mean to Katie.

"Oh, yeah?" Mom asked. She picked up a carrot and began to peel it.

"Maggie put her investigative reporting skills to good use for me and found my daughter. Her name is Carrie Smith."

Mom stopped peeling the carrot. "You found her?"

"I haven't found her yet, exactly," Maggie explained. "But I did figure out where she's from. We still have to make some phone calls."

Katie's eyes were pleading for approval.

Mom put her hand to her heart. "My niece's name is Carrie Smith?"

"Yes," said Katie.

Maggie winced, nervously awaiting her mother's opinion on the matter. She had always had strong opinions about leaving the past in the past. Maggie mentally prepared herself for a confrontation. She would support her aunt through this, though, no matter what.

"This is wonderful news!" Mom cried. She walked around the island and gave Katie a lingering hug. Maggie was taken aback by her mother's reaction. It was not what she'd been expecting.

Katie's eyes widened. "You're happy about this?"

Mom grabbed Katie by the shoulders and looked into her eyes. "Why should my happiness matter at all in this?"

"Because I care what you think! You've always been the smart sister, the one who makes good decisions. I've spent my whole life trying to be more like you." Katie's voice cracked.

"Katie, I'm thrilled for you! When I spoke to Maggie, and she told me she knew, I was surprised, but I've had some time to think about this, and I think you're doing the right thing. Carrie deserves to know she has more people, more family, who love and care about her. I support you, Katie."

Dad opened the back door and poked his head in. "What the hell happened?"

The three women looked at each other and burst out laughing.

Mom wiped her eyes. "These are happy tears, honey."

Dad shook his head. "Can you pass me the barbeque sauce?"

When supper was ready, the four of them gathered around the picnic table to eat. It was the golden hour, the time of day when the sun was near the horizon, glimmering and just about to set. Golden light fell everywhere, making everything glow. The mysterious call of the loon echoed across the lake while the trees swayed in the relaxing wind. Maggie's parents were having a good time, eating, laughing, and thoroughly enjoying themselves. She was in the middle of telling her parents a story about a hoity toity patron of Waldhaus, who had thrown a temper tantrum because oysters were not on the menu, when she noticed their gaze shift past her and over her shoulder. Maggie turned to see what they were looking at.

"I'm sorry. I didn't mean to interrupt," said Thomas. He sheepishly held up a white cardboard box. "I brought dessert?"

"Thomas!" Maggie jumped up from the table. She wrapped her arms around his neck and kissed him on the lips. She was thrilled to see him. He looked as handsome as ever in a pair of straight vintage-washed jeans and a relaxed navy-blue linen-cotton shirt with a crisp white t-shirt underneath. His hair was flawlessly tousled, and he smelled like a mix of wood, fresh air, and Ivory soap. Maggie was captivated by him, unable to look away.

Mom cleared her throat. "Maggie, do you want to introduce us to your friend?"

Maggie flashed a wide grin. She couldn't wait to introduce him to her parents. "I'm sorry. Mom, Dad, this is my boyfriend, Thomas."

"Boyfriend?" her father muttered under his breath.

"Don't," her mother warned through a clenched smile.

Thomas held out his right hand. "Mr. and Mrs. Taylor, it's a pleasure to meet you. Maggie has told me a lot about you."

Her parents stood to greet him.

"Are you hungry, Thomas?" Katie asked. "I could fix you a plate."

"Yes, join us!" said Mom.

Thomas sat down at the end of the picnic table beside Maggie while Katie served him a tender piece of steak that was perfectly seasoned, a baked potato, and a cob of corn wrapped in tin foil. Maggie passed him the bowl of Caesar salad. Dad opened a nearby cooler and handed Thomas a dripping bottle of beer.

"Wow. This is really great. Thank you," said Thomas.

When Dad's eyes narrowed in Thomas's direction, Maggie instinctively placed a protective hand on Thomas's thigh under the table.

"So, Thomas, what is it that you do?" Dad asked.

"I'm a contractor. I'm currently rebuilding the old Evans's cottage on the point."

"That's impressive!" Mom said.

"How are your finances?" Dad asked.

"Dad!" Maggie interrupted. "That's none of your business."

Thomas patted Maggie's hand under the table. "It's okay, Maggie. It's a fair question. Plenty of construction businesses go under because they simply can't cover the costs of their overhead." Thomas turned his attention to Maggie's dad. "Business is good, sir. I pay attention to overhead expenses, and I'm always aware of the additional costs before I accept a job."

Dad, seemingly satisfied with Thomas's answer, took a bite of steak.

"Tell us about how you two met," Mom said.

Maggie, grateful to her mother for changing the subject, giggled. "Well, it's kind of a funny story."

Thomas took a sip of beer. "It all started with a tick…"

Maggie stared in wonder as Thomas told the beginning of their love story. He was incredibly charming, funny, and a great storyteller. When she saw her dad crack a smile, her heart soared, knowing that he liked him, too. It was impossible not to. They spent the rest of the evening drinking and eating, and when the sun went down, Katie lit citronella candles to keep the mosquitoes away. Maggie was over the moon. Her parents loved him as much as she did.

"So, Thomas, tell me, has Maggie told you why she left the internship she worked so hard to get? She refuses to tell me," Dad said. The laughter and chatter around the table came to a sudden halt. The celebratory atmosphere turned serious in an instant. Dad continued. "I spent thousands of dollars on her education and helped her to get the internship of her dreams, only to have her quit and take off on us."

Thomas shifted in his seat. Maggie's palms broke into a sweat.

"All I know, sir, is that she was very unhappy there," Thomas answered.

"Don't," Mom whispered. She gently placed her hand on Dad's shoulder. "We've had a nice evening. Let it be."

Dad shrugged Mom off and pointed his finger at Maggie. "I know my daughter. I know how hard she worked to get to where she was. Elizabeth, she refused to come on vacation with us during spring break so she could get ahead of her class! And now she's going to give all that up for a boy?"

"This has nothing to do with Thomas!" Maggie said, her bottom lip trembling.

Her father ignored her and he stared directly at Thomas. "Listen. I like you, I really do, but you have to see that for Maggie, living out here and working at a summer resort is a waste of her potential. She's throwing away all that talent and education. If you really care about her, you'll talk some sense into her."

ALYSSA DELLE PALME

Chapter Seventeen

As Maggie walked Thomas home that night, he shot her a concerned glance. When they reached the privacy of the trees between their two cottages, Maggie stopped.

"Thomas, please don't look at me like that. My dad doesn't know what he's talking about. Leaving that internship was the best thing for me. Besides, I've realized there's more to life than working eighty hours a week. If anyone could understand that, it's you."

Thomas ran his hand through his hair. "What is your plan, Maggie? The summer is flying by, and you haven't mentioned what you're going to do in September."

Maggie shrugged and leaned back against a tree. "I'm still trying to figure things out."

Thomas stepped toward her, placing one hand on her waist. "I don't want to be the reason you throw away your dreams."

Maggie wanted to tell him that meeting him and falling in love with him had been a dream come true, but she held back. "Thomas, I felt like I was drowning in that life. I was working in a toxic environment, eating antacids like they were candy, and I had become so isolated from all of my friends. Since coming to Cedar Lake, I'm happier than I've ever been."

Thomas's tight expression relaxed.

Maggie reached up, grabbed ahold of his shirt, and pulled him closer. "Can we stop talking about my dad now?"

Thomas nodded, his green eyes meeting hers. He leaned in, and Maggie savored the soft sensation of his lips. A soft sigh escaped her mouth when his lips made their way down to a sensitive spot on her neck.

"I want to take you right here," Thomas panted in her ear.

Maggie glanced over at her grandmother's cottage. The lights were still on. "You know I want you to, but I have to get back."

Thomas groaned. Hearing how turned on he was made Maggie feel like the sexiest woman on the planet. She stepped aside and adjusted her dress. "To be continued on our camping trip." She set off on the short walk back to her cottage.

"I'll pick you up at noon!" he called out.

Maggie smiled all the way back to the cottage. Inside, she found her parents drinking tea and reading the newspaper.

"There she is!" Mom said. "Would you like some tea?"

Maggie nodded. She grabbed a teacup and joined her parents at the kitchen table.

Her mother removed the tea cozy and poured Maggie a cup of vanilla chai. "Thomas is a wonderful young man," she said.

Maggie wrapped her hands around the porcelain cup, waiting for the other shoe to drop.

"And the way he looks at you! My goodness, that boy is head over heels in love."

Maggie grinned quietly to herself and took a sip. "Thomas is incredible. I've never met anyone like him. He's so kind and thoughtful and—"

"Funny!" her dad chimed in.

"Not to mention, handsome," Mom added.

Maggie's shoulders relax. She felt at home when tea was served, and she was delighted her parents could see what she saw in Thomas. "Listen, I know you're both worried about me, but please don't be. I feel like I'm thinking clearly for the first time in a while. I know I'll figure things out. I just need a little more time to—"

"We just don't want you to get hurt," said Mom, placing her hand on Maggie's forearm.

"By who? Thomas?" Maggie asked.

Dad closed the newspaper he was reading and set it aside. "Thomas made it very clear over dinner that he has no intention of ever moving back to the city."

"I know that," said Maggie, her voice fading as the weight of what he said sunk in.

"Are you serious about him?" Mom asked.

Maggie swallowed. She had to be honest with her parents. "Yes."

"Your options are limited here, Maggie. Do you really want all of your education to go to waste?" Dad asked.

"No! Definitely not."

"Your father and I really like Thomas. We just don't want you to make a decision that you might regret later on," Mom said.

"I promise you, I will work things out. I'm saving almost all of the money I'm making at the resort and—"

"Have you talked to Thomas about when and where you'll go?" Dad asked. "He is smitten with you. You need to be fair to him and remind him that your situation isn't permanent."

"He knows…"

Mom quirked one eyebrow questioningly. "Does he?"

Maggie paused. How was Thomas supposed to know what her plans were when she didn't yet know herself?

"We love you, honey. We just want what's best for you," said Mom.

"It's time to make some plans," said Dad.

"Autumn will be here before you know it."

Maggie had a difficult time falling asleep that night. She tossed and turned for hours, kicking off her blankets because she was too warm and then pulling them up to her chin a few minutes later because she was too cold. Eventually, she gave up trying to sleep and went to the kitchen for a glass of water.

"I'm sorry, did I wake you?" Katie whispered. She was standing at the kitchen island in her bathrobe, making herself a piece of peanut butter toast.

"No, I couldn't sleep." Maggie said. She put the kettle on for her aunt.

"What's on your mind?" Katie asked. "It might make you feel better to talk about it."

Maggie sighed. "The truth is, I know what I want, but what I want isn't possible."

"Are you talking about the internship?"

Maggie shook her head. "I would never work for 880 News again, but I do miss the buzz of the newsroom. I miss interviewing interesting people, writing their stories, and the challenge of meeting tight deadlines."

"Honey, that's great! You know, there are plenty of other news stations to work for in Toronto. I don't see a problem—"

"The problem is that I'm not sure I want to go back to the city! I love the peaceful life of cottage country—the fresh air, the sunsets, and the freedom to go for a paddle when the workday is done. Isn't that what life is supposed to be about?"

"I think what you mean is Thomas is in cottage country."

Maggie's eyes focused intently on Katie. "I'm falling in love with him, but he was upfront with me from the beginning. He's never going to leave Cedar Lake. What do you think I should do?"

Katie let out a heavy sigh. She placed her toast and her tea on a tray to take back to her room. "I can't tell you what to do, but as a wise woman of forty-three, I have learned over the years that these things have a way of working themselves out. You'll see." Katie kissed Maggie on the top of the head and went back to bed.

Maggie found Katie's advice comforting. That night, she fell asleep repeating it like a mantra.

These things have a way of working themselves out. These things have a way of working themselves out.

Maggie awoke to the sound of laughter coming from the kitchen. A small smile tugged at her lips. The radio was playing, and she knew her parents were moving about the kitchen, making banana pancakes, just like old times. When she emerged from her bedroom, her shoulders dropped, seeing their packed bags at the front door.

"You're leaving?" Maggie asked.

"Get ready, Maggie," said Dad. He flipped all the pancakes off the griddle and onto a plate like a circus clown. His face crinkled into a smile. "Tada! You're impressed, right?"

Maggie pressed her lips together to keep from smiling. Her dad used to do that trick for her when she was a little kid. It was the best part about making pancakes with him. "You still got it, Dad."

Dad placed two pancakes in front of her, and Mom passed her the maple syrup.

"Our long weekend has been cut short. There's a crisis at the office. Your father is needed back in the city."

Maggie lowered her head. "Maybe you two could come back for the long weekend in September?"

Mom patted her arm. "We'll see, honey."

Later that morning, as her parents drove away, Maggie was overwhelmed with a wave of homesickness.

She hadn't realized how much she had missed them until they showed up out of the blue.

Katie wrapped her arm around Maggie's shoulders as they waved goodbye. "Everything okay?" she asked.

Maggie nodded. "I know now they just want what's best for me." Smoothing things over with her father had brought Maggie comfort.

"So, what's your plan for the rest of the day?" Katie asked.

"Thomas is taking me canoe camping."

"That's so romantic! On Cedar Lake?"

Maggie gave a coy smile. "He reserved us a spot on one of the islands. That reminds me, I still need to pack!"

At 12:01, Thomas pulled up beside Maggie's dock in his green canoe. "Fancy meeting you here," he said.

Maggie's stomach fluttered with nervous energy. Thomas's presence was magnetic. His muscles rippled under his short-sleeved rash guard, quickening her pulse. Maggie placed her backpack into the bow and slowly climbed into her seat, careful not to tip the packed canoe. She unbuttoned and removed her white collared linen shirt revealing her pearl-white triangle bikini top and high-rise denim shorts. As they set off across the glassy lake, Maggie tilted her face to the sky. The sun kissed her cheeks, and Maggie inhaled deeply, enjoying the warm breeze on her exposed skin. The calm that came with paddling out into the lake settled into her body.

"Are you going to tell me where we're going?" she asked.

"It's a surprise!" Thomas called from the stern.

Maggie grinned ear-to-ear. For some, the thought of paddling hard all day, lugging around heavy gear and no showers in sight, would be an unappealing date. For

Maggie, it was thrilling. Thomas made her feel brave enough to venture outside her comfort zone and dive into new challenges. In her experience, most paddling partnerships were far from ideal. When June visited last month, what had started as a fun afternoon out on the water, dissolved into a zig zag ride that left both of them feeling irritated, but with Thomas, everything was effortless. They glided across the water in perfect sync.

The sun shining high above the pine trees reflected in the water, making it shimmer like polished jade. They paddled past granite cliffs and through a series of little islands. It was breathtakingly beautiful. Thomas steered their canoe to the last island.

"Is this where we're camping?" Maggie asked. Her arms felt like Jell-O.

Thomas hopped out of the canoe with ease and pulled their boat to shore, anchoring it in the sand. "This is where we're stopping for lunch."

Maggie collected firewood while Thomas went to work setting up his fishing rod. The island had a small forest just beyond its beach. Maggie explored the woods, collecting dry sticks, fallen birch bark, and bigger branches along the way. When she emerged from the woods, she watched as Thomas reeled in a large Ontario trout. She couldn't help but laugh at Thomas's proud expression.

"What a catch!" she called.

"I hope you're hungry!"

Maggie went to work building the campfire on the beach while Thomas prepared the fish. He scaled and gutted the trout before rinsing it clean and patting it dry. He showed Maggie how to butterfly the fish and discard the bones. He grabbed a few ingredients from the cooler and added fresh dill, garlic, and lemon slices into the center of the fish. Maggie seasoned it with salt and pepper before Thomas wrapped the fish in a layer of tin foil. He placed the fish directly onto the coals and turned it every now and then to prevent it from burning. Thomas added a pot to the fire and filled it with milk, cream, and finely diced shallots. As it simmered, he whisked in butter and fresh dill. When the fish was cooked, Thomas poured the warm butter sauce all over it. They sat on a large piece of driftwood next to the campfire to eat.

"This is the most delicious thing I've ever eaten," Maggie said between bites. Her fingers glistened with butter. "I'm truly impressed."

He smiled with a sense of pride. "I've never been happier, Maggie."

Maggie glanced down at her toes in the sand. She wasn't sure if it was the sunshine or her attraction to Thomas, but she was overcome with lightheadedness. She was falling in love with him, and she believed he deeply cared for her, too, but she worried he wouldn't feel the same once he found out what had transpired at her internship.

"Thomas, I have to tell you something," she blurted before she could change her mind.

He tilted his head, his look uncertain. "Is everything alright?"

"I don't want to ruin this perfect day you've planned for us, but I think I'm finally ready to tell you why I left the internship."

Thomas reached for her hand. "You can tell me anything, Maggie. I'm here for you."

Maggie explained the whole fiasco with Henry Cooper Jr and how her mentor had written her up for it. "It was all a big misunderstanding, but the damage was done. Rumors circulated in the newsroom. It was difficult to show up for work, knowing everyone was talking about me behind my back. I wasn't sleeping, and I was so stressed out I was eating antacids like potato chips, by the handful! Still, I continued to work long hours. I wanted to prove to my boss, Andrew, that he hadn't made a mistake in hiring me."

Thomas squeezed Maggie's hand. She gathered herself with a deep breath and continued.

"At the weekly staff meeting, I told Andrew I was interested in writing a story about the city struggling to cope with a recent increase in homelessness. I had sources from the street and staff from the local shelters who were willing to be interviewed. Andrew told me to write it up. He said he would review it the next morning. I barely slept that night. I stayed up late preparing and writing. I—" Maggie's voice broke.

Thomas wrapped his arm around her shoulders. "I'm here, Maggie. You can tell me."

Maggie leaned into Thomas for support. She was drained of energy, but she continued. "The next morning, I was waiting for him outside of his office. When he arrived, he said, 'Someone is eager to see me.' He invited me in and told me to take a seat. He shut the door."

Maggie's head fell into her hands. If she stopped talking now, she would never tell her story. "I was nervous and rambling on about homelessness statistics like an idiot when I suddenly felt his hands on my shoulders. He said I looked tense and needed to relax. I sat there frozen. I didn't know what to do. I don't remember telling him to stop. I just let him massage me. He went on and on about how he'd like to hire me after the internship. He bent down and put his lips next to my ear and told me I just had to show him how committed I was—"

"Did you?" Thomas asked. His eyebrows drew together in an agonizing expression.

"No! I remember standing up to put some distance

between us. I was scared and shaking so badly I fumbled as I collected my papers off his desk. I remember feeling ashamed, like this was somehow my fault. I must have led him on or something. I couldn't even make eye contact. I mumbled something about how the internship wasn't working out, and I got out of there as fast as I could. Everyone stared as I exited his office. He yelled after me to leave the premises immediately. Later, I snuck into my office to save my portfolio from my work computer, and I overheard people gossiping in the hallway. Rumor had it, I was trying to sleep my way to the top."

Thomas's eyes widened. He shook his head in disbelief. "I'm so sorry that happened to you, Maggie. The nerve of that guy! Have you thought about reporting him?"

Maggie shook her head. "My reputation is ruined. Nobody would believe me."

Thomas grabbed her by the shoulders. His eyes held hers. "I believe you, Maggie."

Relief flooded through her. Carrying the weight of her secret was exhausting. She collapsed into his arms, feeling safe and accepted for the first time in a long while.

Thomas held her, gently stroking her soft wavy hair that framed her face. "When you're ready to start writing again, I have an idea for your next story," he said.

Maggie perked up. "Oh, yeah?"

Thomas nodded. "An exposé on society's sexist narrative about women sleeping their way to the top, when instead, we should be calling out the men who withhold promotions until they receive sexual favors."

Maggie's eyes brightened. "That's it!"

Chapter Eighteen

Maggie stood on a flat rock on the edge of the island and looked out at the open water. A burden had been lifted off her shoulders and she was lighter and more at peace since telling Thomas the truth. Now, she could move forward in life and in their relationship. Thomas came up behind her and wrapped his arms around her waist. Maggie leaned back against his chest. They swayed for a moment, listening to the soothing sound of the water lapping against the rocks.

Thomas pointed out into the lake. "Do you see that island just before the inlet?"

Maggie nodded.

"That's where we're camping tonight. We better get moving. I want to get there before it gets dark."

Maggie and Thomas went to work cleaning up their lunch site, leaving no sign they were ever there. Their campfire had burned completely to ash, but they poured a bucket of lake water on it to ensure it was out. They packed out their garbage with them. As they got into the canoe and pushed away from the shore, a kaleidoscope of brilliant orange butterflies fluttered across the beach.

"Wow! Look how many monarchs there are!" Maggie cried. She stopped paddling to admire their black-veined wings with white spots at the edges.

"From here, they'll migrate thousands of kilometers away to the mountain forests of Mexico," Thomas said.

Maggie stared in wonder as their canoe slowly drifted away from the island. Thomas steered them into the open water, and Maggie paddled with a newfound gusto. Maggie was transformed. Like a butterfly, her wings unfolding.

As they paddled across the lake, they waved to passersby in sailboats, rowboats, and motorboats. It was a sunny day with calm waters, which made for easy paddling. The sun beat down on Maggie's exposed legs, toasting them golden brown. The lake was window clear. Below the surface, soft strands of seaweed danced back and forth with the gentle movement of the water. The sway of the small waves caressed the shoreline ahead.

It was 6:00 when they finally arrived at their campsite. Maggie and Thomas went straight to work setting up their tent. Maggie snapped the poles together while Thomas removed all the sticks, pinecones, and debris from the ground where they were going to pitch their shelter. After he laid out the tarp, they worked together to stretch the tent base across the tarp. Maggie sensed Thomas's eyes on her, and suddenly, she was self-conscious.

"What?" she asked.

Thomas inserted the longest pole into the sleeve on the outside of the tent. "I was just thinking I can't wait to spend the entire night with you."

A wave of heat rushed between Maggie's legs. Before she could respond, Thomas told her to repeat what he was doing with the cross pole.

"I'm going to raise the tent, and then you go around to each corner and fit each pole into the pocket along the exterior, near the ground," he said.

Thomas then showed her how to clip the additional fasteners to the poles and how to stake the corners to secure the tent to the ground.

"We did it!" Maggie said. She tossed their sleeping bags and Therm-a-Rest pads inside the tent.

"We're not finished yet," Thomas said. He pulled a foldable saw from his pants pocket. "We need to gather firewood."

They went to work foraging for tinder—dry bark and small sticks the size of their pinky fingers. They combed the forest floor for kindling about the size of their thumbs and bigger branches for firewood. By the time they had a pile big enough to satisfy Thomas, Maggie was a sweaty mess.

"We should go for a swim," Thomas said. He slowly peeled off his damp shirt.

Maggie looked out into the lake. The sun was setting, a perfect conclusion to their amazing day. Flaming colors of red, tangerine, and yellow collided over the horizon. The lake was quiet. Boaters had tucked their vessels in for the night. Maggie and Thomas had the lake to themselves. Feeling frisky, Maggie slowly removed her bikini top and let it drop to the sand. Her nipples hardened as they met the fresh air. Thomas's eyes raked boldly over her body. He stepped toward her.

"I like where this is going," he said, wrapping his arms around her and pressing his warm, salty body against hers. She tilted her head up and Thomas teased her bottom lip by tracing it with his tongue. When he finally kissed her, Maggie quietly moaned into his mouth. His lips left hers to nibble at her collarbone as he brought his hands to her breasts, circling her nipples with his thumbs. Maggie wanted more. She traced her fingers from his chest down his abs to the waistband of his swim shorts. She tugged at the string to untie them.

"Are we doing this?" he asked breathlessly.

Maggie nodded. Excitedly, they both removed their bathing suit bottoms and took a step back to admire each other. Thomas was deliciously appealing, standing there in the sand. His tall, powerful body was strong with lean muscles. His skin was smooth and tanned from spending so much time outdoors. He held his aroused length with one hand and ran the other hand through his messy mop of curls. A touch of sunset caught his eyes, and they smoldered with his passion.

"You are the most beautiful woman I've ever seen," he said.

Maggie's heart flipped in her chest. She stepped toward him and wrapped her arms around his neck, her breasts tingling against his chest. "I want you to make me come again," she said.

A spark of amusement twinkled in his eye. "I can do that," he promised, licking his lips. He slowly glided his hand down her torso until it was between her legs. Applying firm pressure, Thomas rubbed and stroked until Maggie's breath became quick and labored. She dug her nails into his shoulders as pinpricks of pleasure rushed to her pelvis. Just when she was about to go over the edge, Thomas suddenly stopped.

Maggie let out a strangled whimper. "Keep going!" she begged.

"Not yet," Thomas said in a husky voice. "I want us to come together." He was hard and ready for her. Thomas bent down and quickly grabbed a condom from the pocket of his discarded board shorts, tearing the foil package with his teeth. As Maggie helped him secure it in place, he groaned and tilted his head back. Moments later, his mouth found hers in an insatiable kiss. Thomas swiftly lifted Maggie from her middle, and she wrapped her legs around his naked waist. He moved his hands under her thighs to support her, and with ease, carried her into the lake.

Maggie shrieked with glee as the cool water washed over her warm skin. There was such strength in Thomas's arms. He could quite literally sweep her off her feet. Maggie traced his biceps with her fingers and raised her gaze to find him watching her. Being naked with him in the lake was inherently liberating. She didn't know if it was the adventure or the heightened sense of intimacy, but she was ready for the mystery of wading into unknown waters with him, and she wanted him to know it. She tightened her arms around his body and a guttural gasp escaped her lips as he thrust into her. Thomas rocked back and forth, slow at first, and then quicker until his body was taut with restraint. It wasn't until Maggie shuddered with pulsing waves of satisfaction that Thomas finally released with a low, tortured groan.

After the sun went down, Maggie and Thomas sat beside the campfire, wrapped in large plush towels, drying off. Maggie watched the flames dance, replaying the mind-blowing experience in her mind. Their lovemaking was connective. She'd never experienced anything like it, and she couldn't wait to do it again. Maggie crawled between Thomas's legs and leaned back against his chest.

Thomas kissed the top of her head. "You're incredible," he whispered.

"Me? My whole body is tingling."

Thomas tilted his head back and laughed. "You're not like anyone I've ever met before."

Maggie smiled. It was good to know that she could satisfy him, too.

"Maggie, I feel like I'm so much better when I'm with you."

Maggie turned to face him. "You're my favorite person to spend time with. I trust you."

Thomas cupped her face in his hands and kissed her hungrily. A sudden swoosh sensation filled her pelvis as if she were on a rollercoaster ride. She craved having his weight on top of her. She stood up and let her towel fall to her feet.

"I'm ready for bed," she stated.

Thomas's gaze dropped from her eyes to her

breasts. "I –I'll be right there."

Maggie crawled into their tent and went to work zipping their single sleeping bags together into one larger blanket. The anticipation sent a warm glow through her. Meanwhile, Thomas removed the rain fly from the top.

"What are you doing?" Maggie asked.

"There's no rain in the forecast tonight, and this way, we can sleep under the stars."

Thomas hung their towels to dry on a tree branch before crawling into the sleeping bag with Maggie. They both lay on their backs, admiring the black sky that was splattered with silver. Their tent was surrounded by cedars and white pine on one side, the lake on the other, and the Milky Way above. Maggie glanced at Thomas, longing to have his hands all over her naked body again. She couldn't wait any longer. She rubbed her foot against his calf and ankle. Thomas looked over at her and smiled, which sent her pulse racing. Maggie nodded slowly, but subtly. She wanted more of their wild, outdoor lovemaking. Thomas reached for his backpack and pulled out a condom. Moments later, Thomas was on top of her. Maggie buried her face against his throat and stroked his back with her fingers.

"I want you," he growled into her ear.

Maggie eagerly wrapped her legs around his waist and pulled him in. Thomas moaned, moving slow and heavy, just the way she liked it.

"Does this feel okay?" he panted, moving his hips in a circular motion.

"It feels amazing," she answered, her pulse quickening. She raked his body with impatient hands. "More."

Thomas kissed her deeply. He whispered her name over and over again as he grinded and thrusted until her breath became erratic. Maggie gripped the sleeping bag in her fists as the rush of pleasure rippled throughout her body. Almost simultaneously, Thomas emitted a hoarse groan as he crossed the finish line with her. His body collapsed on top of hers, their hearts pounding in unison. Thomas, sounding short of breath, took a moment to dispose of the condom before rolling over and spooning her. Her body fit perfectly into his. Maggie closed her eyes and drifted off to sleep, listening to the gentle wind that rustled through the trees.

The next morning, the sun was beaming through their tent, causing Maggie to stir. A medley of energetic birdsong played overhead. The scent of coffee brewing on the campfire drifted into the tent. Maggie slipped on her denim shorts and pulled a hoodie over her head before joining Thomas by the fire.

"Good morning, sleepyhead," Thomas said, handing her a hot cup of coffee. It smelled lightly caramelized.

Maggie took a sip. "Mmm, just what I needed."

She looked out at the lake. It was calm and statue-still. She sat down on a log beside Thomas and leaned her head against his shoulder. Dragonflies, with their wings glistening from the morning dew, were perched in the long grass by the water's edge. They needed the sunshine to fly. Once they could stretch their wings, they would spend their day flying around to catch food. She pointed them out to Thomas.

"After Johnny's funeral, we came to the cottage to help my grandmother close it up. There was an abundance of dragonflies, hundreds of them flying around our dock. A swarm. I had never seen anything like it. Grandma said it was a sign that Johnny was with us. Whenever I see one now, I think about that. I think about him."

Thomas took a sip of coffee. "Your grandmother

sounds like an amazing woman."

"The best! She would love you."

Thomas's face lit up with a smile. "Will she be coming to the cottage this summer?"

Maggie shook her head. "She recently had hip surgery and is recovering in a rehab facility. Even if she was well enough to visit, she wouldn't. She hasn't been back since the day of his funeral. It's too painful for her."

Thomas nodded as though he understood. "I guess there's finally a good reason for me to go back to the city then."

Maggie grinned. It touched her heart to know how much he wanted to meet her grandmother. "I'd love to meet your family someday, too."

Thomas stared at his bare feet. "My mom left when I was two."

Maggie brought her hand to her mouth. "I'm so sorry, Thomas. I didn't realize."

Thomas shrugged. "There's no need to apologize. I only have one memory of her. I remember driving my Big Wheel tricycle around the kitchen island as my parents screamed at each other."

"Do you know where she is now?"

"She went to the United States to study to become a nurse. Last I heard, she was living in Oregon."

"Did she ever try to stay in touch with you?"

Thomas clenched his jaw. "When I was younger, she'd call once in a while, always promising to come visit me, but she never did. She never even sent me a birthday card. The random phone calls stopped when I was eight years old."

Maggie gently placed her hand on his forearm. "It's not your fault. You know that, right?"

Thomas offered her a tight-lipped smile and placed his hand on top of hers. "I was lucky to have the amazing father that I did."

"Yes, but it couldn't have been easy growing up without a mother."

Thomas nodded. "It's literally messed with every relationship I've ever had. I have a hard time trusting people. I'm always afraid they're going to leave me. I usually end things before they can."

Maggie swallowed the lump in her throat. A subtle storm brewed in her chest as she wondered if she would be enough to break his cycle of pushing people away. She realized that her indecision about where or what she was going to be doing with her life could be causing Thomas a lot of unnecessary stress. "I would never do anything to hurt you. You know you can trust me, right?"

Thomas brought her hand to his lips and kissed her knuckles. "I hate to say this, but it's time for us to break camp."

"No, already?" Maggie whined, trying to ignore the fact that Thomas avoided answering her question.

"I still have some work to do on the Evans's cottage, and I have to clean up my cabin. I'm hosting a bachelor party this weekend."

Maggie's mouth dropped open. "A bachelor party? I didn't even know you had any friends," she teased.

Thomas laughed. "My college roommate, Nick, is getting married. I'm a groomsman. When he asked if he and a few of his friends could come fishing for the weekend, I couldn't say no. I've been so busy working on the Evans's cottage I haven't had a chance to plan it."

"I could help you!" Maggie offered.

"No. Really?"

"Yes! I love planning parties. I'm good at it, too. I don't have a shift for a couple of days, so I have the time."

Thomas's smile widened, showing his approval. "You're incredible!"

After breakfast, Maggie and Thomas broke camp. They washed their dishes, took down their tent, put out the fire, and packed their canoe. As Maggie dipped her paddle into the lake, a dragonfly landed on the grip.

"Thomas, look," she whispered.

Thomas leaned forward, and they silently admired its turquoise abdomen until it took flight.

"Did you know in some cultures, dragonflies represent good luck or prosperity?" Thomas asked.

Maggie smiled and paddled forward. With her face toward the sunshine, the shadows of the past year fell behind her. Her luck had changed the moment she met Thomas.

Chapter Nineteen

"Hello?" a gentle voice said on the other line after two rings.

"Hi, Grandma!" Maggie said. "It's so good to hear your voice."

"Maggie! How are you, dear?"

Maggie sat down on a cold stool at the kitchen island. "Much better since the last time we spoke. How's your physiotherapy coming along?"

"I can't wait to get out of this godforsaken place."

Maggie laughed. "That bad, huh?"

"They wake me at the crack of dawn to torture me."

"Mom says it's the best rehabilitation in the province. I heard your physiotherapist is quite handsome."

"He says I'll be home soon if I keep up with my daily exercises. Speaking of handsome men, I heard the neighbor boy is quite good looking."

"Mom told you, I guess?" Maggie asked.

"She said you've never looked happier."

Maggie smiled. "Thomas is amazing. He wants to meet you. Maybe when you feel up to it, you could come to the cottage for a visit. It's been an incredibly healing summer for me. I—"

"I'll think about it dear." There was a quieter, sad tone in her grandmother's voice.

Maggie didn't push it. "I miss you."

"I miss you, too, Maggie. I'm glad you're having a good summer. Have you given any thought as to what you're going to do in September?"

Maggie bit her lip. She was blissfully happy, but she still didn't have a concrete answer to her grandmother's question. "Not yet." That answer gnawed at her confidence.

"Don't worry, dear. You're an intelligent and beautiful girl. I have faith you'll know what to do. Listen, Maggie, my nurse just walked in to take me down to chair yoga. I'll talk to you later, dear. I love you."

"I love you, too, Grandma."

Maggie grinned as she hung up the phone. She always felt better after she'd spoken to her grandma. Grandma saw her for whom she truly was, and she believed in her.

"How's my mom doing today?" Katie asked as she entered the kitchen. She opened the fridge door and pulled out sliced turkey, tomatoes, cucumbers, and the mayonnaise. "Would you like a sandwich?"

"Yes, please." Maggie was hungry from the paddle back from the campsite. "Grandma says she'll be home soon."

Katie nodded. "Her doctor says she's making excellent progress. Your grandmother is a strong woman." Katie sliced two fresh white rolls with a bread knife and layered the buns with deli meat and vegetables and sprinkled the mayo with black pepper. Maggie grabbed two glass bottles of sparkling water from the fridge, and they took their lunch outside to the picnic table overlooking the lake.

"How was camping?" Katie asked.

Maggie took a big bite of her sandwich. "Good," she said, covering her full mouth.

Katie raised one eyebrow questioningly. "That's all I get? Good? I want details."

Maggie's cheeks flushed with warmth. She'd grown a lot closer to her aunt over the summer and Katie had become more like an older sister than an aunt. "Thomas makes me feel things I've never felt before."

A slow, secretive smile spread across Katie's face.

"I'm happy for you, honey."

Maggie had the urge to tell her aunt what Thomas had said about his trust issues, but she held back. It was too private to share.

Katie reached across the table and squeezed Maggie's hand. "While you were away, I was able to narrow down the search."

Maggie's eyes widened. "Did you find a phone number or address?"

Katie shook her head. "There are only ten families in the Fox Creek area with the last name Smith."

"Katie! That's amazing news. I can help you make calls—"

"I'm not ready," Katie said quickly.

Maggie's mouth gaped in surprise. "She has to be related to one of these families, Katie. She might still live at home with her parents—"

"What if she wants nothing to do with me?" Katie asked. "What if her parents were awful people and she hates me for putting her up for adoption? I don't know if I can bear it."

"What if she's been waiting her whole life for you to call? What if she wants a relationship with her birth mother?"

A faint smile touched with sadness spread across Katie's face. Despite Maggie's eagerness to connect with her cousin, this was something that Katie had to do in her own time.

"I'll be here to help you make those calls when you're ready, Katie."

Maggie spent the rest of the afternoon sitting on the dock with a notebook in hand, writing a list for the bachelor party. The sky was a brilliant shade of blue, dotted with puffy cumulus clouds. Bird songs blended with the steady hum of a motorboat in the distance. The chop of the boat's wake eventually made its way toward Maggie and slapped against the dock. Fresh earthy scents of cedar and sand mingled with the faint aroma of gasoline. Everything about the summer air was alive and full of possibility.

When Thomas returned home from work, Maggie was eager to share her ideas.

"I called the party store in town, and they sell beer cozies that say, 'He's been hooked!' on them," Maggie said.

Thomas's face lit up. "I can't believe you did all this for me." The warmth of his smile echoed in his voice.

After dinner, Maggie and Thomas headed into town to shop for party supplies and groceries. They pulled into the parking lot of Cedar Grove's year-round costume and party shop. Inside, it smelled of musty carpet and latex balloons. Maggie loaded their cart with bachelor party supplies—paper plates, napkins, and beer cozies. She added themed candy like sour fish and gummy worms to the cart for a "Bait Bar." She also convinced Thomas to buy a light-up custom sign.

"You can write 'Nick's Bachelor Party' on it or something." Maggie placed it into the cart.

"Or 'Nick, the Great Master Baiter,'" Thomas added.

They looked at each other and burst out laughing.

"Can I help you two?" the store owner interrupted.

Maggie covered her mouth with her hand, stifling her giggles.

The store owner glared at them over her reading glasses. "What's so funny?"

Thomas swallowed his laughter and cleared his throat. "I think we've found everything we need."

Before they made their way to the cash register, Maggie begged him to add a package of customizable balloons to the cart.

Thomas shook his head. "I draw the line at balloon garlands."

At the grocery store, they worked through Maggie's long list. She had included everything from appetizers to steaks. "Just in case you don't catch anything."

Their last stop was at The Beer Store. Thomas picked up two cases of Nick's favorite beer, and Maggie helped by lugging one of the crates to the back of his truck. They leaned against the tailgate and watched a mix of townies and summer vacationers lollygag from the parking lot into the store to buy beer or return their empties. Many stopped to chat with one another. The Beer Store was a happening place in Cedar Grove.

Thomas reached for Maggie's hand. "Thank you for helping me out with this." He pulled her to him, and she wrapped her arms around his neck, pressing herself against his solid body.

She swayed her hips into his. "How are you going to repay me?" she asked.

Amusement filled his eyes. "I'll have to take you back to my place to show you."

"Thomas!" a familiar voice called out, interrupting their moment.

Maggie stood up straighter when she realized it was Sadie. Maggie didn't know how it was possible, but Sadie somehow looked even more beautiful than the last time she saw her. The summer sun had highlighted her hair, and the golden strands softened her face. Maggie smiled politely, composed on the outside, but inside her insecurities stirred—fueled by exes who cheated and chipped away at her confidence.

"Hey," said Thomas, wrapping his arm around Maggie's waist protectively. "How's your summer been?"

"Busy," Sadie said directly to Thomas. "You missed the annual beach bonfire this year. Remember that time it was forty degrees, and we stripped down to nothing and—"

"We went camping instead," Thomas interrupted. His eyes flashed with annoyance. Sadie had pressed a button.

"I think about that night ... a lot," said Sadie. Her mouth curved upward as she turned and slowly strutted toward the store. Maggie couldn't take her eyes off Sadie's long, slender supermodel legs. "I'll see you at work, Maggie," she said flatly before entering the store.

Maggie looked down, staring at the chipped nail polish on her toes. She hated how Sadie had the power to make her feel less than.

"Ignore her," said Thomas.

Maggie raised her eyes to find him watching her, assessing her. His mouth was tight. Maggie sighed, leaning into the firmness of his body.

"I could go for some ice cream," Maggie said, desperate to put their run-in with Sadie behind them.

Thomas's lips eased into a smile. "My treat," he said.

The rest of the week went by in a blur. Maggie had a shift to work each day, and for the most part, she was able to avoid the wrath of Sadie. On her downtime, Maggie started writing again. After her camping trip with Thomas, she was inspired for the first time in a long time to put pen to paper. Both Thomas and Katie asked if they could read her work, but she wasn't ready to share.

"Soon," she promised them.

When she wasn't at work or writing, Maggie was with Thomas. They spent most of their evenings paddling across the bay to the tiny island where they could jump off the rocks into the lake below. Sometimes, they lazed in the hammock reading, and on cooler nights, Thomas built a campfire so they could roast marshmallows, or Maggie would brew a nighttime tea, and they'd watch a movie under the stars on the projector. Every night ended the same, making love in Thomas's bed.

Thomas's cottage was a minimalist's dream summerhouse. Maggie admired the architecture, which was sleek and simple and blended in well with the natural landscape. Thomas's king-size bed was made of oak and was layered with pillows and textured throws that gave it that lovely lived-in look. Maggie couldn't help but wonder if Sadie had had a hand in decorating.

"I love having you in my bed, naked," Thomas murmured after another night of sensual lovemaking. "Don't leave me. Sleep over tonight."

Maggie desperately wanted to stay the night and wake up to his face the next morning. But every night, Maggie begrudgingly got out of his bed and made her way back to her grandmother's cottage. For some reason, she felt obligated to do so, and if she stayed the night, Katie would be up worrying. It was best not to stay.

Maggie returned to Thomas's cottage the next morning to help him set up for the bachelor party. She found him down by his dock, washing his motorboat. Thomas preferred to fish in his canoe, but he needed to use the bigger boat for the party. They boarded the boat and Thomas offered Maggie the captain's chair. She sat down on the warm leather seat, and he handed her the lanyard key.

"Let's make sure she still starts," he said. He went to the back of the boat and lowered the motor until the propellers were submerged. He nodded, giving her the go-ahead. Maggie turned the key in the ignition, and the motor purred.

Thomas's mouth twitched with delight. "You look sexy in the driver's seat."

Maggie flashed a seductive grin. "If you're lucky, maybe I'll take you for a ride."

"I wish," he said in a resigned voice. "The guys will be here in a couple of hours."

Maggie turned off the ignition and put the lanyard around her neck. "Something to look forward to then."

Thomas's smile widened, showing his approval. He held out his hand and helped her off the boat. They returned to his cottage to finish getting ready for the party.

"Who's coming again?" Maggie asked. She unwrapped the paper plates from their plastic wrap and placed them on the table.

"The groom, Nick, who was my college roommate, his younger brother, Ryan, who's a really nice guy, and another guy named Drew, who I've never met before. He's Nick and Ryan's older cousin."

Maggie finished the food prep, chopping vegetables and making dips, while Thomas did the last-minute tidying. Maggie made sure the dishwasher was empty and cleared away the remaining clutter on the kitchen island. Thomas came up behind her. He fingered the loose strands of her wavy hair, caressing her neck.

"What would I do without you?" he murmured into her ear.

Maggie turned and watched his eyes sweep over her approvingly.

"Don't get any big ideas," she said, loving every minute of his affection. "Your friends will be here any minute."

"I better go take a quick shower to cool off," he said. He kissed her slowly, leaving her wanting more.

"Are you sure you don't want to come with me?"

Maggie smacked him lovingly with a tea towel. "Go! I'll take the garbage on my way out. We'll see each other next week. Have fun with your friends!"

Maggie went back to her cottage, grabbed her notebook and pen, and made her way down to her own dock. The cedar trees that surrounded the lake looked like they were painted onto the still water. She sat down on the edge of the dock and slowly dipped her toes into the water. A warm breeze sighed gently over the tall grass along the water's edge, and Maggie began to write. For over an hour, she let the words flow from her pen. She didn't worry about structure or grammar. She just wanted to get all her ideas out on paper. She could edit and proofread later. A speckled fish jumped somewhere out in the bay, hoping to catch a fly that buzzed about. Its splash echoed across the bay, pulling Maggie from her writing. She smiled. It would be a good day for fishing for the guys.

Suddenly, Maggie reached around her neck, realizing she had forgotten to take off the lanyard for Thomas's motorboat. She quickly made her way back to his place to return it, but when she got there, she saw the cars in his driveway. His guests had arrived. She pulled her lip gloss from the pocket of her jean shorts and applied a liberal amount. As she walked toward Thomas's front door, she straightened her t-shirt and gave her wavy locks a quick scrunch.

Normally, she would've walked right into his home, but she didn't want to barge in on his party. She knocked three times. As she waited for Thomas to come to the door, the wind whispered across the cedar branches overhead. The hair on the back of her neck stood on end. She bit her lip and looked at her feet while she waited. She hated showing up unannounced.

As the door opened, Maggie handed out the lanyard. "I forgot to give you—" Maggie stopped suddenly, frozen in time.

"Maggie?" the man's voice rang with authority.

Maggie couldn't respond. She was lost in the fear of seeing her former boss, Andrew, for the first time since she quit the internship.

"Maggie!" Thomas came up from behind Andrew. "What's up?"

"I–I forgot to give you this," she said. Her hand shook as she placed the lanyard in Thomas's hand.

"Drew, this is my girlfriend, Maggie," Thomas introduced. "Maggie, meet Drew."

A couple more guys appeared behind Thomas.

"So, this is the famous Maggie!" said the one with black-framed glasses.

"We've been here for all of five minutes, and he hasn't stopped talking about you," said the short guy wearing a muscle shirt.

Thomas laughed. The rich, warm sound soothed Maggie's nerves. Thomas was oblivious to her discomfort.

"Maggie, this is Nick," Thomas said, pointing to the guy wearing the glasses. He gestured to the shorter guy in the muscle shirt. "And this is his brother, Ryan."

"Come in for a drink, Maggie!" Nick called out as he headed back into the kitchen.

Maggie shook her head, but before she could refuse the offer, Thomas took her by the hand and pulled her inside. As she passed by Andrew, *Drew* she reminded herself, a sour smile spread across his thin lips.

Chapter Twenty

"Thomas, this girl is a keeper!" Nick said. He pulled a charcuterie board that Maggie had made from the fridge and placed it on the kitchen counter.

Ryan handed Maggie a beer. "Do you live next door, Maggie?"

Maggie's hand trembled as she took a sip. She struggled to swallow. She sensed Drew's eyes stalking her. "I'm staying at my grandmother's cottage for the summer."

Nick placed a piece of brie on a cracker and popped it into his mouth. "What do you do, Maggie?"

Maggie's shoulders hunched. "I—I work in the restaurant at the resort on the lake."

Drews lips twisted into a cynical smile. Maggie's heartbeat accelerated. She needed to get out of there. When Thomas placed his hand on the small of her back, Maggie's pulse slowed a little.

"Maggie is a talented journalist," he said. "She's been writing a freelance piece this summer."

Drew's smile vanished and was quickly replaced by a frown. "Gaining experience through internships and building a strong professional network is crucial for aspiring journalists," he warned.

"Maggie, you should talk to Drew about your career goals. He works—" Nick stopped short. The mustard he had dipped his piece of salami in had dripped onto his shirt.

Ryan laughed. "I can't take you anywhere."

As Nick went to change and Thomas marinated the steaks, Drew slithered his way next to Maggie. Ryan had busied himself with pouring a round of shots.

"You look fantastic," Drew whispered with staid calmness.

Maggie wrapped her arms around herself. Despite the warm weather, her arms were covered in goosebumps.

"I'm guessing your boyfriend doesn't know about the effect you have on men."

"What are you talking about?" she asked, her voice faint.

Drew just stood there for a moment, breathing. His breath smelt like garlic.

"I'm talking about how you flirt, lead guys on, and then leave them in the dust. You're such a tease."

Maggie grabbed her beer off the counter and took a big swig. The beer warmed her body. She chugged the rest of the bottle. Drew had a way of mixing her up, confusing her.

"Aren't you a little young for Thomas?" Drew asked.

Maggie's body stiffened. She didn't like where this conversation was headed.

"What'd I miss?" Thomas asked, interrupting Maggie's thoughts.

"Maggie and I were just talking about how you're a cradle robber," Drew sneered.

Maggie bit her lip and glanced at Thomas.

Thomas threw his head back and roared with laughter, oblivious to Drew's dig. He playfully patted Drew on the back. "At least I'm not as old as you, my friend!"

"There's only a four-year age difference between us," Maggie muttered quietly.

Drew smiled blandly, uninterested in Maggie's presence. "You'll be thirty before you know it, Thomas. You'll want to settle down and have kids in the next few years. If Maggie is the talented journalist you say she is, she's going to leave you in the rearview as she drives her career forward."

Thomas's smile vanished. His eyebrows drew together in a heart-wrenching way. Maggie was silenced by his hurt expression.

"Shots are ready!" Ryan called. He handed everyone a shot glass of tequila and a lime wedge. They each licked their hand in the space where one's thumb and index finger meet and sprinkled some salt on top.

"Remember, Maggie, the mantra is 'lick, shoot, *suck*," said Drew.

Unaware of Drew's jab, Thomas raised his shot glass. "To Nick! I wish you nothing but a lifetime of happiness, man."

"To Nick!" the guys cheered. Maggie raised her glass hesitantly but downed the shot in one gulp.

After a couple more rounds, Maggie transformed into a more confident, vibrant being. The buzz of the alcohol had warmed her entire body. She found it easier to ignore Drew's presence and was becoming fast friends with Nick and Ryan. They laughed at another one of her jokes.

"Where did you find this girl?" Ryan asked Thomas.

Maggie was killing it with his friends. She downed the rest of her third beer.

"Do you have any available friends for me or Drew?" Ryan asked. His eyebrows arched impishly.

"I think my best friend, June, could totally be into you!" she said to Ryan.

"What about me?" Drew asked. His glassy eyes were filled with a strange, eager look.

Maggie crinkled her nose and shook her head. "You're too old!" She leaned closer to Ryan. "And he's balding!" she drunkenly whispered to him but was loud enough for everyone to hear.

A low, throaty laugh emerged from Ryan's throat. He threw his heavy arm around her shoulders. "I love this girl!"

"I'm only a few years older than Thomas," Drew muttered under his breath. He ran a hand over his greasy scalp.

Nick playfully slapped Drew on the back and shook his shoulders. "Don't worry, man. Your girl is out there. Ryan can still be your wingman."

"Good luck," Maggie whispered loudly to Ryan. "His teeth are so bad he could eat an apple through a fence—"

"Maggie!" Thomas interrupted. He had a stern expression on his face. "Can you come help me with something?"

His tone brought her back to her high school days when one was called to the principal's office. Maggie slowly stood up and followed Thomas onto the screened-in porch.

"What are you doing?" he whispered. He placed a handful of empty beer bottles back in their box to return at a later time.

Maggie leaned against the doorframe for balance. The room was spinning. "What do you mean?" she slurred.

"You're insulting my guest."

"I'm not insulting him!" Maggie crossed her arms. "I'm describing him." Her tone was matter of fact.

"Listen, Mags, I think you've had a bit too much to drink—"

"We've all been drinking! Including you!"

"Maggie, I've had one shot. I'm sober. I need to drive the boat later. Listen, I think it's time you went—"

"You're kicking me out of the party?"

"Would you keep your voice down," he hissed.

"I'm not kicking you out. I just think it's time you went home before you say something you regret. It's almost time to take them fishing anyway—"

"This is about what Drew said, isn't it? You're pushing me away because you think I'll leave you." Her voice tremored. Now was the time to be honest with Thomas and tell him who Drew was, but she didn't have it in her to ruin Nick's party.

"Everything okay out here?" Drew interrupted.

Maggie blinked. Her mouth tightened with anger. "Don't worry about us. Worry about your eyebrows," she mumbled under her breath.

"Everything is fine," Thomas said over top of her. "Maggie, on your way out, do you mind bringing the tackle box down to the boat?"

Maggie folded her arms. "I'd rather not."

A frown set into Thomas's handsome features.

"No worries, man, I got this." Drew grabbed a tackle box in each hand and awkwardly balanced a fishing rod underneath his armpit. Thomas held the screen door open for him.

"Thanks, Drew. I appreciate it. I'll go wrangle the other two, and we'll meet you down at the dock in a minute."

Relief flooded Maggie's body as soon as Drew left the cottage. She released her breath, realizing she had been holding it in, frozen in fear the entire time she was in the same vicinity as Drew.

"What's the matter with you?" Thomas whispered as soon as Drew was out of earshot.

Maggie kept her features deceptively calm. "Nothing."

Thomas threw his hands up in frustration. "Nothing? Really? Cause you're acting kind of nuts."

"Yeah, well, being crazy is better than being an

asshole."

Thomas's body stiffened. "Did I do something to piss you off?"

Tell him.

Maggie opened her mouth to speak, but her brain couldn't form the words.

"Listen, I've got a house full of guests, and I'm trying to throw my buddy a party. I can't do this right now. This is the type of shit Sadie used to pull."

Maggie swallowed. Comparing her to his ex was a low blow, even if Maggie was acting insane. Thomas opened the screen door for her. There was something distant in the way he looked, and it frightened her.

She stepped outside and brought her hands to her temple. She was lightheaded and it was as if the world was spinning around her. "Thomas, I—"

"Now is not the time."

The screen door shut with a *swack*. Maggie flinched. The blood drained from her face as she realized she and Thomas had just had their first fight. Suddenly, she didn't feel very good. She ran toward her cottage but had to stop midway to retch in the ferns. When she could finally stand up straight, she reached into her back pocket and pulled out her phone.

"Maggie, slow down, I can't understand what you're saying," June said. The line crackled.

Maggie walked through the front door of the cottage and raced to her room to avoid coming face-to-face with Katie. She kicked off her shoes and curled up in her bed. "I've never been more embarrassed in my entire life!" she wailed. "June, I ruined everything!"

"Take a breath and start at the beginning."

Maggie told June the whole story, including the part about Drew's behavior at the internship.

"What a sicko! This all makes sense now. I get

why you left the internship. I can't believe you didn't tell me this earlier."

Maggie hated hearing the hurt in her best friend's voice. "It wasn't because I didn't trust you. I was mortified. I get confused, too, like this is all somehow my fault. I must have led him on—"

"No, Maggie! You could have worn miniskirts and low-cut blouses around the office, and this still wouldn't be your fault."

"I've destroyed the good thing I had going with Thomas."

"So what? He's friends with a sexual harasser."

"He'd never met him before," Maggie said, suddenly defensive.

"Did he not realize that something was wrong?"

Maggie thought back to the party. "I was so distressed. I remember not wanting to ruin the party, pretending everything was fine when it wasn't. So, it's not really Thomas's fault. I—"

"He should have sensed something was wrong."

Maggie shut her eyes tight, wishing she could forget everything that had happened. "When I tried to tell him what was wrong, it was too late. He shut me down." Maggie started to cry again. "I need to get out of here. I can't face him."

"Where will you go?"

Maggie paused for a moment, thinking through her options. Seconds later, it occurred to her exactly where she would go.

Maggie spent the entire next day in bed, sleeping off her hangover. Her head throbbed from too much tequila, and her throat ached from being sick in the bushes. Her eyes were red and puffy from crying.

"I don't want to talk about it," she called out when Katie knocked on her bedroom door around supper time.

"I'm worried about you, Maggie. You've been inside all day. I'm here if you want to talk about—"

"I said I'm fine!" she yelled beneath her duvet.

"I'll just leave this grilled cheese outside your door then," Kaie said, hurt echoing in her voice.

Maggie was weighed down by a sense of guilt, but she didn't want to burden her aunt with another problem. Katie had enough on her plate. When Maggie was sure Katie was gone, she grabbed the tray outside her bedroom door. Katie had buttered white Italian bread, just enough to turn the outside of the sandwich a perfect golden brown. She had cut it in half, and the cheddar cheese oozed onto the plate. A kosher pickle and a squirt of ketchup sat on the side. The greasy meal helped to settle her upset stomach and gave her the energy she needed to pack a small suitcase.

It was midnight by the time Maggie pulled up to her grandmother's house in Ottawa. Her grandmother's home was only an hour's drive from the cottage, but Maggie had waited to leave under the cover of darkness when the possibility of running into Thomas and his friends was slim. She wasn't taking any chances. Her grandmother's neighborhood was unique, it had an old-fashioned suburban feel. It was in an area with a lot of old trees, plenty of parks, and where people said "hi" to each other while out for a walk with their dog. Maggie worried her visit would be too much for her grandmother, who had only been released from the rehabilitation center a couple of days earlier.

"Maggie, dear, you sound upset. What's wrong?" her grandmother had asked when Maggie called to see if would be okay to stay with her for a few days.

"I'm feeling a little homesick, and I miss you," she said. It wasn't the whole story, but it was true. She missed her grandmother terribly.

"Did you and Katie get into a fight?" Grandma asked, her tone skeptical.

After Maggie reassured her grandmother that her leaving had nothing to do with Katie, Grandma insisted she come stay. "I could use the company," she said.

From the driveway, Maggie looked up at the two-story dwelling with its unique characteristics. The only light on in the house emanated from her grandmother's bedroom. Using her key, Maggie let herself in. She found her grandmother in bed dozing, while the television played a rerun of *Bridget Jones's Diary*. A small bowl of plain potato chips sat on her bedside table next to a miniature box of *Smarties*. As Maggie crawled into bed, her grandmother's paper-thin eyelids fluttered open.

"Oh, good, you made it safe and sound," she said. Her voice was hoarse with sleep. "I was just resting my eyes."

Maggie gave her grandmother a kiss on the cheek and snuggled in close. Her bedding smelled fresh like Ivory Snow, a gentle laundry detergent made for babies and people with sensitive skin.

"I'm glad you're here, dear," Grandma said. She patted Maggie's bare arm and began to trace the paler, sensitive skin of the underarm of Maggie's forearm with her arthritic fingers. For the first time that day, Maggie relaxed. Her grandmother had a special way of making her feel like everything would be okay.

"Katie says she thinks you may have had a fight with Thomas."

"She called you?"

"No, I called her. I wanted to tell her where you were going in case you forgot to tell her yourself. We're mothers. We worry."

Maggie was ashamed. She hadn't even left her

aunt a note.

"I did have a fight with Thomas. I think I ruined everything."

"Do you want some old-fashioned wisdom?"

Maggie nodded and inhaled deeply to prepare herself.

"You'll catch more flies with honey than vinegar," Grandma stated.

"What do you mean?"

"The way we speak to each other matters, Maggie. Your grandfather and I always put in the extra effort to watch our tones and speak to each other with kindness and respect."

Maggie tried to think back to her argument with Thomas, but their conversation was a drunken blur. All she had left was a feeling of helplessness that she couldn't shake. "Thomas asked for space. I'm giving it to him."

Maggie's phone buzzed in her purse.

"You know," Grandma said, closing her eyes and drifting off to sleep, "your grandfather and I never let the sun go down on an argument…" A moment later, she was snoring softly.

As quietly as she could so not to wake her, Maggie reached for her cellphone. Thomas's number flashed across the tiny screen. Maggie thought about what her grandma had said about resolving things in a timely manner, but the hurt and confusion she was feeling was almost too much to bear. She wasn't ready to speak to him. Before she could change her mind, she hit the ignore button and slipped her phone back into her purse.

Chapter Twenty-One

"I should be the one making you breakfast," Maggie said. She was consumed with guilt, watching her grandmother slowly putter around the kitchen, fixing her something to eat.

"I already told you. I need to do these things on my own to keep my strength up. Just enjoy your tea while it's hot."

Maggie took a sip of the warm breakfast blend while Grandma pulled two pieces of white bread from the toaster and buttered them with shaky hands. She cut the toast into soldiers, straight uniform strips for dipping, and added soft boiled eggs to delicate little porcelain cups on the plates. Maggie stood up to help.

"Sit down, Maggie! I've got this." Grandma carefully placed both plates on her walker and slowly maneuvered her way to the table. "You're my guest. Let me make you breakfast."

Maggie was impressed with how well her grandmother was doing. "I'm sorry, Grandma. This looks delicious!" Maggie sprinkled black pepper on her egg and dipped a soldier into its warm yellow yolk. The dippy egg held a special place in Maggie's food memories. Her grandmother had perfected the art of buttering toast and always spread it right to the edges.

"I love staying with you because it feels like I'm on vacation at a cozy bed and breakfast. There are always fresh towels and face cloths left for me in the bathroom, and you make the best breakfasts."

"Don't get too comfortable here, Maggie. I love you and you're always welcome, but September is only a few weeks away. Have you made any decisions about what you're going to do? You could apply at another radio station or go back to school or—"

"Actually," Maggie interrupted, "I've decided to apply somewhere." The other day, during her lunch break at Waldhaus, Maggie had been flipping through the local newspaper when she spotted an ad announcing that Lake 88.5 in Cedar Grove was looking to hire a reporter. She'd kept the news to herself. She didn't want to jinx anything.

Grandma placed her teacup back in its saucer. "Maggie, that's wonderful. Tell me about it."

Maggie fidgeted with her napkin. "I hate to be vague, but I don't want to get my hopes up."

Grandma raised her right eyebrow. "Is it a position that requires some of the education you've acquired?"

"Yes. I haven't told you this, but being at the cottage inspired me to begin writing again."

Grandma smiled knowingly. "I knew it would."

"I recently finished writing an article and sent query letters to a few national newspapers and magazines. So far, I've received two rejections, but I'll let you know if anything comes of it."

"Maggie, that's great! Don't let the rejections get you down. I once read about a famous writer who wallpapered his entire bathroom with rejection letters."

Maggie smiled and settled back into the upholstered bench in her grandmother's cozy breakfast nook. The wall of windows brought in the sunshine, which added to the room's happy atmosphere. Her grandmother's enthusiasm about her article and job application made her feel more at ease. Grandma's approval was important to Maggie, and her encouragement boosted Maggie's confidence.

"I was up all night thinking. My fight with Thomas put everything into perspective," said Maggie. "I know what I want to do moving forward. For me."

After breakfast, Maggie went to her

grandmother's office. Only once the door was shut did she allow herself to take out her cellphone and flip through its photo album. She had an abundance of pictures of her and Thomas camping, canoeing, and cuddling in bed. Maggie was finding it difficult to cope with not seeing, speaking, or kissing Thomas every day, but she also wasn't ready to call him back. Her stomach hardened when a photo of her and Thomas at the drive-in movie theater flashed across the screen.

A few weeks earlier, while out for an evening paddle, Thomas told Maggie he had a surprise for her.

"I'm taking you out after your shift tomorrow night," he said. A mischievous look captured his eyes.

Maggie stopped paddling. "What should I wear?"

"Nothing fancy."

The next evening, Maggie settled on wearing her favorite pair of denim shorts, a ballet-pink t-shirt, and white Keds. As the sun was setting, Thomas picked her up in his truck.

"Are you going to tell me where we're going?" she asked.

He clamped his mouth shut and shook his head. "Not a chance."

Maggie climbed into his truck and relaxed into the passenger side seat. A peaceful nighttime drive was just what she needed to escape the hustle and bustle of work life at the resort. The roads in Cedar Grove were less crowded at night, the air was cooler, and the light from the setting sun created a serene atmosphere. Maggie didn't really care where they were going. She was happy to go anywhere with Thomas.

When they arrived at their destination, Maggie couldn't believe her eyes. She sat up straight in her seat. "How did you find this place?"

Thomas's eyes twinkled with amusement. He

pulled up to a little white booth at the entrance to the property.

"Welcome to Port-Perth Drive-In! How many?" asked the friendly attendant with a receding hairline.

"Two adults, please," Thomas said, handing the man a twenty-dollar bill.

The attendant accepted the cash and passed Thomas a receipt. "Enjoy the show, folks!"

Thomas drove down the dirt road and into the outdoor theater. He parked backwards in their designated spot in the grass so that the bed of his truck faced the big white screen. "Are you excited?"

Maggie nodded. Her insides were vibrating.

"I know how much you like classic films, and it just so happens to be Old-School Night at the drive-in. They're playing *The Breakfast Club*," he said.

"Shut up! I love Molly Ringwald."

Thomas lightly rapped his fingers on the steering wheel. "It gets even better. Close your eyes," he instructed before getting out of the truck.

Maggie did as she was told and waited impatiently. When Thomas finally opened the door, she turned to face him with her eyes squeezed shut. He took her hands and slowly guided her out of the passenger side seat and led her to the back of the truck.

"You can open your eyes," he whispered.

Heat radiated out of Maggie's chest when she saw what Thomas had done for her. The back of his truck had been transformed into a cozy nook for watching movies with a puffy white duvet, pillows, and twinkle lights.

"I brought all the fixings, too." Thomas opened a cooler. "I've got buttered popcorn, beer, and Twizzlers because I know those are your favorite."

Maggie bounced lightly in place. "I can't believe you did all of this for me!" She grabbed her cellphone from her back pocket and wrapped her arm around Thomas's waist. "Let's take a picture. I want to remember this moment forever."

A knock at the office door pulled Maggie back to the present moment. "Yes?"

"Do you need anything, dear?" Grandma asked from the other side of the door. "I'm going to take my bath."

"I'm good, Grandma. Thank you!" Maggie called. She looked down at the blissfully happy photo of her and Thomas one last time before she exited the gallery. Maggie didn't know where she stood with Thomas anymore, but she couldn't help but feel like she was the one left to pick up the pieces of an ended relationship. It was time to move forward with her life, and that meant looking for a position in her field as a full-time job.

She bit her lip as she picked up the office phone. The pale blue walls made for a calming backdrop, but they did nothing to settle Maggie's nerves.

"Waldhaus, Cedar Lake's House in the Forest, how may I direct your call?" the receptionist asked in a friendly voice.

"Sadie Miller's office please."

Sadie picked up after the second ring.

"Sadie, hi, it's Maggie."

"Maggie, hello." Sadie sighed. "What can I do for you?"

Maggie swallowed. The fear of disappointing someone caused the familiar knot in her stomach to tighten. "I'm calling to resign. I apologize for not giving you more notice, but I need to quit immediately."

Sadie tsked. "You're leaving me high and dry on the tail end of our busiest season! Figures." Sadie paused. "Trouble in paradise, Maggie?"

Maggie cleared her throat to compose herself. "I

would like to thank you for the opportunity. I'm currently out of the city, but I will need to make arrangements to pick up my final check and my belongings from my locker."

"Quitting like this isn't going to win you a good reference or any recommendation from me."

"I understand." Maggie imagined Sadie's sour expression through the phone. She wouldn't be surprised if Sadie decided to stop by Thomas's place after work to "check in" on him. Maggie shook the image of Sadie and Thomas's reunion from her head.

"Your personal items and check will be held here until Human Resources receives an official resignation letter for their records."

"Thank you, Sadie. I—"

Click.

Maggie grabbed a tissue from the box on her grandmother's desk and pressed it against the inner corners of her eyes, blocking the waterworks. She refused to let Sadie make her cry. Confrontation was difficult, but she'd stood her ground, and a spark of courage ignited within her. Maggie took a steadying breath as she picked up the phone to make another call.

"Hey, Rooney, it's Maggie. I was wondering if I could still get that letter of reference from you?"

A couple of hours later, Maggie was prepared to hit the "send" button on her computer screen. She reread her cover letter and made sure her resumé and demo reel were attached. Lastly, she made sure Rooney's glowing letter of reference was included in her application. When she'd spoken to him, she'd thought for a moment he didn't remember who she was.

"How could I forget the best intern I've ever had? I'm just surprised to hear from you," he had said in his booming radio voice. "I'd be happy to write you a recommendation letter."

After Maggie triple-checked to make sure all of her attachments were there, she clicked the mouse and sent the email. A few minutes later, her cellphone rang. An unknown number. Her heart rate sped up. This could be it.

"Maggie Taylor speaking," she said in her most professional voice.

"Maggie, it's Katie."

Maggie let out a disappointed sigh.

"Everything okay, Maggie?"

"Um…" Maggie turned from the computer to give Katie her full attention. "Yes. I'm sorry, I thought you were someone else."

"Thomas?"

"No, I was just in the middle of something. Never mind. What's up?"

"Well, since you left, I've been mulling it over, and I've come to the conclusion that I'll never be ready to find my daughter, but I'm going to do it anyways."

Maggie's ears perked up. "Really? That's great!"

"I'm so relieved to hear you say that. To be honest, I'm terrified, but the thing I'm most frightened of is living a life of regrets. I'm ready."

"What's your plan? Do you still need my help? I could really use a distraction."

"That's why I'm calling. I'm at a gas station just outside of the city. My cellphone died, and I forgot the charger at the cottage. Can you let Mum know I'm on my way? I'm going to need your support when I tell her."

Maggie nodded. "Of course."

That evening, Grandma sat in her walker in the kitchen, calling out orders to Maggie and Katie as they attempted to recreate her infamous roast beef dinner.

"Not like that!" Grandma scolded them. She

slowly stood up and made her way to the stove. She grabbed the wooden spoon from Maggie's hand. "You have to stir the gravy consistently or it will become lumpy."

Maggie stepped aside. Who was she to argue with the best chef in the family? The kitchen smelled of her childhood, of Sunday suppers when the weather was damp and cold. Maggie went into the dining room to set the table. Behind the head of the table, there stood an antique hutch cabinet that contained all of the good china, crystal, and silverware, all family heirlooms that once belonged to her great-grandparents.

Growing up, family dinners were so full and overflowing with guests that Maggie and her cousins had to sit at a children's table in the front foyer made up of a foldable card table that her grandmother would use when she hosted Bridge Club. However, Grandma would cover it with an ironed white linen tablecloth. At Grandma's house, even the children ate off the fine china and drank red punch out of crystal wine glasses. Grandma wouldn't have it any other way.

The dining room table looked lonely when it was only set for three people.

"Roast is ready!" Katie called from the kitchen.

Silence fell over the table when the three of them sat down to eat. Grandma didn't make them pray with her, but before she ate, Grandma bowed her head and silently whispered a short prayer. Afterward, the clink of the silverware against the plates, the sniffs, and the lip smacks were deafening. Their silence gnawed at Maggie, amplifying every worried thought in her head. She wondered if her grandmother had yet to forgive Katie for the separation from her husband.

"How are the twins doing?" Maggie asked Katie in an attempt to get the conversation flowing. She already knew Mathew and Joshua were having the time of their lives working as lifeguards at summer camp.

"They love it! I spoke to Mathew last week, and he told me that Joshua has a girlfriend."

"What about Mathew? Any love interests for him?" Maggie asked.

"If he did, he wouldn't tell me, but he did tell me he and the other lifeguards have been busy pranking the counselors at night. They rigged the camp director's car so that when he pressed on the brakes, it would sound the horn."

Maggie laughed. "It sounds like a scene straight out of the movie *The Parent Trap*."

"Mom, you've barely touched your roast beef. Is everything all right?" Katie asked.

Grandma lifted the linen napkin from her lap and pressed it against her withered lips.

"How is Stuart doing?" Grandma asked. A tremor touched the corner of her mouth.

Embarrassed, Katie set down her fork and stared at her plate. "He still refuses to speak to me. I—"

"Grandma, did I tell you I applied for that job today?" Maggie said in an attempt to change the subject.

"Maggie, don't interrupt. Katie's here to tell me she's getting a divorce." A frown was set into her grandmother's wrinkled features.

Maggie's eyes darted nervously from her aunt to her grandmother.

Katie shook her head in dismay. "I'm not sure if Stuart and I will be able to work things out, but that's not why I'm here."

Grandma quirked one thin eyebrow questioningly as she cut a small piece of roast beef.

Katie's eyes met Maggie's. Fear added shine to her eyes. Maggie gave her aunt a tense nod of support.

Katie cleared her throat. "Mum, I know you think some things are better left in the past, but I've decided to find my daughter. Her name is Carrie Smith. With Maggie's research and technology skills, I've been able to locate where she lives."

Grandma swallowed her roast and took a tiny sip of red wine to wash it down. "That's what this visit is about?"

Katie nodded eagerly.

"Does Carrie want to meet you?"

Katie nervously flicked a bit of lint from her dress. "I don't know yet."

"You haven't spoken to her?"

"We've only been able to narrow down the search," Maggie piped in. "We still have a few phone calls to make."

"Mum, your blessing is important to me," Katie said.

"Katie, dear, what if she doesn't want to reunite with you?" Grandma asked. "Are you prepared for that kind of rejection?"

Katie shrugged. "All I know is that I'll regret it my entire life if I don't try."

Grandma reached across the table and rested her hand on Katie's arm. "All I've ever wanted for you is to be happy. Go find our girl!"

Katie flashed a thankful smile, and her eyes glowed with purpose.

After the kitchen was cleaned and Grandma was helped up the stairs and into bed for the evening, Maggie and Katie went into the office and shut the door. Katie restlessly tapped the arm on the office chair before finally picking up the phone and dialing the first number on Maggie's list. She put it on speaker.

"Hello?" a man answered in a grudging voice.

"Yes, hello. I'm calling to speak to Carrie Smith," Katie said. Her voice was shaking and fragile.

"Wrong number." The man hung up.

Maggie dialed the next number.

"Fox Creek Auto Repairs, how may I help you?" a woman answered eagerly.

"Er, yes, hello! Is Carrie Smith there?" Maggie asked over the noise of the power tools in the background.

"Who, dear? I'm having trouble hearing you."

"Carrie. Carrie Smith!" Maggie yelled into the phone.

"I'm sorry, you've got the wrong number." *Click.*

Maggie sighed as she hung up the phone. She watched the emotions play over Katie's face. She worried her aunt was going to give up hope already. Maggie pushed the phone toward her, an encouragement to keep going. Together, they worked through seven more phone numbers on the list. All dead ends. Only one phone number remained on the crinkled piece of paper. The corners of Katie's mouth turned down in sadness.

"What if this isn't the number either?" Katie asked.

Maggie squeezed her shoulder. "Then we'll start from scratch. We're going to find your daughter, Katie."

"I feel like I can't breathe. You'll have to do it. I'm too nervous."

Maggie picked up the phone and punched in the number. It rang five times. Maggie bit her lip.

"Hello?" answered a deep, jovial voice on the other end of the line.

Maggie cleared her throat. "Hi, yes, hello. Is Carrie home?"

"I'm sorry, hon, she's out in the chicken coop doing some chores. Would you like me to take a message?"

Maggie tightened her grip around the receiver. They had found her! She covered the mouthpiece with her hand. "Katie! I think I'm talking to her dad," she whispered. "He wants to take a message."

Katie bolted out of the armchair and hit the speaker button. "Y–yes, hello, Mr. Smith," Katie said bravely. "My name is Katherine Edwards. I'm—"

"Carrie's mother," he interrupted. His voice was warm.

"How did you know? I—"

"My wife told me you would call one day. You sound like my daughter. You sound just like Carrie."

"I don't want to cause any upset or trouble, but if it's all right with you and your wife, I would love to be put in touch with Carrie. Only with your blessing, of course."

"My dear wife, Erin, passed away when Carrie was ten. Breast cancer."

Maggie's hand flew to her chest. She couldn't think of anything more heartbreaking than an adopted child losing the only mother they'd ever known at such a young age.

"I'm so sorry," Katie whispered.

"Listen, Katherine. Carrie had a wonderful ten years with her mother, and even though she's an adult, she still needs a mother. I will let her know you called, but it will be up to her if she wants to call you back. Is there a number where she can reach you?"

Katie gave him her cellphone number and address, just in case Carrie preferred written correspondence first.

"Thank you so much, Mr. Smith. I—"

"Please, call me Peter."

"I can't thank you enough, Peter."

"It's the least I can do after all you've done for us, Katherine. Since it was a closed adoption, Erin and I never had the chance to thank you for all the joy and love you brought into our lives."

Katie managed a small trace of a smile. "Peter, just in case Carrie decides she doesn't want to speak to me or have a relationship with me, how is she? Is she okay?"

"She is as happy as a ray of sunshine."

ALYSSA DELLE PALME

Chapter Twenty-Two

"You're going where?" Maggie's mother asked.

"Alberta. For two nights. Katie asked me to go with her, and Grandma offered to pay for my ticket."

"I'm worried about Katie. Do you think she's emotionally ready for this?"

Maggie paused. Her aunt had been a bit of a hot mess since Carrie had returned her phone call. "Don't worry, Mom. I'll be there to support her."

"What about your job?" she asked.

"I quit."

"What? Your father isn't going to be pleased when he hears about this."

"I'm not going to be pleased when I hear about what?" her father asked in the background.

"Maggie, hold on, I'm putting you on speaker phone."

Maggie held the phone between her ear and her shoulder as she folded laundry on her grandmother's guest bed, which used to be her mom's childhood bedroom. Maggie grew impatient. She didn't have the time or the energy to be reprimanded by her parents.

"Maggie, what's going on?" her father asked.

Maggie placed a folded white t-shirt into her suitcase. "I quit my job at the resort."

Her parents fell silent. Maggie sensed her father seething on the other end of the line.

"Maggie, I want to make myself clear. Just like I told you when you quit the internship, we're not going to support you financially while you let your education go to waste. An education I paid for, let me remind you."

Maggie's mouth tightened with determination. "I'm not asking you for money. Besides, I already have a job interview lined up for a position in my field," she lied.

"You do?" her parents asked in unison.

Maggie folded a sweatshirt and added it to her suitcase. "Um, yes. In a couple of weeks. I'm also hoping to hear back about some queries I sent out to a few publications."

"Maggie, that's wonderful!" Dad said. "Where did you apply?"

"I'll have to tell you about it later. Our flight leaves in a few hours, and I have to finish packing. I'll call you when we land. I love you!"

Maggie ended the call and tossed her cellphone on the bed. She had to focus. They were leaving in less than an hour. She held up another shirt from the clean laundry basket and a wave of despair washed over her when she realized it was Thomas's t-shirt. He had given it to her on their date at the drive-in. Seeing it again transported Maggie back to that night.

They had been halfway through the movie when thunder rumbled in the distance.

Thomas groaned. "Damn. I should put a tarp over the truck bed. We can watch the rest of the movie from inside the cab."

"I'll help you," Maggie had offered.

They'd barely begun to unfold the tarp when the downpour started. They worked quickly to cover the truck bed. A flash of lightning revealed that Maggie's ballet-pink T-shirt had become transparent.

"Get inside!" Thomas yelled over a roar of thunder. He took a bungee cord and pulled it tightly over the tarp to secure it in place. "I'm almost finished!"

Inside the cab, Maggie shivered as she waited for Thomas. Her clothes were soaked through. The rain was coming down straight and hard. It was so powerful it felt as though she was inside a car wash. Maggie couldn't see anything outside. Moments later, Thomas jumped into the driver's seat and slammed the door shut.

"That storm came out of nowhere!" Thomas said, shaking the raindrops from his messy curls. He turned on the windshield wipers. "I'd take us home, but I don't think it's safe to drive." He turned to Maggie and opened his arm. "Your teeth are chattering. Come over here."

Maggie scooted across the bench, and Thomas gathered her in his arms and held her. She looked up at him longingly, wanting him to kiss her.

"You're soaked," he said. His voice husky. He reached on the floor for his gym bag. "Here. Put this on." He handed Maggie an oversize *New West* t-shirt. "It's clean. I promise."

As Maggie stripped off her wet t-shirt and bralette, Thomas didn't look away. His eyes raked over her body. Suddenly, feeling shy, she pulled his dry shirt over her head. It was so big it almost fell to her knees.

"It's such a turn on to see you in my clothes," he said.

Maggie unbuttoned her denim shorts and peeled them off. Thomas's tormented groan was her invitation. She slipped out of her panties and glanced over at Thomas's drenched jeans. As though reading her thoughts, Thomas quickly unbuttoned his pants and wrangled them off his hips, exposing his thick shaft. A sultry smile danced on her lips. Maggie reached into the glove box for a condom before straddling Thomas in the driver's seat. His hands skimmed up her shirt, cupping her breasts firmly. Maggie clutched his shoulders for balance as he brought his mouth to hers. He tasted sweet and fruity like Twizzlers. Moving his lips to her neck, he left a trail of warm kisses to her collarbone.

"I want to feel every inch of you," she said,

gasping as Thomas gently pinched her nipples.

Thomas looked up at her, a cocky smile spreading across his face. "I'm so hard for you."

Maggie covered his mouth with hers and sucked on his bottom lip as she reached down and wrapped her hand around the warm length of him. She moved her hand up and down until he gripped her hips.

"Slow down," he said, his breathing heavy. "I want this to last."

Maggie let go, slowing the tempo by planting little kisses along his jawline. She nibbled his earlobe, her nipples hardening against the soft material of his t-shirt. A mighty crash of thunder shook the truck. Maggie sat up straight and widened her straddle. She gazed down at Thomas. "You're the most gorgeous man I've ever been with," she said.

Thomas let out a strangled groan, squeezing her hips and pulling her firmly down against him. A bolt of pleasure filled Maggie's pelvis. She moaned, leaning forward, her wavy hair falling over his face like a curtain. His fingers tangled in her hair as he kissed her, parting her lips with his tongue. Maggie flattened her hands against his wet chest, moving her hips up and down, harder and faster, until Thomas peaked with a wave of shuddering force. Moments later, Maggie's climax followed as furious and electric as the torrential downpour that pounded down outside the truck's fogged-up windows.

A knock at the door pulled Maggie back to her mother's childhood bedroom.

"Are you almost ready, Maggie?" Katie asked.

"I'll be out in a minute!" Maggie called. She quickly folded Thomas's t-shirt and placed it inside her suitcase. She wasn't ready to leave it behind. She had the urge to pick up the phone and call Thomas, but she wasn't sure what she'd say, and there wasn't enough time to talk. It was time to leave. Maggie was still surprised this trip was actually happening. When Carrie hadn't called Katie back that first night, her aunt was devastated.

"She must hate me," Katie cried. "Should I try calling again?"

Grandma patted Katie's hand gently. "Carrie doesn't hate you. You have to be patient and give Carrie the time and space that she needs to gather her thoughts and feelings. When she's ready, she will call you."

The next day, the three of them sat down to lunch at Grandma's kitchen table. Grandma continued to refuse their help in preparing their meals. Her grandmother's strength was gradually returning. Grandma had made Maggie's favorite lunch—salmon sandwiches on soft white bread with a side of sweet pickles. Before they took their first bites, Katie's phone rang.

"It's an Alberta area code," she said.

"Answer it!" Maggie encouraged.

"Put it on speaker," Grandma whispered.

"Hello, this is Katherine Edwards speaking."

"Hi, um, Katherine? This is Carrie Smith calling."

Katie's face lit with a friendly, open smile. "Please, call me Katie. I'm so glad you called. There are so many things that I want to say to you. I don't even know where to begin."

"I don't want to rush things. I know this first conversation probably won't answer my deepest questions—"

"You mean, you'll want to talk again?" Katie blurted out.

Grandma patted Katie's arm gently. "Patience," she mouthed.

"I'm sorry, I didn't mean to interrupt," Katie said. "I'm just so thrilled to hear your voice."

"I'm not really good on the phone," Carrie said. "I was thinking—"

"You want to meet in person? I would pay for your flight, of course. You could meet your extended family here and your brothers—"

"I have brothers?" Carrie asked.

"Yes. Well, technically they're your half-brothers. Twins."

"Actually, I was thinking you could visit me here, in Alberta. You could meet my dad."

"Yes," Katie answered quickly. "I would like that very much."

Days later at the airport, Katie paced up and down the seating area of their terminal.

"Would you sit down?" Maggie hissed. "You're making the other passengers anxious."

Katie fell into the seat beside Maggie. She bounced her knees and chewed at a hangnail on her thumb.

"You need to relax," Maggie said. "Everything is going to be fine."

"I just want everything to be perfect. Do you think I look okay? Maybe I should have worn a dress. I want to make a good first impression."

Katie looked sophisticated in a light blue and white striped linen picnic jumpsuit. Her tousled blonde bob was both laid back, yet full of personality. The truth was, Katie looked fantastic.

"You look stunning, Katie. She's going to love you."

Katie seemed satisfied with Maggie's answer. "We still have half an hour before our flight leaves. I'm going to go to the coffee shop. Do you want anything?"

Maggie shook her head. Once she was alone, Maggie pulled her phone from her purse. Thomas had texted her several times.

Call me back. Please. Thomas wrote.

The voicemail notification flashed across the screen. Thomas had called her every day since she'd left. Maggie missed him terribly, but she was terrified to hear what he had to say. She took a slow, deep breath, carefully entered her voicemailbox password, and put the phone to her ear.

"You have three new messages. To listen to your messages, press one," said the monotone voice of the operator.

Maggie's heart was beating so loud in her chest she was certain the other passengers could hear it. Before she could change her mind, she pressed one.

"Hey, Maggie, it's Thomas. Call me back." *Click.*

Maggie hit the delete button. The next message began to play.

"Hey, Maggie, I've been trying to reach you for a couple of days. Please call me back." *Click.*

Maggie's hand shook as she hit the delete button once more. There was only one message remaining.

"Mags … it's me … again. I get it, you don't want to talk to me. I wouldn't want to talk to me either, but I need you to know what happened the night you left. While we were fishing, Drew was talking about his job, and I quickly pieced two and two together. He admitted he was your old boss. If it wasn't for Nick and Ryan, I would've pummeled the guy and thrown him overboard. When we got back to the cottage, I kicked him out. If I had known who he was, I never would have let him step foot on my property. Maggie, I'm so sorry. I hope you can forgive me."

Maggie quickly exited her voicemail and dialed Thomas's phone number. He answered on the first ring.

"Maggie?" His tone was filled with hope.

"Thomas! I'm so sorry. I acted like an idiot. I should've told you what was wrong. I was in shock and—"

"I can't believe I let that asshole into my home!"

"You didn't know."

"This is the pre-boarding announcement for flight 1212B to Edmonton. We are now inviting those passengers with children and any passengers requiring special assistance to begin boarding at this time," the gate agent read clearly into the intercom.

"Where are you?" Thomas asked.

"The airport. It's a long story, and I can't wait to tell you all about it. We found Carrie, and we're flying to Alberta to meet her!"

"Are you serious? That's amazing, Maggie! I'm so happy for your family. When will you be back?"

"In a couple of days."

"Will you be coming back to the cottage? I miss you, Maggie. I want to see you." A huskiness lingered in his voice.

"I want to see you, too," she answered over the thundering of her heart.

The flight to Alberta was ordinary, but after her conversation with Thomas, Maggie was flying high. Luck was on their side that day as one of the flight attendants, an old friend of Johnny's, recognized Katie and upgraded their economy seats to first class.

"He was my favorite person to work with," the flight attendant, Kim, said. "He was always smiling and eager to help me put the heavier suitcases in the overhead bins. He also had this incredible gift when dealing with irate passengers. He would just kill them with kindness until they were smiling, too. Gosh, I miss him. Anyways ladies, I have a pre-flight briefing with the pilot. I will check on you later. It's so good to see you again, Katie."

Hearing other people's stories about Johnny always made Maggie smile. Most people had a misconception that talking about him would upset her or her family when, in fact, talking about him always made Maggie feel good.

As the plane accelerated down the runway, the feeling of being pushed back into her seat gave Maggie butterflies. She enjoyed looking out the tiny window as the Boeing 737 cut through the sea of clouds, making her window fog up. During the final approach and landing in Edmonton, Katie passed Maggie a pack of gum to help pop her ears as the plane descended. There was something really satisfying about touching down, when Maggie's feet could feel the wheels of the plane make contact with the earth.

Katie had booked them a room in a hotel located in the downtown core that was adjacent to the Arts District.

"The Royal Alberta Museum and the Citadel Theatre are within walking distance," Katie said, placing her suitcase on the luggage rack in their hotel room. "There are plenty of restaurants and shops in the area, too."

Their suite had two queen-size beds, a full kitchen, and a separate living area. It was indulgent and much more than they needed.

"Katie, this is too much!" Maggie said. She opened the curtains and looked out the floor-to-ceiling windows at the ribbon of green below. "Wow!"

"That's the River Valley," Katie said. "There are over one-hundred-sixty kilometers of trails and parks. Edmonton really is a vibrant city in the heart of the wilderness."

"Maybe that's where I'll go exploring when Carrie comes to visit."

Katie and Carrie planned to have their first face-to-face meeting at the hotel. It was the reason Katie had sprung for the suite. It had been decided that Maggie would give them their space and meet Carrie another time.

"Do you think this room is nice enough? Will Carrie be comfortable here?"

"It's perfect. I mean, look at that view! There's a coffee machine and tea in the cupboard, and there's plenty of space to sit and get to know one another. The concierge told me there's a bakery across the street that sells melt-in-your-mouth pastries. I could go grab some before I head out if you like."

"Thanks, Maggie, but I still have time to go and get them myself. The walk will help calm my nerves." Katie pulled Maggie into a hug. "I can't believe you traveled all this way with me. I can't thank you enough."

"I'm so happy for you. Just remember, keep it light until you're both more comfortable. Don't force it and just be yourself. It's going to go well."

Maggie went off to explore the River Valley. The summer air was cooler than in Ontario, but the sun was bright and cheerful. The canopy of trees was lush and green, and wildflowers decorated the edges of the paved path she walked along. Chipmunks and squirrels scampered in nearby undergrowth. Maggie eventually passed by a golf course and then a large six-lane bridge.

When she stopped to take a break, she looked down toward the shore and spotted a swing hanging from a tree below. Curious, she peered over the edge of the trail. It was a steep dirt hill, but someone had set up a makeshift railing with a rope to help explorers climb down. It had rained in the last few days, making the hill muddy and slippery, but Maggie managed to make it down to the bottom in one piece. A gentle breeze carried the algae-scent of the river. The secret swing had a large flat seat that had enough room for two people. It hung high off the ground, so Maggie had to jump to get on, but the reward was soaring over the river! The views were stunning. In the distance, the skyline of the city rose high above the trees. Below her feet, the river rushed over smooth, slippery rocks.

Maggie couldn't wait to tell Thomas about the hidden gem she had found. She wished he was there with her in the seat next to her, swinging over the river. She was overwhelmed with how much they had to discuss. She didn't know what their relationship would look like moving forward. All she wanted was to be with him. She wanted to make it work. First though, she needed to get a job.

Maggie's cellphone buzzed in her purse. She didn't recognize the number. "Hello?" she answered.

"Hi, I'm looking to speak to Maggie Taylor," said the man on the other end of the line. There was a rich timbre to his voice.

"Speaking."

"Hi, Maggie, my name is Larry White. I'm the News Director at Lake 88.5, and I received your application, resumé, and demo tape."

"That's great!" said Maggie. She gripped the rope of the swing with her free hand tightly, afraid she would fall off in excitement.

"Miss Taylor, I have to say, I'm impressed with your education, but I don't usually bring someone in for an interview with so little experience." His voice was firm and final.

Maggie's courage gave her the resolve to try to persuade him. "Mr. White, if you would just give me a chance to show you—"

"No, Miss Taylor. I said I don't *usually* bring

someone in for an interview with so little experience. However, your demo tape is excellent, and your reference letter from Rooney didn't hurt. You've got great potential. Would you be available for an interview early next week?

Maggie nodded her head.

"Miss Taylor?"

"Yes! I'm nodding my head yes!"

"Great, I've penciled you in for Tuesday afternoon at 3:00."

"Wow! Thank you, Mr. White."

"Don't thank me yet. You still have to impress the Station Manager, Angie Perkins."

Maggie smiled when she heard that the Station Manager was a woman, a rarity in the radio business. "Yes. I'm looking forward to it, Mr. White. I will see you both then."

Maggie pumped her legs, swinging herself higher and higher over the river. Her heart was sent soaring like the eagle she just spotted overhead, sailing across the pale-blue sky. Things were looking up.

Chapter Twenty-Three

When Maggie returned to the hotel, Katie couldn't stop gushing about how wonderful Carrie was.

"She's incredibly smart and fun," Katie said. "I think she looks like me, too."

Maggie took off her purse and joined her aunt on the stiff pebble-gray sofa. "You have to tell me everything."

Katie flipped through a stack of old photos that Carrie had brought for her to keep. When she found the one she was looking for, she handed it to Maggie. "This is where she grew up."

Maggie looked at the elegant farmhouse. It was surrounded by an expansive vegetable garden and hedges. A veranda wrapped around three sides of the white timber house. In the photo, chickens roamed freely on the sun-drenched lawn. "It's beautiful. Their home exudes history and charm."

A small smile of relief rested on Katie's lips. "You can feel all the love that went into this home. A magical place to be raised." Katie handed Maggie another photo. "Here's a recent photo of Carrie with her dad, Peter."

Peter was tall with a grand, self-confident presence. He had a full head of gray hair and seemed much older than Katie. His big smile was full of warmth. Maggie couldn't believe how much Carrie and Katie looked alike. It wasn't just their looks that were similar, but it was their mannerisms, too. "See how she's standing with all the weight on her back leg? Katie, you do that, too!"

Katie met Maggie smile for smile. "I do stand like that, don't I?" Katie took the photo and held it to her chest. "She has a boyfriend named Paolo. He's a firefighter. They're going to Europe at the end of the summer, and she told me her dad thinks Paolo might propose!"

Maggie could see how proud Katie was to be able to share information about her daughter. "That's wonderful."

"I can't thank you enough for traveling with me. I know it was a long way, and you didn't even get to meet her. We talked about it, and Carrie's going to fly to Ontario in October for Thanksgiving. She wants to meet the whole family."

Maggie crossed her legs. "I'm really looking forward to meeting her, too, but have you spoken to Stuart about it?"

Katie shook her head. "I realized on this trip that it's time for me to ask Stuart for a divorce."

Maggie swallowed. "Are you sure?"

Katie nodded. Her face lit with an inner strength. "I've thought about it a lot since we separated but today confirmed my decision. Stuart and I don't communicate. We can never find the time to talk, and when we do, he doesn't listen. We're incapable of meaningful conversation. We just don't connect anymore. I haven't felt close to Stuart in years. I've tried talking to him about my feelings, but I never felt understood. I completely disrespected him when I had the affair, and now, he doesn't trust me. It's over."

Maggie sensed Katie didn't want to talk about it any further. She excused herself to use the washroom, and when she emerged, Katie was dressed in workout attire.

"I'm going to go to the hotel gym," Katie said. "I won't be able to sleep unless I go for a run."

After Katie left the room, Maggie got into bed and flopped backward onto the mountain of puffy pillows behind her. She was restless and unsettled. Maggie wondered if she and Thomas had what it took to have a long-lasting relationship. Maggie grabbed her phone from the bedside table and dialed Thomas's number.

"Hey, you," Thomas answered, his voice warm.

"It's so good to hear your voice." Maggie snuggled deeper under the covers. "I miss you."

"Is everything okay?" There was a hint of concern in his voice.

"Yes! Katie and Carrie had a wonderful reunion, but that's not why I called."

"What's on your mind?"

Maggie inhaled deeply. "Thomas, how do we know this is real? Us." She wrinkled her nose as she waited for him to answer.

Thomas sighed. "I knew you were having doubts. After you left without saying goodbye—"

"No!" Maggie interrupted, kicking herself for leaving the way she did. She wondered if it stirred up memories of his mother leaving. "I'm so sorry, Thomas. I was scared. It wasn't a rejection of you—"

"I do worry that I'm not enough for you, Maggie." There was a solemn tone to his voice.

"But I think about you all the time," Maggie admitted. "It's kind of ridiculous."

Thomas quietly chuckled on the other end of the line. "I've wondered if you think of me half as much as I think of you. When I walked past The Book Nook in town today, I saw the new display in the window and thought how much you'd like to go in with a cup of coffee in hand and wander through the aisles of books! Everything reminds me of you."

Maggie released a blissful sigh. "That does sounds like my idea of a perfect date night. But what about my quirks? There must be something about me you don't like."

"Maggie, you drive me crazy. In a good way. I like you just the way you are."

Maggie pulled the covers over her head and pinched her lips together. She was ready to tell him that she was in love with him, but she wanted to wait until she could tell him in person. "So, we're good?"

"Sweet dreams, Maggie."

The hesitation in his voice was so slight that Maggie wondered if she had imagined it. "Goodnight, Thomas."

The flight back to Ontario was uneventful. Katie helped Maggie practice for her upcoming job interview by asking her a series of questions. Maggie sailed through them but was stumped when Katie asked her where she saw herself in five years.

"I'm not sure," Maggie responded. "I can't envision it yet."

Katie placed her list of mock interview questions down on the tiny airplane table that unfolded from the seat in front of her. "Do you think you'll be satisfied being a small-town reporter?"

Maggie shrugged. She wasn't sure. What she did know was that the opportunity to work for Lake 88.5 would allow her to have hands-on experience in a community she had fallen in love with. "I want this job, Katie. I'll have more responsibility than the internship ever gave me. I'll learn a lot and improve my skills."

"You have so much potential, Maggie. I don't want you to throw it all away to be with a guy, even if he is a great one."

Maggie nodded. What Katie said didn't upset her. Her aunt was coming from a place of love and only looking out for her best interests. She reached out and squeezed Katie's hand. "I promise to thoroughly think things through before I make any big decisions."

"Does he know about the interview?" Katie asked.

Maggie shook her head. "I didn't want him to get his hopes up, and I don't need any added pressure. What if I don't get the job?"

Katie offered her a sympathetic smile. "I think there's a really good chance that you do."

Once the plane landed, Maggie turned on her cellphone and saw an email notification from the national newspaper, *The Ottawa Post*. Maggie quickly opened the email and scanned through it. Maggie grabbed Katie's arm. "*The Ottawa Post* has accepted an article I submitted. They're going to pay me three-hundred dollars!"

Katie stood up and grabbed her carry-on from the bin overhead. "That's fantastic, Maggie! I'm so happy for you!"

Maggie had barely read through the attached contract when she was interrupted.

"Ahem!" A man huffed, impatiently waiting for Katie and Maggie to move out of the way so that he could exit the plane.

"I'm sorry, sir!" Maggie gathered her belongings and followed her aunt down the tiny aisle. She added her signature to the DocuSign agreement and sent it back to the editorial pages editor from *The Ottawa Post*. She could reread the contract later. Maggie didn't really care what it said. She was going to have her first byline in a national newspaper! Maggie couldn't wait to tell Thomas.

Maggie and Katie collected their luggage and found Grandma's car where they had left it in the long-term parking lot. Maggie dropped Katie off at her car, which was still parked in her grandmother's driveway, before driving the familiar scenic route back to the cottage. Maggie was enveloped in a sense of peace, like she was going home. The flat cornfields alternated between green hills and dense patches of forests. All Maggie could think about was Thomas. Pedal to the floor, the wind whipped through her hair. Memories of their time together over the summer flew by with the scenery. She was counting down the minutes until she'd be in his arms and smell his familiar scent.

When Maggie pulled into the driveway, she left her suitcase in the trunk and dashed between the trees that separated their cottages. When she reached Thomas's front door, she took a second to straighten out her cotton summer dress. She tucked her wild, wind-blown hair behind her ears. She wondered if maybe she should have gone back to the cottage to freshen up, but the excitement of seeing Thomas again overruled those thoughts. She knocked on the door and tapped her foot as she waited. When he didn't answer a minute later, she knocked again. Louder this time.

"I'm coming, I'm coming! What's the emergency?" Sadie said, swinging the porch door wide open. She was wearing nothing but a towel. "Oh, hey, Maggie." The corners of Sadie's mouth lifted in silent satisfaction. "Thomas is, uh, indisposed. What can I do for you?"

Maggie's hand flew to her chest. The sharp pain of seeing Sadie wearing next to nothing at Thomas's door sent shockwaves through her body. Maggie stumbled backward down the front steps. Without a word to Sadie, she left.

Chapter Twenty-Four

When Maggie woke up the next morning, there was a brief, disoriented moment where she thought her old life with Thomas still existed. Sleep had provided her with a short reprieve from the pain he had caused. Fresh memories of Sadie in a towel hit Maggie with a vengeance. A heavy sadness weighed on her chest, which made getting out of bed even harder. Even though it was still dark outside, Maggie had to get up and do *something* to ensure her brain was focused and at top capacity for her scheduled interview later that day. Despite what Thomas had done, Maggie still wanted the position at Lake 88.5. She *needed* it and wasn't about to let Thomas ruin her chances.

Maggie rubbed her tender, swollen eyes and got out of bed. The idea of getting through the day without crying would be like climbing an insurmountable mountain, but she was determined to do it. She slipped into her black one-piece Speedo and grabbed a clean plush beach towel from the linen closet in the bathroom. A sunrise swim would not only help her clear her mind, but it would help reduce any puffiness in her face from crying herself to sleep the night before.

Down at the dock, Maggie admired the dawn. It was that special time of day when light first appeared in the sky, but the sun had not yet risen. Blackbirds, robins, and thrushes sang their morning chorus. Others would soon join in. The clear sky was suddenly enveloped in the most vibrant colors of coral-pink and bright pumpkin. The magic of the sun rising was about to happen at any moment.

"The best way to start the day is to watch the sunrise with an open heart," Johnny had once said to her when she was younger.

Maggie smiled at the memory. She removed her towel and stood at the edge of the dock with her head held high. Just as the sun bloomed over the horizon, Maggie dove into its golden reflection across the lake's surface. The cold water unlocked a shift within. As Maggie swam across the bay, she was able to switch off the part of her brain that needed to know what her future would hold and instead replaced those thoughts with the simplicity of being exactly where she was. When she reached the other side of the bay, Maggie stood on a big, slimy rock next to a bobbing yellow buoy that warned boaters of shallow water. In that moment, she was reminded that when her life was in flux, the lake had always been there for her.

The swim back was more difficult. Her lungs burned, but the release of endorphins helped push her forward. By the time Maggie made it back to her dock, she had the strength to face whatever life was going to throw at her. It was in the stillness of the sunrise that Maggie remembered that it was at the lake where she was most at peace with herself. She was ready to face the day head-on.

Back in the cottage, Maggie's cellphone buzzed on the kitchen island. She picked it up and was consumed with disappointment. Three missed calls and a series of text messages from Thomas. She leaned over the counter, holding her phone in a way for Katie to read along with her.

Hey! How was your flight? Thomas wrote.

Did you get in late? You can come over. I'm awake.

Good morning! Are you awake? Come over. I'll cook you breakfast.

Maggie placed her phone down on the kitchen island and cradled her head in her hands. "I can't believe he's going to pretend like nothing happened with Sadie. How could he do this to me?"

Katie quickly circled the island and enveloped Maggie in a sympathetic embrace. "I can't believe it either. You deserve so much better than this."

"You should've seen the smug look on Sadie's face. Like she was happy I found out about them the way I did. She didn't even try to deny it."

Katie pulled away and reopened Maggie's phone. She reread the text messages. "From the looks of it, she didn't even tell Thomas they'd been caught in the act."

"She didn't need to. She knows she won." Maggie's chin trembled. "I shouldn't have left him the way that I did. I broke his trust, and now he's chosen Sadie."

"You should talk to him—"

"No!" Maggie interrupted. She was done. Every lie and manipulation from past boyfriends came crashing down on her. She didn't want to hear Thomas's excuses. He didn't get to apologize or pretend their relationship hadn't meant anything. She refused to give him the time of day. "I'm not doing this again," Maggie said, her voice firm and final.

"What are you going to do now?" Katie asked.

Maggie held her fingers to her stinging eyes. She refused to let the pain of what Thomas had done stop her from pursuing her dreams. She could collapse later, but not now. She needed to stay focused. "I'm going to get ready for my job interview."

"You're still going to go through with it? Honey, why would you want to stay here after what Thomas has done?"

Maggie bent her head and studied her hands, willing herself not to cry. "Because I need a job."

"You could move back to the city. There is so

much opportunity there."

"Competition for jobs is fiercer in the city. Besides, I want hands-on experience. I want to learn everything I possibly can about the radio business. In the city, I'll be put in charge of everyone's coffee orders."

Katie smiled faintly, but it was touched with sadness. "I'd hate to see you here all alone."

"Living in the country has made me a stronger and more independent person. I love it here. I always have."

"Are you sure you want to do this?" Katie asked again.

The nod of Maggie's head was her only gesture.

Later, as she primped for her job interview, Maggie's cellphone buzzed every few minutes. She ignored the messages, brushing her teeth until her gums bled. She rinsed her mouth and spat in the sink. Suddenly, Maggie heard a knock at the front door. She froze with the hand towel to her mouth. When she heard the knock again, she opened the bathroom door a crack. She had a direct line of view to the front door. She saw Katie walking toward the front door. Katie's eyes revealed an angry spirit.

Katie sighed before opening the door. "What are you doing here, Thomas?"

"Uh, Katie, hi. Is Maggie around?" His voice sounded confused.

"She doesn't want to see you."

Katie began closing the door, but Thomas held it open with one hand. "Wait! Can you at least tell me why? She won't take my calls. I don't understand."

Katie shook her head silently and slowly closed the door.

Maggie breathed a sigh of relief when she heard Thomas's footsteps leave the deck. She hadn't realized she'd been holding her breath the entire time. Angry tears threatened to escape, but Maggie gripped the bathroom sink and willed them to stop. She wouldn't let Thomas get in the way of her future. She needed to focus on this job interview. Maggie gave her hair one final scrunch before exiting the bathroom.

"Wow, Maggie. You look so professional!" Katie said, eyeing her up and down.

Maggie twirled in her black pantsuit, grateful that Katie chose to ignore what had just happened with Thomas. "It's the outfit. I think it serves up some empowered working girl vibes."

"I'm impressed. Now, go get 'em!"

Maggie wasn't nervous until she walked up to the front doors of Lake 88.5. The radio station was located in an old 19th century home on Main Street. The house had been converted into a radio station in the late eighties, and it looked like it came straight off the pages of *Anne of Green Gables* with its white siding and forest green shutters. A large blue and green Lake 88.5 sign hung on the outside of the house. The logo was a combination of blue waves, gray rocks, and two pine trees.

Maggie straightened the wrinkles from her pants and went inside.

"You must be Maggie Taylor," the receptionist said. She had a raspy voice and welcoming smile. "I'm Nancy."

"Nice to meet you, Nancy. Yes, I'm here to see Larry White and Angie Perkins."

Nancy stood up and walked around the overwhelmingly large L-shaped desk, which was almost bigger than Nancy. "Follow me. They're waiting for you in the conference room."

Maggie followed her down a blue carpeted hallway. Pictures of musical artists lined the walls. When they entered the room, Larry and Angie stood to greet Maggie. After shaking hands, Maggie sat in the chair across from them. Nancy hustled around the boardroom table, filling their empty glasses with water before exiting the room and closing the door behind her. Angie slowly flipped through *The Ottawa Post* as Larry began the interview.

"Like I said on the phone, Maggie, we are impressed with your demo reel and reference letter. I guess what we want to know is, why Lake 88.5?" Larry asked.

"I know smaller radio stations take an all-hands-on-deck approach, and I think Lake 88.5 will offer great opportunities for further learning and career progression," said Maggie, her voice steady and confident.

"How do you feel about managers being more closely involved in your work at a smaller station?" Angie piped up, keeping her eyes on the newspaper.

Maggie folded her hands on the table. "Direct mentoring that includes a woman Station Manager is why I'm here. I want the hands-on responsibility."

"Mmhmm," Angie said as she continued to read on.

Maggie bit her lip. Her answer was strong, but she didn't seem to be making an impression on Angie. "I know in a small business environment, it's likely I'll work side-by-side with colleagues across all departments. I'm looking forward to this effective collaboration."

Angie's continued silence gnawed at Maggie's confidence.

Larry looked at Angie. His brows drew together in a questioning expression, but when Angie didn't reply, he continued with the interview. "Listen, Maggie, in the past, we've hired reporters who only stayed for six months before moving on to a bigger radio station in a larger city. The training costs us a lot of time and money. Are you committed to staying with Lake 88.5 for at least a year, if not longer?"

Maggie swallowed. This was her last chance to catch their attention. "I love Cedar Grove. There is an overall connection to community and nature here that you don't get in the city. I am committed to staying here."

Larry's smile widened, showing his approval. When Angie didn't take her eyes away from the newspaper, Larry gave a soft, uneasy cough. "Um, thank you for your time, Maggie. We still have a few candidates to interview. So, we'll be in touch soon with—"

"Wait." Angie held up her hand as she continued reading. Moments later, she looked up and pointed to the newspaper. "Did you write this?"

Maggie leaned against the table to get a better look at what Angie was talking about. The headline read, "Toxic Workplace Cultures in the Radio Industry." Maggie gulped, reaching across the table for the newspaper. The byline read, *by Maggie Taylor.* "Yes, I did. I didn't know they were going to publish it so soon—"

Angie stood up, walked around the oak table, and held out her hand. "Well, Maggie Taylor. You're hired. Welcome to the Lake 88.5 team."

The drive back to the cottage was a blur as Maggie replayed the sequence of events in her mind. One minute, she had thought she'd blown the interview, and the next minute, she was offered the job. She didn't snap out of it until Katie popped a bottle of champagne.

"Congratulations, Maggie!" Katie poured them each a glass of shimmering bubbles on the back deck. "I knew you'd get the job." She handed Maggie a glass.

"I haven't said yes yet."

"What. Why?"

"They told me to sleep on it."

"Are you going to say yes?"

Maggie paused. She looked out at the lake, admiring its calm and steady waters. The warm summer breeze carried the sweet scent of cedar, and the hum of the cicadas reminded Maggie of all her happy childhood summers spent up at the cottage. Her body relaxed, and she knew in that moment she was making the right decision. "I'm going to say yes!"

Katie's eyes were present and proud. She raised her glass. "Cheers to Cedar Grove's newest reporter!"

Maggie clinked her glass against Katie's before taking a sip of the light and fruity drink. "I'm going to need to find an apartment before it gets too cold!"

The next day, Maggie began apartment hunting, and so far, it had been a frustrating ordeal. She couldn't stop thinking about Thomas and Sadie, and her feet were tired from walking all morning. She grabbed a latte from North Folk, the best and most popular café in town, and found a seat outside on an empty green bench to enjoy it. She called her mom for the third time that day.

"So, did you like it?" her mother asked, referring to the last apartment Maggie had viewed.

"It smelt like cat pee, and the carpets were red," Maggie whined.

"Listings can change and hit the market by the hour. Don't panic," her mother instructed.

Maggie took a sip of her latte. The barista had sprinkled a little cinnamon on top of the froth, and it tickled Maggie's tongue. "People usually start looking for apartments months before their target move-in date. I start my new job in two weeks!"

"You know, you could stay at the cottage with Katie a little bit longer."

Maggie couldn't bear the thought of living next to

Thomas any longer than she had to. Every time she heard a car, she imagined it was Sadie visiting him for another rendezvous. "No, I need to find an apartment today."

"What's next on the list?"

"A two-bedroom in the heart of Cedar Grove. The ad says it's spacious and bright with hardwood flooring throughout."

"Wonderful! Stay positive, sweetie. And remember, go with your gut. If you have a bad feeling about the apartment or the landlord, skip it."

"Thanks for the pep talk, Mom. I love you." Maggie hung up and placed her phone back in her purse. She begrudgingly got off the bench. She drank the last drop of her latte and tossed the paper cup into a nearby recycling bin, ready to continue the pursuit.

Hours later, she returned to the cottage emptyhanded. She found Katie outside on the deck, setting the table for dinner.

"How'd it go?" Katie asked.

Maggie sat down at the picnic table with a huff. "I had to tell the last landlord that a kitchen and a kitchenette are not the same thing! There were also the issues of low water pressure, broken windows, and rotting floors."

"I'll get the wine," Katie said, squeezing Maggie's shoulder as she passed.

As Maggie waited, she stood up and walked to the edge of the deck and leaned against the wooden railing. The lake was choppy today. Two loons bobbled in the middle of the bay, drifting with the current. Despite telling herself not to, Maggie peered over the railing to get a better view of Thomas's cottage. Sweet memories of being with him hit her like a phantom boot to the gut, but those images were suddenly replaced with the memory of Sadie wearing nothing but a towel. Her thoughts teased her like a puzzle that was missing the last piece. She couldn't figure out where she had gone wrong or how she hadn't seen this coming.

Katie returned wearing oven mitts and carrying a bubbling lasagna in a glass casserole dish. A bottle of red wine was tucked under her arm. "Dinner is ready!"

Maggie took a seat, but she had lost her appetite. She pushed the steaming square of lasagna around on her plate. "Do you think he misses me?"

Katie tilted her head to one side. Her eyes glistened with sympathy. "You should call him. I think you need some closure."

Maggie placed her fork down. "I just don't understand why I feel so haunted this time. When I broke up with Brody, I breathed a sigh of relief!"

"Because Brody wasn't right for you. You're in love with Thomas, Maggie. You're mourning what you thought the two of you shared. It's normal to be hit with waves of memories and emotions. Trust me, I know."

"I can't stay here anymore. I need distance between me and Thomas. I need to find an apartment."

Katie took a sip of red wine. "I can help you look tomorrow if you like?"

Maggie gave a thankful nod. "Yes! I really appreciate everything you've done for me over the summer." Maggie picked up her fork and took a nibble of the homemade lasagna. "Mm, this is really good."

Katie smiled. "I knew you needed comfort food. Oh! Speaking of moving, Stuart called me today."

Maggie's jaw dropped. "What did he say?"

"He wants a divorce. We agreed I will move back home next week to help get the house ready for sale."

Maggie's shoulders stooped. "I'm so sorry."

Katie shrugged. "It's for the best, really. We both just want to be happy. We'll tell the boys when they come home from summer camp. Also, even though I'm in my forties, I've been thinking about going back to school. I've always wanted to study environmental science."

"That's a wonderful idea, Katie! When it comes to education and learning, it's never too late."

Katie couldn't contain her grin. "I'm ready for a fresh start."

"I'm going to miss living with you, Katie."

"Me, too, Maggie. I'm proud of us, though. We both came here, running away from life and relationships, yet here we are today, knowing our worth and facing our challenges head on."

"Avoiding Thomas feels a bit like running away," said Maggie.

Katie reached across the table and placed her hand over Maggie's. "You're just taking time to honor your pain. You accepted the job, and you're moving to Cedar Grove. You are most certainly not running away."

Maggie raised her wine glass. "To finding a love that chooses us!"

Katie clinked her glass against Maggie's. "Over everyone else and under any circumstances."

Maggie smiled. "To becoming the best versions of ourselves!"

Chapter Twenty-Five

Last night's bottle of wine turned into this morning's hangover, which made apartment hunting even more of a drag. Maggie almost lost her breakfast when she opened the kitchen cupboards in one apartment to find mouse droppings scattered everywhere. She and Katie left the apartment in a hurry.

"I don't know if I have it in me to look at any other places today," Maggie whined.

"It's too early in the day to give up," said Katie. "Let me buy you a coffee. I think we need the fuel to power us through the next apartments on your list."

Maggie and Katie walked down the block to North Folk. When they stepped into the coffee shop, the smell of freshly ground beans helped soothe the tension in Maggie's shoulders. Maggie and Katie joined the long line of locals and summer tourists waiting for their lattes and cappuccinos. Maggie was focused on reading the menu written in white chalk on a large blackboard behind the counter when Katie tapped her shoulder. Katie pointed to the woman standing in front of them. Sadie. She was speaking to someone Maggie had never seen before.

"The initial cleaning and demolition is complete," Sadie explained to the woman beside her. "Now they're working on the plumbing connections before they can install the drywall and tiles."

"It will be worth it once the renovations are finished," Sadie's friend replied. "Then you'll be able to enjoy your bathroom to its full potential."

"I can't wait," said Sadie. "I'm getting tired of showering at other people's houses."

Suddenly, Maggie was all ears. Before Katie

could stop her, Maggie joined the conversation uninvited. "You showered at Thomas's house because you're renovating your bathroom?"

Sadie turned and narrowed her eyes. "Yes." Her expression remained unsympathetic.

Maggie's face was suddenly scorching. She clenched her hands into fists at her sides.

Katie wrapped her arm around Maggie's shoulders and quickly guided her out of the coffee shop. "Just take a breath."

Maggie wriggled away from Katie's arm. "I'm upset! She let me believe that something happened between her and Thomas! He was just being a good friend."

"Sadie's a bitch. Do you really expect anything less from such a conniving person?"

Maggie's hand flew to her chest, struggling to take a full breath. "Do you realize what this means? I've been terrible to Thomas for no reason! I broke things off with the best thing that has ever happened to me without even giving him the chance to explain. He'll never forgive me."

"I'm going to drive you back to the cottage. You need to talk to him."

The drive back to the cottage passed in a haze. When Katie pulled into the driveway, she hadn't even put the car in park before Maggie opened her passenger side door and hopped out of the moving vehicle. "Thanks, Katie!" she called as she dashed between the pines that separated the cottages.

Maggie reached the other side of the pine grove in record time and ran up the steps to Thomas's front door. She knocked incessantly. When he didn't answer, Maggie looked around helplessly. His truck was in the driveway, so he must be home. She bounded down the stairs that led to his dock. She found Thomas sitting at the end with his feet dangling over the edge. His gray sweatpants were pulled up to his knees, and he was staring off into the distance. If he had heard her rushing down the stairs, he was choosing to ignore her.

Maggie swallowed hard and lifted her chin. "I'm so sorry, Thomas."

Thomas's body stiffened as though he was surprised to hear someone behind him. When he turned to look at her, his face darkened with unreadable emotion.

Wild anxiety ripped through her, but Maggie took a step toward him. She had to make him understand. "I ran into Sadie at the coffee shop, and I overheard her talking to a friend about her bathroom renovation and—"

"You don't answer my calls, you refuse to come to the door when I call on you, and now you're here and want to talk about Sadie's bathroom renovations?" His voice was heavy with disapproval.

"I'm here to apologize! I made a terrible mistake. When I got back from Edmonton, and Sadie answered your door in nothing but a towel, I just assumed—"

"Wait, you came to see me after you landed?"

Maggie paused. The memory saddened her. "Yes, I couldn't wait to see you, but Sadie had made it seem like something had happened between the two of you. She didn't tell you I came by?"

"No," he said in a resigned voice. Anger blazed in his eyes. "I can't believe she did that. Nothing happened between us. I told you we were over a long time ago." Thomas stood up at the end of the dock. His feet were wet from the lake, and his messy curls played in the gentle summer breeze. His broad shoulders carried the burden of their miscommunication. "I should've told you she was coming over, but you didn't even give me a chance to explain! When my mom walked out, I waited for her to come back and call, too. That kind of silence messes with your head."

A cold weight dropped into Maggie's chest. "Thomas, I'm so sorry! I've been cheated on in the past and Brody was so manipulative—"

"I'm not them!" Thomas yelled. "When you shut me out, I felt like a scared little kid again, Maggie. It was that same punch to the gut, like I wasn't worth staying for." Thomas's voice cracked.

The crumpled hurt in his eyes was too much for Maggie to bear. "I screwed up!" she said quickly, desperate to repair the damage she had caused. "You're nothing like my exes and I shouldn't have treated you the way that I did. I'm so sorry!"

Thomas remained quiet for a moment. A deep furrow formed between his eyebrows. "How can I trust you now?"

A twist of dread curled in Maggie's stomach. "I made a mistake! I hate myself for hurting you, but Thomas, I'm not leaving you." Her voice trembled. "I'm staying in Cedar Lake."

Thomas's eyes widened as the weight of her words sunk in. After a beat, he shook his head. "No. I won't let you throw away your career for me."

Maggie stepped toward him. "I'm not. I made this decision when I thought you were back together with Sadie. I'm doing this for me, but I'd love to do this with you by my side. Please don't push me away."

Thomas stood silently as Maggie's plea hung in the air between them like a held breath.

Maggie swallowed. "Look, I understand if you want nothing to do with me."

Thomas's guarded gaze melted away and was replaced by something tender and soft. "Nothing to do with you? Maggie, I'm in love with you," he said.

A rush of relief flooded her chest, and a quiet laugh slipped out as Maggie stepped toward Thomas and wrapped her arms around his neck. "I love you, too!"

Thomas smiled, wiping away all traces of hurt. His eyes smoldered as he smoothed her wavy hair, tucking a loose strand behind her ear. "I know we still have a lot to figure out, but I don't want to push you away, Maggie. You're it for me. I want to make this work."

Maggie couldn't pull her eyes away from him, captivated by his tall, athletic form. She had an overwhelming desire to be with him. She pulled him roughly against her and stared longingly at his lips. She wanted to kiss him, but first she had to tell him the good news. "There isn't much to figure out anymore. I accepted a job offer from Lake 88.5."

Thomas's face split into a wide smile. "What?" He picked her up and twirled her around before placing her back down on the dock. He exhaled with contentment as he held her in a tight embrace. "Congratulations, Maggie! You deserve this."

Maggie's heart leapt at his response. She gazed up at him, admiring the firm set of his jaw. "We can be together," she whispered in a silky voice. She clutched the back of his neck, pulling him closer.

Thomas's mouth hungrily took hers. He swept her into his arms as if she were weightless, and as his lips left hers to nibble at her earlobe, he murmured, "I'm taking you to bed."

But they didn't quite make it there. Once inside his cottage, Thomas pinned Maggie against the front door, pressing his hips into hers. "I can't believe you're with me," he said, his eyes darkening to a deep shade of green.

"I'm yours," she whispered, her chest rising and

falling.

His lips found hers in a ravenous kiss. Maggie's nipples tingled as Thomas's hands fumbled with the zipper on the back of her white cotton dress.

"Here, let me help you," she said, turning around and sweeping her long hair off her neck. Her body trembled with anticipation as Thomas slowly unzipped her dress. He pulled the straps off her shoulders, kissing the nape of her neck as the dress fell to the floor. Maggie stepped out of it, and stood before Thomas in her strapless, nude-lace bra and matching cheeky panties.

Thomas ran a hand through his untamed curls. "You have no idea what you do to me," he said in a gravelly voice, full of desire.

Maggie's gaze lowered to the hard ridge of arousal straining against his gray sweatpants. Her lips parted. She walked a few steps into the kitchen and leaned over the counter. "I want you to take me right here."

Thomas exhaled out of pursed lips and quickly ran to his bedroom to grab a condom. When he returned, he not only took her in the kitchen, but he also pleasured her on the couch in the living room, before bringing her back to his bedroom. As Maggie fell back on the mattress, the springs squeaked under her weight. She stretched her legs open. The buildup was becoming so intense, the sweet spot between her legs throbbed for release.

"I'm not going to last much longer," Thomas said, lowering himself on top of her, supporting his muscular frame on his forearms. "Come for me, Maggie."

Maggie shook her head, biting her lip, resisting. Not until he came first. He sunk into her deeply, and peaked moments later with a low, guttural groan, sending an explosion of blissful warmth detonating throughout

Maggie's body.

"That's it," he stimulated as she continued to summit. "I love you," he whispered in her ear, over and over again until the pulsing waves of pleasure petered out of her system.

A couple of hours later, Maggie was gathered against Thomas's warm body. She was the happiest she had ever been in her life. Maggie settled back into him, enjoying the feel of his bare chest against her naked back.

Thomas's lips brushed against her shoulder as he spoke. "I wasn't lying when I said I want to be with you every day. Move in with me."

Maggie didn't answer. She reached back and combed her fingers through his curls. She pulled his head toward hers and kissed him as gently as a whisper. "Yes, I'll move in with you."

It wasn't until the sun began to set that they finally emerged from the bedroom.

"I don't want to be out of bed," Maggie groaned as Thomas led her to the kitchen. He was wearing gray sweatpants, and she was wearing his t-shirt.

"We need nourishment. All that lovemaking has made me hungry."

Maggie leaned against the counter and crossed her arms, pretending to pout.

"You look cute when you're mad," Thomas said. He pulled two pieces of bread from a brown paper bakery bag and placed them in the toaster. He plugged in the kettle and proceeded to cut a ripe avocado in half. He removed the pit, emptied the green flesh into a bowl and mashed it with a fork.

When he opened the fridge and reached for a tomato, Maggie gasped. There, on the door of his fridge, was her article. "You cut out my article?"

Thomas closed the door and placed the tomato on

the cutting board. "I'm proud of you. I bet that article will help a lot of women in the same position. They'll know they're not alone."

Maggie grinned with the kind of pride that only comes from meaningful achievement. "You know, I wouldn't have had the courage to write that article if it wasn't for you."

Thomas popped the toast and put each piece on a separate plate. "I appreciate you saying that, but this was all you, Maggie."

Maggie grinned ear-to-ear. "I found my voice again."

"Your article may have started a movement. Did you read about that big-time morning show host in Vancouver who is being accused of abusive behavior toward the female staff? He apparently spat in one of his colleague's faces! There's going to be an investigation."

"What? No! When did you hear about this?" Maggie asked.

Thomas spread the avocado on the toast and added sliced tomatoes on top. "In yesterday's paper." He nodded his head in the direction of the newspaper on the counter.

Maggie had been too focused on apartment hunting to read the news yesterday. She grabbed the paper and flipped through its pages until she saw the headline. *Investigation into Workplace Harassment Allegations at Vancouver's Radio Planet.* "I'm glad those women came forward. Did I tell you my new boss is a woman? I think she runs a tight ship. I'm not worried about a toxic workplace environment at Lake 88.5."

Thomas added a light drizzle of balsamic glaze to the avocado toast and sprinkled chopped basil on top. He poured boiling water over chai bags that were resting in two ceramic mugs. "Let's take our snack outside. The humidity is gone, so I know the colors of the sunset will be vibrant."

They brought their meal to the hammock that hung between two pines near the top of the stairs that led to Thomas's dock. Maggie and Thomas placed their dishes down on a stump that acted like a coffee table and sat down in the middle of the hammock. They sat sideways, turning the hammock into a swinging chair.

Once they were stable, Thomas handed Maggie her toast and tea.

Maggie took a bite. She enjoyed the combination of textures with the crunchiness of the toast and creaminess of the avocado. "Mm, I could get used to this."

"I hope you do. Moments like this is what I'm looking forward to most with you," said Thomas.

Maggie took a sip of the ginger and cardamom spiced tea. She let out a sigh of satisfaction and comfort. The sky was an abstract painting of sweeping lines and rhythms with lush colors of pink, orange, and lavender. Maggie couldn't help but compare this moment to her old life in the city. She had been so busy and distracted there that she never had time to stop and admire a sunset. Besides, city sunsets weren't as wonderful as country sunsets because of the light pollution. Maggie was eager to share the news about moving in with Thomas and her new job with her family and June. They'd be thrilled for her.

"I see us getting married on our dock one day," Thomas said, interrupting her thoughts.

Maggie paused. It was thrilling to not only hear that Thomas wanted to marry her someday, but he had called it *our* dock. "I'll wear daisies in my hair and walk down the aisle barefoot."

Thomas threw back his head and roared with a

rich, warm laugh. "Do you remember when I first met you? You were wearing high heels! My, how things have changed."

His laughter was wonderfully catching. Maggie wiped a happy tear from her eye. "When I arrived, I was such a mess! I think I've always been this girl, though. I just needed time in this special place to rediscover her."

Thomas reached for her empty plate and mug and placed it on the makeshift coffee table. He wrapped his arm around her shoulders. "Do you see us having kids in the future?" His tone was filled with respect and touched with curiosity. His eyes were a story of love and passion.

Maggie leaned her head against his shoulder. "At least three!"

Thomas rested his head against hers. "I have to say, we'd make some good-looking babies."

Maggie smiled as she imagined three little kids with Thomas's curls running through the pines and across the property. They swayed in the hammock, watching as night cloaked the shoreline cedars across the bay.

From somewhere deep in the forest, a sedge wren sang, "All is well."

The End

ACKNOWLEDGEMENTS

I'd like to start by acknowledging the powerful voices of women in radio, past and present, who paved the way and inspired generations of storytellers.

To the men of radio, who helped shape my journey, thank you for your belief in me when I was finding my voice in a male-dominated space. Dylan Black, Jeff Larocque, Tony Orr, Terry Parker, Tony Smith, and Jody Tedford, thank you for your mentorship and guidance.

I am deeply grateful to my publisher, Evernight Publishing. A huge thank you to Stacey Adderley and Sofia Aves for believing in this story and helping it come to life.

To my editors, Carrie Clauson, Laurie Clayton and Corinne DeMaagd, thank you for your thoughtful guidance, sharp eye and encouragement.

I have immense gratitude for my mom, Meg, my biggest supporter. Thank you for being my first reader, and always believing this book would be published.

To my late grandmother, June, and Uncle Peter—your love and wisdom have shaped so much of who I am today. Parts of this book are a tribute to you both, and I will forever carry your lessons and spirit in my heart.

To my dad, Patrick and Caleigh. I will treasure our childhood cottage memories forever!

A big thank you to my best friend, Jerin, for manifesting this book into reality with me.

To my three amazing children, Henry, Rosie and Hubert. This book was written between your adventures and laughter. You give me more love, joy and motivation than you'll ever know.

Mike, my incredible husband. Thank you for your unwavering belief in me. I love walking this life, and this dream, with you by my side.

Last but never least, a massive thank you to my readers. I'm endlessly grateful to you for bringing this story to life with your time, your attention and your support. Your belief in me as a writer means the world to me.

EVERNIGHT PUBLISHING

www.evernightpublishing.com